GRAHAM CAWLEY joined
his first branch being P
Following retirement as
James's Street, London, branch, he took up writing as a hobby and has had numerous financial articles and short stories published. His first crime novel, CHAIN OF EVENTS, relates back to his banking roots in South Devon and FATAL RETRIBUTION is the second book in his series featuring bank manager, David Goodhart. Each book depicts little-known-about banking-related crimes and also encompasses Graham's love of jazz, golf and the fortunes of Torquay United Football Club.

# GRAHAM CAWLEY

## FATAL RETRIBUTION

*To Jenny
with my very best wishes
Graham*

**SilverWood**

Published by Silverwood Books 2008
www.silverwoodbooks.co.uk

Copyright © Graham Cawley 2008

The right of Graham Cawley to be identified as the author of this work
has been asserted by him in accordance with the Copyright,
Designs and Patents Act 1988.

All characters and situations portrayed are fictitious and are not based on actual persons
whether living or dead.

All rights reserved. No part of this publication may be reproduced,
stored in a retrieval system, or transmitted in any form or by any means,
electronic, mechanical, photocopying, recording or otherwise,
without prior permission.

ISBN 978-1-906236-04-5

British Library Cataloguing in Publication Data
A CIP catalogue record for this book is available from the British Library

Set in 10pt Stempel Graramond by SilverWood Books
Printed in England by Biddles Ltd

*For Katie and Lucy*

My grateful thanks to the many readers who expressed kind words about CHAIN OF EVENTS, thus inspiring me to write FATAL RETRIBUTION. In particular, I am indebted to my family, to my great friend, David Trower, and also to Helen Hart of SilverWood Books, for their unstinting support and encouragement.

# CHAPTER 1

'This branch will be raided at 2.30.'

Numb with apprehension, David Goodhart re-read the terse message. Had he now come to learn the real meaning of fear?

The pencilled scrawl stared back at him, as if challenging him to doubt its significance. The piece of yellow blotting paper on which the threat had been written had been set out that morning on a desk in the banking hall. It was there to soak up ink from the steel-nib pens put out for customers' use. Instead, it bore a message of unconcealed menace.

Across his desk, he looked up at his young cashier, Trevor Smith. "Tell me everything that's happened," he said. "We must get the facts right before I start making my calls."

In all his twenty-five years with National Counties Bank he had only heard of two bank raids in Devon. The worst, five years ago in 1952, had been at a sub-branch on Dartmoor when a gunman had shot dead the guard in front of his cashier. No money had been taken, the raider having fled in panic. The cashier never recovered from the shock and had not worked again.

But a bank raid here? In Barnmouth? In this peaceful seaside town? In the middle of April? Never mind at his own bank! Until now, almost three years since his appointment as manager in 1954, his only other unwelcome visitors had been bank inspectors on their two-yearly snap inspection of the branch.

After charging into the room, Trevor's hands had visibly shaken when he passed over the blotting paper. Now he sat opposite, tense and upright. He clasped his hands together, clearly trying to steady his nerves. But he had every reason to be afraid. Last year, he had been the victim of that other raid in Devon.

"Everything had been quite normal," he began, the knuckles

of both hands now whitening, as he dug his nails into his palms.
"We'd been really busy, sir – as usual on a Wednesday morning."

That was not unexpected. Early closing day consigned most transactions to the morning.

"Had customers been sitting at the tables?"

It was not a large banking hall – as if in keeping with the branch itself, David's first managerial appointment. But there was room for two tables and accompanying chairs where customers could complete their credits and cheques.

"Most of the time," Trevor replied, frowning, as if trying to recall the customers concerned. "But it was difficult to see. The queues often cut out my view. I did notice old Mrs Grimes. She always needs to sit down to write out her cheque. And Mr English used the same table."

David groaned inwardly at hearing John English's name. But this was not the time to go over that old ground. Unless…

"Then, just before eleven, sir," Trevor continued, "there was a lull and Bernard asked me to go into the public space and tidy up the tables."

Really?

It was hardly likely. Bernard Groves was not notable for having his eyes open for such things. As first cashier, he preferred not to demean himself by getting involved with that sort of menial task. More likely, Trevor had used his own initiative. He was far more alert to his manager's requirement of keeping the banking hall tidy at all times.

"That's when I noticed the scribble on one of the blotters. It was on the table opposite my till – the one used by Mrs Grimes and Mr English. And others, of course. At first, I thought it was doodling. Then I read the words. It scared me stiff. I'm sorry… that's why I barged into your room."

"And quite right, too," David said. At the very least, the boy needed consoling. He was visibly shaken. No wonder, after his experience at Chagford.

That attractive market town on the edge of Dartmoor bristled with thatched buildings, quaint narrow streets and wild ponies on its outskirts. Nothing dramatic ever seemed to happen in Chagford. Until a year ago.

Trevor had gone there as relief cashier – just for a week. On the Wednesday afternoon – also early closing day in Chagford – he had apparently been tidying up his till, when an armed robber had burst in. The villain had leapt over the counter, almost into Trevor's actual till, then rifled through the cash, before escaping into the street with all he could carry.

The whole operation had taken no more than thirty seconds, but it had been months for Trevor to get over the shock. No wonder he was so disconcerted by his discovery this morning.

And he was not alone.

David scrutinized the note again. Could it just be a hoax? The writing certainly looked childish. Yet, unaccompanied children were unlikely to come into the bank. In any case, the schools had not yet broken up for Easter. And the handwriting of such a message was bound to be disguised; why not by way of a child's hand?

"Could it just be a sick joke?" Trevor asked, as if he was on the same wavelength. He certainly seemed to be pleading that this might be the case.

David shrugged, the action relieving some of the tension in his shoulders. "I was just wondering if it could be a hoax. But why? Why would anyone want to do such a thing?"

"Yet, if it's genuine...?"

"If it's genuine, why give advance warning? It would clearly put us on full alert... not to mention calling the police. Would a serious raider risk that happening?"

Trevor shook his head and even looked a little relieved.

But the written threat still stared out from the blotting paper. If a raid did take place, Trevor would be right in the firing line – possibly literally. For him to have experienced one raid was one too many. How was he really coping with the prospect of another?

"What about Regional Office?" Trevor then asked. "Are you going to phone the RM?"

The RM? Spattan? That was a good one. His Regional Manager should have been his first point of contact. After all, he was his immediate boss – and number one confidant in difficult circumstances. Spattan's predecessor had been just that. A great man. Yet, somehow, since taking over, nine months ago, Spattan had appeared to have chosen David to be his least favourite manager. But why?

"Perhaps not the RM, himself," he simply said. "But I'll speak to his office. Also to the Chief Inspector."

Now, how different had the Chief been? Based in London, as opposed to just up the road in Exeter, he was responsible for branch security throughout the country. Yet, after last year's frauds and violent crime which had rocked Barnmouth, he had been the one to go out of his way to praise David for his handling of the situation. Strangely, it was after this that Spattan's antipathy towards him had become evident.

"And the police?" Trevor asked.

David nodded and smiled at the youngster. "Of course. But it's deciding on what order to place these calls."

"I'd say the order you just said," Trevor replied. Bearing in mind the circumstances, it was good that he was thinking logically. But how was he really coping within himself? There was a clear case for moving him off the counter right away. He was an extremely capable lad and could turn his hand to plenty of the back-office jobs. But would that be fair to whoever took his place as cashier? Someone would certainly need to support Bernard Groves.

"But what about you, Trevor?" he asked. "Are you okay? I mean…"

David let his words tail off and the boy's Adam's apple moved up and down as he considered his reply. But his actual response could not have been more positive.

"I'm fine, sir," he said, actually smiling, "really. And I must get back to Bernard. He'll be going spare if customers are flocking in."

It was clearly not the time to express any further doubts and David sent Trevor on his way. But he would keep a close eye on him. Any sign of anxiety and he would come off the counter straight away.

Yet, it was not just about young Trevor on the counter. What about Bernard Groves? How would the first cashier be bearing up under the threat? In theory, better than Trevor, if only because of his age and experience. But, last year, he had been found wanting in the mishandling of a customer's credits. At one stage, his action had appeared to have been complicit in the fraud which had caused such a stir. But this had remained unproved and he had only suffered a severe reprimand. Since then, he had been doing his best to keep a low profile. A bank raid would hardly help that particular cause.

As he pondered over a man he could not warm to, David glanced up at his Great Western Railway wall clock. Eleven-thirty and there was much to do. But he had never before been conscious of the clock's regular ticktocking. How ominous was that? It was like a ticking time bomb – one that was primed to go off at two-thirty.

# CHAPTER 2

It was now two-fifteen precisely. Trevor Smith had heard St Mary's clock strike the quarter hour and that particular timepiece was never wrong.

With sweaty palms, he attempted to count the bundle of fivers, but his hands shook badly as his fingers rustled through the white parchment-like notes. Not for a year had he been so nervous.

He had hoped that memories of that dreadful day in Chagford were well behind him. The recurring nightmares had certainly stopped; they had gone on for months. A hooded creature – neither man nor beast – sprang across the bank counter, teeth bared and spitting flames. Destruction, not theft, seemed to be its objective and Trevor's ten shilling notes were the first to char from the creature's searing breath; then the pound notes and fivers. For some reason, he was naked at his till and when the flames spat forth in his direction, he would always awaken, sweating in his pyjamas, not from the heat, but from the horror of the bad dream.

And now he might face another raider.

Finding the note that morning had sent a chill through his bones, but he had tried to exhibit a calm equilibrium in Mr Goodhart's room. He could tell the manager was anxious about his reaction and he had to appear strong and dismiss any suggestion that he might have failed to put Chagford behind him.

Last year, it had taken him months to do just that. It was not the same as getting on a bike again, immediately after falling off. His nerves had been too shattered for him to carry on cashiering and only people who had suffered physical harm or psychological distress from a bank raid could understand that. At the time, well-meant assurances that 'time would be the healer' simply did not help, yet such prophecies had eventually been proved correct.

But fresh nerves now engulfed him as he finished counting the fivers, then slipping the bundle into the back of his till. It was unlikely they would be needed before dispatch to the cash centre, customers much preferring the handier lower denomination notes.

He cast a furtive eye around the banking hall which was devoid of customers. That was not unusual on early closing day but the presence of one or two familiar faces would have helped to ease his mind. At least he had Bernard Groves by his side.

"You're sure your till's as empty as possible?" his first cashier asked, not for the first time.

"Of course," Trevor replied. Bernard was probably as nervous as he. It was always prudent to transfer surplus notes into the strong room – even more so having been forewarned of a possible raid. He had done this just before lunch and the afternoon had been quiet. "Hardly anyone's paid in since lunchtime."

Bernard Groves nodded. "I can't remember a quieter afternoon."

That really was a good one.

Most days could be considered quiet for Bernard. He was of the old school – over fifty and fastidious in the extreme. In the time it took him to serve one customer, Trevor could handle six.

But at least his previous arrogance had been knocked out of him. Last year, he had incurred Mr Goodhart's wrath at the way he had handled some fraudulent transactions. Since then, working alongside him had become far pleasanter. And, this afternoon, his presence at the next till was certainly comforting.

"Let's hope the Council don't pay in," Trevor said, looking at his watch which now displayed two-twenty.

It was always bad news when the representative of the Council's treasurer showed his face in the late afternoon. It was not just the large amount he paid in, but the notes and coin were always in such a jumble. Why could he not be better organized?

But the front door remained steadfastly shut. The only person entering the banking hall was a tall man of military bearing. He had emerged from the manager's room and gave Trevor a brief nod before positioning himself at the customers' table nearest to the bank's entrance.

With his Brylcreemed hair, DC Pound resembled Denis Compton and Trevor imagined him wielding a cricket bat at any would-be raider. Instead, sitting at the table, his chosen implement was a slender wooden-handled pen. He dipped its nib into the black inkwell and started to fill in a credit slip, giving it the attention Trevor wished all their customers would exhibit.

As the minutes ticked onwards towards two-thirty, Trevor felt the tension to be almost palpable. A glance over his shoulder told him that his nervousness was not only shared by the chief clerk, Norman Charlton, but also by the girls in the machine room from where the usual mechanical clatter had suddenly stopped. He imagined them huddled over their machines, sharing anxious glances and conscious that the church clock was about to strike the half-hour.

DC Pound continued to pore over his credit, but Trevor noticed his sharp eyes also taking in all that was around him. Every now and again he thrust his hand inside his jacket, as if to check that his wallet was still safely ensconced in its pocket.

There could now be less than a minute to go and the wording of the warning expunged all other thoughts from Trevor's mind.

'This branch will be raided at 2.30'.

It was such a cryptic message. But was it a hoax? Thank goodness Mr Goodhart had taken it seriously; it was such a comfort to have DC Pound in the banking hall. If only he had been there in Chagford.

At last, the clock chimed.

Then, total silence.

Trevor glanced at Bernard, whose eyes flitted between the front door and the detective. The only other movement in the branch was DC Pound's hand being plunged inside his jacket.

Chagford flashed before Trevor. Although he had never talked about it, the other staff knew what he had been through. He now felt their unspoken support as he stood behind his till, right there where any offensive would take place.

But this concern for him now increased his anxiety. He was bearing a heavy burden of responsibility. Whatever might be about to happen, he must not let the others down. Their support must encourage him to be strong.

But the time had now passed two-thirty and nothing had happened.

DC Pound rose from his chair, glanced at Trevor and raised his eyebrows. Was this a sign that he felt any danger had passed? He moved towards the front door and glanced surreptitiously through the window on to the High Street.

He stayed there as the minutes ticked by. Trevor now wondered if all the security arrangements had been for nothing. His nervousness was all but gone when Roger Singleton, the office junior, went to lock the front door at three o'clock. Trevor smiled with relief at Bernard Groves. It was also the cue for DC Pound, with his holstered pistol not called upon, to make his way back to Mr Goodhart's room.

But as Roger reached the front door, it swung open with a fearful crash.

# CHAPTER 3

From his room, David heard the commotion in the banking hall and rushed to his door. He immediately spotted and recognised its cause – a small weasel-faced man, dwarfed by the detective at his side.

"I thought I'd never make it," the Council's man was saying to Trevor Smith as he spilled a jumble of notes and coin on to the mahogany counter. "I was all set to come half an hour ago and then, would you believe, a rent collector arrived at the very last minute. Why some people leave things so late, I'll never know."

Despite all the tension, David could not help but smile. Trevor's despair at the man's late arrival would be more than tempered by the unintentional irony of his words. It was extraordinary that such people could never recognise another person's faults or actions in their own particular deeds. It was like someone with BO complaining about the smell surrounding a smoker; or a chatterbox bemoaning the inability of getting a word in with another windbag. But any concern of Trevor's would be quickly dissipated by relief that the new arrival had not been a raider. David could only share such feelings.

Retreating into his room, he was thankful he did not have Trevor's task of sorting out the half-crowns from the florins, shillings and sixpenny pieces. The lad would be wise to give the man a stack of paper bags in the hope that he would sort the coins into denominations before leaving for the bank. How much easier and quicker it would then be for the bags simply to be weighed on the scales.

Smiling broadly, DC Pound, soon joined David in his room. "I thought we were going to have some real action then," he said, as David motioned him to sit down on one of the two chairs on the other side of his desk. The chair was barely suitable for a man who must stand six-feet-five in his socks, but it did not seem to bother him. In the last hour David had come to like and respect the attitude of a policeman who would probably be in control of any situation. "And I now reckon," DC Pound continued, "that the threat on the blotting paper was probably a hoax."

"But why would anyone want to do that?" David asked. "Particularly in a place like Barnmouth. The holiday season hasn't started yet and the town's hardly overflowing with strangers. Who might do such a thing?"

"Why just strangers?"

"I doubt if locals would play such a prank – especially customers."

"You never can tell. It might be more than just a prank. There could be a motive behind it; someone making mischief for a purpose."

David shook his head. It did not seem likely.

DC Pound scrutinized him carefully. "Have you seen anyone recently who might bear a grudge against the bank – or you personally, for that matter?"

David pursed his lips. Surely not? "I don't always agree to lending propositions. But turning down a customer? That would hardly lead to threatening the bank."

The detective raised his eyebrows.

"What about a youngster?" David added quickly, not wanting to have his lending decisions closely analysed. It was bad enough having that done by inspectors, never mind by Spattan. "It might be a case of infantile mischief. The writing was certainly childish."

"Maybe," DC Pound acknowledged. "But people can alter their handwriting. Anyway, you'd better all stay on full alert – and keep your Head Office in the picture."

"I'll certainly do that," David said. This morning the Chief

Inspector had already been most supportive. At this stage, he had decided to leave things in the hands of the police; his Department would become involved if a raid did take place. Otherwise, he simply wanted a follow-up report. From Spattan? Nothing. Although one of his assistants had seemed genuinely concerned.

"And many thanks for all your help," David added, then grinning. "And please don't take this the wrong way, but I hope we never have to meet again."

DC Pound was smiling broadly as he left. At least, the episode had ended in good humour.

One other good thing was that he knew his staff would be even more security-conscious than ever; there was nothing like a threat such as this to concentrate minds. Nevertheless, he would again stress the need for strict control of cash, valuables and keys. Last year, they had fallen down badly on the front door opening procedures. Proper use of the spy-hole and security chain was paramount. Unfortunately, there was no accounting for human fallibility, but this was now unlikely for a little while, at least.

He leaned back in his chair and took a deep breath. With all the tension gone, he realized how much it had taken out of him. If only he could go home now. A cold light ale with his beloved Sarah would go down very nicely. He might even further relax by getting on his hands and knees with train-mad Mark. It was his turn to be signalman. Everything had to run strictly to order on his nine-year-old son's Hornby 'Dublo' layout.

But he still had much to do here.

With the front door now locked for further business and the man from the Council gone, leaving Trevor to sort out his mess, it was time to call in his assistant, Jane Church. Although it was impossible to put to one side his continuing concern about a possible raid, normal work still had to go on and Jane should be well into the assignment he had given her that morning.

Ah, Jane – most definitely one of his success stories.

The girl had blossomed out of all recognition from the shy twenty-one-year-old who had arrived at the branch about nine months ago – foisted on him by the regional staff controller who had become keen to see girls holding down positions traditionally held by men. Her shyness and in-built lack of confidence was now behind her and she had steadily developed into her role as his assistant. Perhaps, after all, the staff controller's forward thinking had been spot on.

Within seconds of answering his call, she breezed into the room. After all his recent anxiety, she was like a breath of fresh air. Typical of her new-found aura was her recently-acquired pert bobtail. It swayed across her shoulders, only coming to rest when she sat down. Could the staff controller have possibly foreseen her turning out like this? When he interviewed her, she must have worn her previous attire: dreary grey cardigan and matching straight skirt. Now, her primrose blouse with collar and cuffs edged in blue was as striking as Torquay United's latest strip.

"I know we've had other things on our minds today," David said, forcing his mind to concentrate on the matter in hand, "but how have you been getting on with those dormant accounts?"

On an annual basis, he monitored accounts which had been inactive for a number of years. Such dead wood cluttered up the ledgers and did not give him any opportunity of establishing contact with the respective customers.

Banking was about people dealing with people, but he could not create and encourage successful relationships if customers were effectively non-existent. In the case of very small dormant balances, debit or credit and with no response from customers to letters, it might be as well to write the amounts off. The accounts could always be resurrected should such customers eventually turn up.

"Very well, sir," Jane replied, caressing the frames of her newly-acquired modern glasses in the manner of a man getting used to a recently-grown moustache. She certainly never gave the same attention to her previous steel-rimmed National Health spectacles.

"But it's all rather strange," she continued, frowning. "There are fewer dormant accounts than we had a year ago. I also checked back on previous years and we usually see a year-on-year increase."

"Sounds like good news to me," David said. "The more active accounts we have, the better."

"I know, but it still seems a little odd. Why a change this year?"

This was the new Jane – using her head and not simply accepting information as it stood. He had stressed that to be an effective manager's assistant, she must question things and look deeply into any investigation he might put her way. Not many problems were positively black or white and he needed to know the full picture before making a decision. And he also wanted Jane to share the decision making. That would be effective training and experience for what now looked to be a successful career ahead of her.

"Are you suggesting we should look into it more deeply?"

"I'm not sure, sir. Probably not at the moment. After all, it's not a matter of life or death."

"That's certainly true." But having had an armed policeman in the branch this afternoon, Jane's phraseology might have been better chosen.

"But if I get a free moment in the next couple of weeks, I'll delve around."

"Yes, that sounds good."

"If I find accounts have become active, we could drop the customers a line. It might be worthwhile to try and meet them face-to-face."

"Agreed. But even though it's not urgent, don't wait too long. We're now well into April and the holiday season's only round the corner."

"But that won't be until July and August."

"You're forgetting the OAPs. Their coach parties will be here next month."

Pensioners were not the best visitors as far as hotels and traders were concerned, but they did help to extend the main holiday season.

"I'll make a start next week, then."

"Good. And I want your help with something else."

"That sounds ominous."

David grinned. That response would not have crossed her lips a while ago. But this was no laughing matter and he looked at her seriously. "I'm still worried about this threat of a raid. I'm going to call everyone together before we leave tonight. I want to make sure we all keep on our guard."

"After today, I don't think that'll be a problem," Jane replied, as if springing to the defence of the other staff. "We've all been feeling for Trevor. No-one's going to put a foot wrong, if only for him. He's been such an inspiration."

Her eyes actually shone with pride as she said this. If David had not known she was going steady with the young assistant professional at the golf club, he might have visualized an office romance developing.

"Anyway," he replied, "I must make the most of this opportunity to emphasise the question of security. And then I'd like you to help."

Jane's forehead furrowed.

"Just keep an eye on what's happening out there. You know, proper control of keys, security of cash, that sort of thing."

Jane now looked alarmed. "You mean to spy on everyone?"

"Good heavens, no! Nothing as dramatic as that. But another pair of eyes would help – to make sure things are done properly. I don't want anyone to be put at risk."

Jane soon left his room looking rather disturbed. Perhaps, on reflection, he was asking her to spy, but that was not his intention.

As well as the threat of possible raids, so many other things could go wrong – without his knowing.

Such as tills being left unattended and slackness over the control of keys. Any such negligence could encourage light fingers. He could not imagine any of his own staff dipping into someone else's till, but any laxity in the observance of laid-down rules could lead to temptation. It had certainly happened elsewhere.

Far better to have proper control in place and if this meant calling upon Jane's assistance, so be it. She might have looked a little askance at his instruction, but it was part of her training. Anyway, he was confident about her using tact and discretion.

Yet it was a little odd that he should instinctively consider young Jane for such a task, rather than his deputy, chief clerk, Norman Charlton. But, on this occasion, Jane was definitely the one to help him out.

Norman was generally an able deputy. He handled much of the day-to-day running of the branch, including most aspects of security. But he displayed little evidence of leadership qualities. And that was strange. In the war, he had been a Spitfire pilot and a successful one at that. After all, he had survived. But now, in his mid-forties, he seemed to be devoid of ambition. Perhaps he had burnt himself out and had settled for a quieter life. That might be understandable, but it was difficult to accept.

Yet Norman was supportive and evinced great charm with the elderly customers who always sought him out for investment advice. He was able to woo them to their evident delight and it certainly led to worthwhile business for the branch.

There was a knock on his door and, at his call to come in, long-time supervisor Barbara Bolton entered the room. "Are you ready to call your ledger, sir?" she asked.

After the day's excitement, a request like that was enough to bring him down to earth. Each day, the balances calculated on statement sheets had to be compared with those recorded on the respective ledger sheets. This ensured that the customer's statement was a true record of the bank's ledger. Pairs of staff carried out this tedious task of 'calling' the balances and David felt it was only equitable to take his turn.

"I suppose so," he answered. Barbara would understand his lack of enthusiasm. She had been at the branch for over thirty years and none of his predecessors would have relished calling ledgers.

"But one other thing," he added. "Don't let your girls nip off early this evening. Before we leave, I'm going to hold a staff meeting... about security. It won't take long."

"Of course," Barbara agreed, frowning. "But, before then, make sure you don't keep me waiting with that ledger calling."

After admonishing him, her frown turned to a smile and she left for her machine room. Perhaps she was justified in laying down the law. She always ran her section like clockwork. In fact, he considered her to be the office lynchpin, knowing customers intimately – not personally, but from their accounts and files.

There was only one problem: she would soon be leaving. And it was partly his fault – following a decision he had made some nine months ago.

"I need a loan of £30,000," her husband, Geoff, had said when he came in to see him last June.

"£30,000?" he had exclaimed. That was enough to buy thirty new limos.

"I'm going to southern Spain – Marbella," Geoff replied.

"I'm setting up a company to build holiday homes."

"Why would the Spanish want holiday homes in Marbella?"

Geoff grinned. "Not the Spanish. They're for the Brits."

What on earth was he talking about? Blackpool, Newquay, Torquay – not forgetting Barnmouth – were the chosen holiday destinations for the Brits.

"I think you'd better explain," he simply said.

"I reckon there's going to be an expansion in air travel," Geoff said. "Jets are going to replace the propeller jobs. Getting to places like Spain will then be much quicker. And think about the weather. Two weeks lying on a beach, without that rain of ours."

"But people won't be able to afford it."

"They will when it starts to get popular. Prices will then come tumbling down."

"Be that as it may," David said, almost shuddering at the sheer speculation of the scheme, "why do you need as much as £30,000?"

"Set-up costs and then building the first stage of the development."

"And after that?"

"It'll all be self-financing."

It had always been bad enough getting Regional Office to sanction facilities for developments in this country, never mind Spain. And from what he had heard about this project, it was a non-starter for him, never mind Regional Office.

"How much are you putting up front?" he asked. In any borrowing proposition, customers were normally required to put in a third, or even half, of a project's costs. Investing such a stake certainly helped to concentrate minds.

"Me? Well… nothing, actually. That's why I've come to you."

David had feared the worst. "What about security?"

"There'd be the holiday homes, of course."

"Out in Spain?"

"That's where they're being built."

Never mind the sarcasm, getting effective security over partly-built properties in another country? A thousand miles away? In itself, this made the proposition a non-starter. So, he turned the request down flat – without even reference to Spattan.

Now, nine months later, the venture was under way. Geoff had, apparently, managed to raise funds from a Spanish bank. But not enough. So Barbara had been saving hard and was selling their Barnmouth house. She would then leave the bank in June to help run the company.

What a sad loss she would be to the branch. Foregoing such experience was also a further reason for getting Jane more involved in all aspects of dealing with customers' accounts.

As he contemplated calling that ledger, he considered what he would say at his security-meeting with the staff. But, almost immediately, Katie Tibbs came through on the telephone.

Katie Tibbs.

This girl really was a one-off. Still only nineteen, she managed to combine the ebullience of youth with maturity far beyond her years. And she certainly turned heads. Yet there was nothing voluptuous about her. Yes, boys queued up to date her, but last year 'plain Jane' had been her main concern. She was anxious for the older girl to share in the attention she enjoyed herself. To that end, she had been behind Jane's makeover. Since then, Jane had been going steady with John from the golf club. And Katie was now the one without a boyfriend. How ironic was that?

She had been his secretary for only six months. Yet, how could she have become so efficient in such a short time? She had certainly disproved the staff controller's opinion that the position demanded someone more senior. But David had stood his ground.

Her predecessor had been more senior and look what had happened to her. Miss Harding's formidable and forbidding persona had shielded an unsuspecting vulnerability. So much so, that it had led to her suspension and eventual sacking. David could never imagine Katie getting involved in financial irregularities. But until it happened, he had also thought the same about Miss Harding.

There was only one problem with Katie: she was such a chatterbox.

"You're wife's on the phone, sir," she said, when he lifted the black Bakelite receiver. "She wants to speak to you, but didn't say what it's about. I suppose she wouldn't, would she? And I certainly wouldn't ask, sir. But she sounds ever so worried. I hope she's all right. It could be about the threat of the raid. That was enough to make anyone worried. She'll be so relieved nothing's happened and…"

"All right, Katie." This was hardly the time to encourage her chit-chat. "Just put her through."

"David," Sarah gasped, as she came on the line. "It's Mark. I've had a threatening letter – an anonymous one. It was at work – this lunch time… Darling… I'm going out of my mind with worry."

# CHAPTER 4

Speed was now the essence.

With winter well behind them, David was thankful he had resurrected his Raleigh sit-up-and-beg for his journeys to and from the bank. Walking would normally take him about twelve minutes, but it was more like three or four on his bike.

With Sarah's distraught words ringing in his ears, it would be even quicker this afternoon. Speeding past the amusement arcades, he hardly heard the cacophony emanating from the pinball machines and other contraptions which relieved punters of their pennies and sixpences.

Back in the office, Sarah's call had shaken him badly. He had never known her so agitated. But his own initial distress soon turned to anger. Having received the threatening note at lunch time, why on earth had she waited until late afternoon before ringing him? What could have been so important to delay her telling him immediately? For God's sake, Mark was his son, as well.

He now regretted being sharp with Jane. She did not deserve that. He had bluntly said he had to go; he had a problem at home. The staff meeting would be postponed until the morning. And Barbara would need to find someone else to call his ledger.

He was still seething as he reached the promenade, impatiently ringing his bell at a pedestrian who had the temerity to attempt to cross his path. His blood was boiling – and not from pedalling so hard.

Cycling along the hotel-lined promenade, he dwelt on the brief words he had exchanged with Sarah. He had not quizzed her comprehensively; far better to do this face-to-face. The writer of the note had not been specific; Mark was about to come to some harm, whatever that meant. Pure intimidation appeared to be the immediate motive. But one thing was specific: on no account should Sarah alert anyone – especially the police or her husband. Yet she had told him – eventually. Thank heaven for that. Throughout their ten-year marriage, they had always sought one another's support and comfort in times of crisis. Today was clearly no exception. But why had she delayed telling him?

Strangely enough, as he made towards their three-bedroom semi, he started to cool down. Perhaps it was the calming influence of the aromatic cherry blossom which infused the road at this time of the year. Whatever, it was no bad thing. He would need kid gloves when he got in the house. If any shoulder was to be leaned on, it would surely be his.

A few minutes ago, he had visualized himself throwing his bike down in the small front garden of their house and hurtling through the front door. But as he reached their home, his new-found inner calm enabled him to lean the cycle against the porch before carefully inserting his Yale key into the front door lock.

As soon as he was through the door, Sarah rushed from the kitchen and fell against his still-heaving chest. She wrapped her arms around him and he grasped her tightly. Their intimacy made him wonder how he could have possibly been so cross with her those few moments earlier.

It took much to break Sarah's resolve. But when matters might adversely affect their only child... Perhaps, it was because they could not give him a brother or sister. No matter, nothing must hinder his well-being. Not that they wrapped him up in cotton wool. He got into the normal scrapes of any growing child, but Sarah's protective instincts were always well to the fore.

David could feel her stifling her sobs against his chest and she eventually drew back from him, seeking his attention through glistening eyes. "Thank goodness you're here," she said, her normal composure already returning. "I've been going out of my mind. What are we going to do?"

"First of all," he replied, pecking her pert nose and leading her towards the lounge and the haven of their Grieves and Thomas settee, "you better tell me exactly what happened. When did you actually get the note? And where did it come from?"

"It suddenly appeared on my desk," Sarah replied, wiping her eyes with a cotton handkerchief she had withdrawn from the sleeve of her cardigan. "It was in a plain envelope – with my name on it. I'd taken a batch of work to the machine room and when I got back, it was there."

"But when? What time was it?"

"Half the girls had just gone off to lunch, so it must have been just after twelve."

"Twelve?" David exclaimed, drawing back from her, his anger returning. This was madness. "And you waited until four before phoning me?"

Sarah's eyes flashed at his sharpness. "You had your own problems at work. Remember?"

He did not need to be reminded of that, but now regretted letting her know of his own worries. If he had not phoned her before lunch about the possible raid, she would surely have immediately told him of the threat to Mark. A threatening note about their only child far outweighed anything linked to work – even the warning of a potential bank raid. No, her answer was not the one he sought.

"And I was frightened," Sarah added hastily, correctly gauging his reaction which he clearly had no further need to voice. "The note said I must tell no-one – not even you. And I feared the worst... if I didn't do what I was told."

David drew her back to him. His impulsive reaction had been unfair. What would he have done in her place? Rational thinking was far easier after the event – here, in the comfort of their own home.

And it was not as if Sarah was in familiar surroundings at work. She had only started at the bank's Newton Abbot branch a few weeks earlier and was still finding her feet. From day one, her peers had viewed her with suspicion. They all knew her husband was manager at Barnmouth. Was she one of them?

"I'm so sorry," he said, stroking her hair. "Of course, I understand."

"And I still feel like a new girl," Sarah said, her eyes glistening again.

And that should never have been so.

Prior to Mark's birth, Sarah had been enjoying a successful career with National Counties. When he had turned five, she felt she needed to return. Although working mothers might well be rare, she only wanted to work part-time. But the bank refused; it was only recruiting full-timers – despite its previous high regard for her.

Then, a few months ago, the powers-that-be relented. They offered her a ten-till-two casual/clerical post, mainly to provide lunch-time cover in the busy market town branch of Newton Abbot.

"But you started last month," David said, feigning a look of puzzlement and pointedly counting his fingers. "You must have been there… let me see… it must be all of three or four weeks, by now. How can you possibly still feel like a new…"

Sarah drew back from him and gently slapped him on his cheek. Although she immediately re-buried her head in his chest, he knew that his riposte had helped to lighten the dark mood which had engulfed them.

"But what did you do next?" he asked, believing that she now felt able to continue.

"I rang the school straight away," she said, pulling back from him and wiping her eyes again with her handkerchief. "I just asked how Mark was. I said he hadn't felt a hundred percent at breakfast. They said he was fine. I phoned again before I left work and again when I got home. Typical neurotic mother they must have thought," she added, able to smile at the school's supposed reaction.

This was more like the old Sarah.

"And I made sure I was at the school gate well before Mark was due to come out."

"And then you phoned me?"

"Yes, as soon as we got home. By then I knew for certain that Mark was all right. Until then, it was enough for me to go through it all – without you having to share it."

It was typical of Sarah's innate consideration for him, but on this occasion, he had to question her judgement. It was far too traumatic for her to bear alone. Once she knew that Mark was unharmed, she should have told him.

But no more recriminations.

Yet where was the boy now? And, for that matter, Dad? In all the tension, he had completely overlooked the obvious.

"Mark's upstairs," Sarah replied, smiling quizzically at his embarrassment. "He's looking through his football programmes – yet again. And your Dad went out to get the Herald Express. He should be back soon."

That was a relief, then.

Poring over his beloved Torquay United programmes would keep Mark out of the way. They had started going to matches together at the beginning of this season. Mark was convinced that it was his influence that, for the first time ever, the team was vying with the leaders of the 3rd Division (South). United had even scored seven goals in successive home games in February. That had buoyed Mark's enthusiasm no end.

As for Dad, thank goodness he was out. Following a car

crash in which Mum had been tragically killed, he had lived with them for the last seven years. But it had not been easy. He had developed extraordinary behavioural traits. These had eventually been diagnosed as the result of an incurable head injury, caused by the accident. Excessive use of the wireless was one of Dad's more annoying foibles. It was as well that they were not having to battle with the airwaves during this heart-to-heart with Sarah.

"Let me see the note," David suddenly said. Another major oversight! He was supposed to be the logical one of the family, yet he was disregarding the most obvious points.

Sarah delved into her handbag and retrieved it surprisingly quickly from the myriad contents. The message was brief, but irritatingly unspecific.

'Keep a close eye on Mark if you don't want him to come to any harm. And don't even think of telling anyone about this – especially the police or your husband.'

The warning might not be specific, but the intent to scare was clear enough. No wonder Sarah had been so frightened.

"This could easily be linked to the threat at my branch," David mused, re-reading the wording in his hand. "Even though the handwriting's different, it's too much of a coincidence. What do you..."

"Darling," Sarah suddenly blurted out, her face etched with concern. "I'm so sorry. I never asked you... about your own problem. I've been so caught up in myself. What happened?"

"Nothing, thank God."

"Was it a hoax?"

"Could be. Especially as my warning was specific for this afternoon. Can we draw comfort from that?"

"I don't know," Sarah replied, frowning. "But I can't take any comfort from this one. Whatever harm he's talking about could come at any time."

"He?"

Sarah shrugged. "He? She? Who knows? But you'd assume this sort of threat would come from a man."

Not necessarily, but he could see her point. "But you don't know who put it on your desk?"

"No. I asked the other enquiry clerks and the cashiers, but none of them had been given it by a customer. I couldn't ask everyone, though. The office is too big. And quite a few had gone off to lunch."

David was not surprised at the answer. Anyone could have taken the envelope in over the counter, possibly in a batch of other items. It would have been far easier to identify the source at Barnmouth where he had only ten staff. There must be over fifty at Newton Abbot.

"Did you give anyone an inkling that something was wrong?"

"I don't think so. It said don't tell anyone and I didn't want to give any impression of being worried."

Good girl. That must not have been easy.

"But Greville thought something was wrong," Sarah added.

"Greville?"

"Yes. He came by my desk at about half-twelve and asked if I was all right. He said I looked off-colour."

"I'm not surprised," David said. No doubt she was as white as a fiver. "But you didn't say anything to him?"

"Of course not."

No, but in other circumstances, Greville Gladstone, or GG as he was always affectionately known, would have been another shoulder to lean on.

'Best friend' might be more applicable to school chums, but Greville had continued to be David's best friend long after they had left Torquay Grammar. They had then joined National Counties together. Their careers had followed similar paths until

GG's had stalled at Newton Abbot where he was still in charge of the securities department. Management did not seem to be beckoning – probably because he was too technically minded. The bank was not seeking boffins for its managers. Just as well, as far as David was concerned. But the situation had not affected their deep friendship and they regularly had a convivial pint or two at nearby Coombe Cellars Inn on a Friday evening.

"But now you've told me, what about the police?"

"The note says I mustn't."

"But you've told me."

"That's different."

"I don't see why. And the police are bound to be discreet. What's more, they'd know exactly what to do. They'd also expect us to tell them."

Sarah looked unconvinced.

"This afternoon," he continued, "I was really impressed by the police. It was a DC Pound and…"

"Pound? He was the one I saw last year. The one who came to see your Dad in December – with Inspector Hopkins. Remember?"

How could he forget?

Yet he had not made the connection this afternoon. After all, his dealings had only been with the inspector. Dad had unwittingly been a witness in respect of the murder which had rocked Barnmouth. That irrational behaviour of his had bizarrely provided the vital clue to the killer's identity.

"Well, DC Pound was great this afternoon. I'd put my complete faith in him. If the two notes might be linked, he's clearly the man we should speak to. What do you think?"

Sarah's mouth opened and closed as she struggled to seek an answer.

That was not surprising. They were effectively re-enacting a scene they had recently witnessed at the Odeon in Torquay. In the film, the police had been brought in on a kidnapping and the perpetrator had eventually been apprehended. But not before all manner of traumas had beset the family of the victim.

"I don't think we have any option," she eventually replied, her eyes moistening. "If not, we'll go out of our minds with worry... waiting for something to happen... or expecting a follow-up threat."

She was right; there really was no option. He needed to call DC Pound now, before Dad returned.

Nodding in acknowledgement of Sarah's wise counsel, David rose from the settee and went to the telephone in the hall.

## CHAPTER 5

Taking her time and relishing her return to the familiar town she had not seen for ten years, Doris Martingale reached her destination – Barnmouth's branch of National Counties Bank.

She had always admired this particular bank which stood majestically on the corner at the bottom of the High Street. The York stone construction was so different from the stark concrete structures which dominated the avenues and streets of her new home town of New York.

How she loved the Manhattan skyline, but she did miss the quaintness and charm of English towns and villages.

Typical was the route she had taken to the bank from St Mary's at the top of the town, an area devoid of day trippers. Their Royal Blue and Wallace Arnold charabancs would simply deposit them at the sea-front attractions.

The church dominated the upper part of the town and its dignified presence seemed to survey everything that stretched below. It was as though it were trying to maintain a sobriety which modern custom did its best to eschew down by the sea. Doris thought of the church almost as a Mother Goose, its train of goslings being the mishmash of properties which cascaded down the street to the promenade.

The houses and shops certainly needed maternal care, their infrastructures no doubt requiring constant attention. Yet all had somehow survived the passing centuries, history oozing from nooks and crannies, peg-tiled fascias, old oak beams and faded thatched roofs.

New York, this definitely was not.

Doris found the bank little-changed after these past ten years, except for a smart white flagpole which had been erected over the doorway. For some reason, the fluttering blue and yellow flag had Torquay United's name emblazoned on it.

Averting her eyes to the entrance, Doris mounted the steps to the oak front door. She would be sorry to leave behind her the aroma of freshly-made bread which wafted through her nostrils from the adjacent Western Bakery shop.

Although she had previously lived in Totnes, she had kept her account at Barnmouth. She had transferred it there just before the war. It was when Arthur had opened his accountancy business in the town. Since then, there had been no reason to change. She never needed to see the manager and the bank had set up a perfectly acceptable open credit arrangement for her to cash cheques at Totnes.

On the other hand, it had meant a train journey today; she had felt it better to visit the bank personally to sort out why she did not now appear to be getting her bank statements. It also gave her the chance to renew acquaintance with her beloved Barnmouth.

She was pleased to find the banking hall bereft of other customers and made her way past a couple of small tables and accompanying chairs to the mahogany counter. A smart young cashier, stacking half-crowns and florins in neat one pound piles on a shelf within his till, looked up, smiled broadly and asked how he could help her.

"My name's Doris Martingale," she replied, returning his smile. She resisted the urge to preface her words with "Hi", this salutation now coming so naturally from her acquired Americanism. "I've had an account with the bank since I left school... my goodness, that's nearly sixty years now. But it's only been here in Barnmouth since just before the war. I've not been in here for the last ten years, but..."

"Was it something we said?" the cashier interjected, his good humour matching his smile.

"No, no, of course not," she answered, immediately striking an affinity with the cashier who she now saw from the nameplate on the counter was called Trevor Smith. In only a few words, he had put her at her ease. "I went to live in New York – straight after the war."

"New York?" Trevor exclaimed, his blue eyes shining. "It's always been my ambition to go there. 52nd Street – that's where I'd make for."

"You like your jazz, then," Doris replied, having enjoyed several visits to the street which had spawned an array of jazz clubs. It all started there after be-bop had introduced itself to its incredulous fans.

"My idol's Sonny Rollins," Trevor said, warming to a topic that she had not expected to be raised in National Counties Bank. "I play the tenor sax a bit myself, but it's so dispiriting hearing what Rollins can do."

"He probably felt the same when he first heard Coleman Hawkins."

Trevor's eyebrows almost broached his hairline. "Are you into jazz?"

"And why not, young man?" These youngsters! Yet, he could hardly expect a seventy-five-year-old to be the hippest swinger in town. "When I was your age, Louis Armstrong was my idol. And once you're hooked on such wonderful music... But I didn't come in here to talk about jazz; I have a problem. I've not been getting my bank statements. Do you think I could see someone about it?

"Of course," Trevor obliged. "I'll get our supervisor to come out and see you. Her name's Barbara Bolton."

"Mrs Bolton? Is she still with you? I've known her since before the war."

"That's before my time," Trevor said, grinning.

There was that sense of fun again. Doris smiled. Trevor Smith must be popular with customers, not to mention the other staff.

"I'll go behind and have a word with her," he added, locking his till carefully before leaving his position.

At least her query would be handled by someone she knew. Mrs Bolton had always been extremely efficient. She had dealt with Arthur's business accounts until they were closed down after he had been killed in the middle of the war. His death was the prime reason why Doris had eventually gone to New York.

As she waited, she thought back to how their daughter, Alison, had met Hank, a GI based at Slapton Sands prior to the Normandy landings. The whole South Hams area had been requisitioned under defence regulations to accommodate thousands of American soldiers. This led to three thousand residents being evacuated, having only six weeks to find alternative housing. Being bereaved and living nearby in Totnes, Doris thought it would do her good to take in one such family and it was through them that Alison had got to know Hank in a Totnes pub.

When he returned from France, a casual relationship developed into a serious romance. With marriage then on the horizon, Doris was thrilled when the youngsters pleaded with her to join them in New York and, being widowed, she thought "why not?" Her only stipulation had been that they must live on their own and she would rent an apartment of her own.

Her thoughts were broken into when Mrs Bolton appeared and beckoned her over to the enquiries counter. The supervisor seemed visibly shocked at seeing her. But being away for ten years, it was a wonder Mrs Bolton even recognised her.

"How nice to see you again," Barbara Bolton said, quickly regaining her composure, colour brushing her cheeks. "It must be all of eight years…"

"Ten, actually," Doris said, offering her hand. "But walking down to the bank, I found that little seems to have changed in Barnmouth. And to find you still here is a real bonus."

"Some things never change," Barbara Bolton replied, smiling. "It's a good job I've enjoyed working here. Anyway, how can I help you?"

"I don't seem to be getting my bank statements. I know I'm living abroad now and don't use my account, but I should still get my statements... if only occasionally?"

"Of course you should. But you're sure you've not overlooked them?"

"I suppose that's possible. I am getting rather forgetful these days. But could you please check my address... to make sure you've got it down correctly?"

"Of course. I'll do that right away."

"Oh, and can I have my latest statement now, please?"

"You certainly can," Barbara Bolton replied and then disappeared into the back office.

As Doris awaited her return, she exchanged smiles with young Trevor Smith and surprised herself by thinking how she might have reacted if she had been fifty years younger.

It was as well she could not dwell on this, Mrs Bolton soon returning with the address card. It duly confirmed the bank had the correct details recorded. "But I'm sorry," she then said, "I can't let you have your up-to-date statement. The ledger and statement sheets are held alphabetically in cans and the M–R section is in with Mr Goodhart, our manager. I really can't disturb him. Would it be all right if I put your statement in the post?"

How frustrating! And such a wasted journey. "I suppose I don't have any option," Doris replied, seeing no need to try and hide her frustration. "I certainly can't wait until your Mr Goodhart can be disturbed. I've got to get my train back to Totnes. I'm staying with my sister, so you'd better take down her address."

That done, she turned to leave, still peeved at the inconvenience. But her mood eased somewhat when a smartly-dressed man in his early forties came into the bank and held the front door open for her. He gave her a cheery Trevor-Smith-style grin which made her now wish she were only thirty years younger.

His appearance certainly helped to reduce the disappointment of her wasted visit, but as she made her way out of the bank, she was disconcerted to hear, behind her, Trevor Smith's words of surprise that they had not expected Mr Goodhart to return that afternoon.

# CHAPTER 6

David had certainly not expected to get back to the branch that Thursday afternoon. Even though he had other things on his mind, he grinned at Trevor Smith's obvious surprise.

"I suppose you were hoping for an early finish," he said. In the absence of the manager, staff would always aim for an early getaway.

"The thought never crossed my mind, sir," Trevor replied, looking pained at the suggestion. "Why ever would I want to leave early?"

"All right, all right, let's take your dedication as read. But that lady who just left... who was she? I didn't recognise her."

"Mrs Martingale. You wouldn't know her, sir. She's over from New York."

"Not a customer, then?"

"Oh, yes. She's been with the bank for nearly sixty years. But she went to the States straight after the war. I think she's back here on holiday. But, you know what?"

David waited. It was the sort of rhetorical question that did not expect an answer.

"She's just made my day," Trevor duly obliged.

Made his day? This Mrs Martingale must be in her seventies. "Not a bit old for you, Trevor?"

The cashier grinned. "You've a one-track mind, sir. No, you'd never believe it. She's into jazz."

Now, that was certainly something; music to David's ears and a shared interest with Trevor. Foot-tapping rhythms set both their pulses racing. Yet his love of the music had resulted in severe misgivings. It went back to his youth – back to a bequest from dear old uncle Wilfred. His favourite relation had meant well, but at the time, no self-respecting teenager would have wanted to be seen in possession of his uncle's prize possession.

A banjo.

The instrument was symptomatic of the roaring twenties; but by the mid-thirties, jazz had moved on. It was more sophisticated: Ellington, Goodman, Basie – not a banjo in sight. No, if he had still been alive, Uncle Wilfred would have understood. Ditching his beloved banjo – consigning it to the dustbin – had been the only option. Right?

Wrong.

But how was he to know that the current trad-jazz craze would resurrect the plucked stringed instrument? How could he have predicted that he might have become a rival to Lonnie Donegan? Fame and fortune could have been at his command; his other natural talents would have been denied to National Counties Bank.

It was almost enough to drive David to drink. Instead, he had cast his attentions to listening to modern jazz, often frequenting his favourite haunt – the Walnut Grove Club in Torquay's suburb of Chelston. It was there, a Friday night only two months ago, that he had the surprise of his life.

Trevor had emerged from back-stage, tenor saxophone clasped to his chest. Joining the rhythm section, he roared into his interpretation of *Lady Be Good*. Notes cascaded from his horn in the best traditions of Coleman Hawkins and Lester Young. Eyes closed in concentration, it was as if he was trying to prove that the music had lost nothing in its three thousand mile journey across the Atlantic.

And he was quite oblivious of his manager sitting in the audience.

At the end of the set, they came face-to-face. Trevor was visibly shocked. It was probably not so much at finding his manager there, but that his evening endeavours might be construed as taking on additional employment – something prohibited by National Counties.

But he had no need to worry. David's main concern was whether their musical empathy might influence his judgement of the boy's banking capabilities and career prospects.

Now, it seemed that Mrs Martingale might be a partner in crime. "How on earth did you find that out?" he asked, re-focussing on Trevor and seeing the old lady in a new light. Jazz was not an expected subject matter between cashier and customer – particularly with someone like Mrs Martingale.

"She said she lived in New York and I told her my ambition – to go to 52nd Street. She seemed to know all about it. I couldn't believe it."

"Lucky her." 52nd Street was the Mecca of modern jazz. The Three Deuces; Hickory House; Downbeat – these were names of clubs to drool over, but at least Torquay had the Walnut Grove. "I'd better meet this lady."

"You might not be lucky, sir. Barbara told me she's staying with her sister in Totnes, but she's going home soon."

"Perhaps next time she's over, then. At least, I could drop her a line."

Mrs Martingale might even be among the dormant accounts Jane was looking into. Not that her living abroad meant her account was inactive. He would mention it to Jane. No doubt she would also be surprised at his unexpected return to the branch.

His visit to Torquay's police station had been quicker than expected. The threatened raid was naturally on the agenda; that was what he had told his staff at this morning's meeting on security. In actuality, his prime concern was the threat to Mark.

Yesterday afternoon, he had managed to speak to DC Pound who readily acknowledged there might be a connection between the two threats, so much so that he wanted his boss to attend the meeting which he fixed for early this afternoon. The timing clashed with Sarah's working hours and David did not want her to make excuses for leaving early at Newton Abbot. Tongues could easily start wagging. So it was agreed this initial meeting would be with him alone.

He had taken the winding coastal road to Torquay and reached the police station in about twenty minutes. He was immediately ushered into a sparsely-furnished interview room. A bare wooden table accommodated two chairs on one side and a solitary matching chair opposite. A fourth chair was positioned next to the door and the only other item in the room was a long mirror fixed to the wall behind the table.

Left to his own devices, David sat down on the single chair at the table, thankful he was not awaiting a grilling following his own arrest for some crime or another. Having said that, he was not in the most relaxed frame of mind. It was as though the venue, never mind the room, created a self-induced guilt. Yet, he had arranged the meeting himself; he was here to obtain the support and guidance of the police. On that basis, faces would not, surely, be scrutinizing him through what must be a two-way mirror. And the chair at the door would hardly be required by a policeman on guard.

He had not long to wait before the door behind him opened and he turned to face the comforting hulk of DC Pound. He was also pleased to see that the detective's boss was Inspector Hopkins. They had developed a good rapport at last year's trials and tribulations.

"Inspector Hopkins," he said, smiling, as he rose to greet the two men. "How good to see you again."

"Shall I tell him, or will you?" DC Pound asked the inspector, his eyes twinkling.

"It'd better be you," Inspector Hopkins said. "You know I'm

not one to blow my own trumpet."

DC Pound turned to David. "It's Chief Inspector now."

"Down to last year," Hopkins added, as David thrust out his hand and proffered his congratulations. "And due in no small part to the considerable help you and your staff gave me."

"On that basis," David replied, feigning hurt, "you better have a word with my Regional Office. They haven't seen fit to give me any promotion." And were not likely to, if Spattan had anything to do with it.

"You're probably indispensable at Barnmouth," Hopkins said, smiling. He and DC Pound then took the seats opposite, the fourth one at the door remaining unoccupied – thankfully. "Derek here," he added, "has put me in the picture as to what happened at the bank. I must say I don't like the sound of it."

So much for the hoax theory.

"Of course, it could be a hoax," Hopkins added, as if reading David's thoughts, "but in my experience of such matters – a fairly limited experience I have to say – there's usually more behind these kinds of threats than mere hoaxes."

"You might imagine that gives me little comfort," David said. He was glad Sarah was not present.

"And you can imagine that we're not in the comfort business," Hopkins said. "Not trying to offer false comfort, that is. A dose of realism and pragmatism doesn't do any harm."

"This is all starting to look too real for me."

"Then that's a good start. But don't forget the pragmatism."

"That's not a problem. It's how I've been trained. Looking at the practical angles. Trying to use common sense."

"I could see that last year," Hopkins said. "Do you think there might be a link to what happened then?"

David had already turned that one over. It was possible. But who? There had certainly been bank robbers involved, but their raids all took place around London. Down here, the principal characters were either dead, in jail, or, in Miss Harding's case, self-imprisoned in her mother's home following dismissal. All except John English. The hotelier had appeared to have been involved, but nothing could be proved. And he had been in the bank yesterday morning. Could he be the link?

"It's possible," he replied. But this was getting frustrating – concentrating on the potential raid. When would they get round to the threat to Mark?

Not yet, apparently, as Hopkins continued, "I gather Derek's already put to you the possibility of a grudge factor."

And it had not left his own mind. Names had come to the fore from dark recesses of his mind, but he had dismissed them all. If he had declined an advance, it might have resulted in a snub in the street, or a cold shoulder at Rotary. But threatened violence? Not a chance.

"I really can't see that happening," he said. "Especially in a place like Barnmouth. And I always say "no" with a smile!"

"That might be the problem," Hopkins said, seriously. "Some years ago, I was an impoverished constable and sought a loan for a second-hand Vespa. The bank manager turned me down flat. Maybe I couldn't afford the repayments, but I could have afforded a less smug and sanctimonious way of being declined."

He had a point. The trick was declining with good reason and good grace.

"What about John English?" Pound then asked, as if feeling left out of the exchange.

"I don't think so," Hopkins said, before David could answer. "He knows we're still looking at him closely. He'd be a fool to step out of line now."

And English was no fool. David could not stand the man, his unctuous arrogance being hard to bear. Sarah disliked him even more. She called him slimy, but that was a female thing; something about how she and her girlfriends felt he wanted to paw them at their coffee mornings in his hotel. But a fool? No.

And Hopkins was right. David knew the police still suspected English of some crime or another. Last year, the criminals had used his hotel as a base. But there was no proof of his actual guilt. Not yet, anyway.

"I've an open mind about him," David said, anxious to get the subject changed to Mark and Sarah. After all, that was the prime reason he was here; why he had rung up yesterday to arrange this meeting. "But what about my son? That's what I'm really worried about."

"Tell me what happened," Hopkins said, apparently quite happy now to move on.

David recounted every detail. He had concentrated so hard on what Sarah had told him that it now seemed that he, himself, had suffered all her torment at Newton Abbot branch and with the school.

To give him credit, Hopkins gave his full attention to the evolving tale – as did DC Pound. Were they as worried as he? But the Chief Inspector's response was a disappointing anti-climax.

"I don't know what to think" he eventually said. "I've seen the odd case like this before and I've heard of others. But they've never come to anything. I've not known anyone experience any harm – physically, that is. That's the stuff of films."

Oh, yes? David thought irritably. But your son is not the one being threatened. Your wife is not at the end of her tether. Your home life has not been targeted, as well as the bank. This was certainly not the answer he had been seeking. Hopkins would not get further promotion with such woolly thinking.

Once again, the Chief Inspector seemed to anticipate his thoughts. "But as I said earlier, I still don't like the sound of it

– even though past evidence dictates otherwise. So, we'll certainly keep an eye on things."

More platitudes. Where was the help and support? Hopkins did not seem to have anything substantial to offer. At the very least, Sarah would be expecting to hear about a positive plan of action.

"So what do we do, now?" David asked. Something definite must, surely, come out of this meeting

"For a start," Hopkins said, "we're going to get the handwriting of the two notes analysed."

Well, that was something.

"And I want you to keep alert – and that means your wife, as well. Be especially aware of what's going on around you. It might be blatantly obvious, but, for whatever reason, someone has actually written these notes."

And that was about it – for the time being, anyway.

As David sought out his two-tone blue and white Hillman Minx in the car park and then started the drive back to Barnmouth, deep dissatisfaction hung over him like a storm cloud. But was he being unfair to the Chief Inspector? Was there more he could have done at this stage? Hopkins had said he was not there just to provide comfort, but where was his guidance? Perhaps he was right to play it low key and keep the meeting short. Perhaps he had a more pressing case to attend to. Whatever, David had the distinct feeling that it would be primarily down to him to sort out what was going on. If that proved to be the case – the police only providing a supporting role – he might even be the one in line for promotion this time. Not that the bank was likely to think along those lines.

He started the Minx's descent towards the river which separated Barnmouth from the coastal road to Torquay. The drive had actually done him good. Despite his overall dissatisfaction at the meeting, somehow, he felt up to the challenge. And he knew that Sarah would be, too. In normal circumstances, they both liked to view things positively. So, why not this time? One way or the other, they had to overcome these threats.

At least, he had not received a call from Sarah. He had given her strict instructions to phone him at the bank, or the police station, if anything – anything at all – untoward had happened.

After parking the car, he was also relieved to find all was quiet in the bank. It was now past two-thirty and he soon learnt from Trevor Smith that the only stranger in the branch had been Mrs Martingale.

But throughout the journey from Torquay and, now in the office, he could not forget the Chief Inspector's parting shot. It was the only tangible thing to come out of the meeting: someone – or even two people? – had actually written the two notes.

But who?

## CHAPTER 7

Doris Martingale left the bank in a better frame of mind than she had first expected. She might be well into her seventies, but the allure of the opposite sex was not entirely dormant. Two men – one without even speaking – had effectively distilled her chagrin at not being able to get her bank statements sorted out.

What if it had been fifty years ago? She really would have wanted to court the attractions of young Trevor Smith. His appeal had such a potent mix: craggy good looks; charm; intelligence; and a quizzical sense of humour that burst from him like the sun emerging from a leaden sky. She might not have got a look in, but, by heaven, she would have tried.

As she might have done, years later, for the equally attractive Mr Goodhart. There could be no doubt that he was the man who had opened the door for her. Yet his manifest appeal failed to eclipse from her mind the words of Mrs Bolton. How could the supervisor not disturb him in his room when, there he was, coming into the bank from the High Street?

There had to be a reason; Mrs Bolton would not have made up the excuse. She was simply not that sort of person, someone who had always epitomized the bank's efficiency – from way before the war. No problem on Arthur's business accounts had ever been too hard for her to rectify. She knew her banking procedures intimately, not to mention all the legal requirements. Doris smiled to herself as she recalled how Mrs Bolton had once quoted verbatim the Bills of Exchange Act when Arthur had queried why a particular cheque could not be paid into his account. From that day on, he had called her his legal seagull, reflecting his admiration for the gulls that swooped and soared along this South Devon coastline.

As she passed the amusement arcades and ice cream parlours, including her favourite, Pelosi's, Doris quickened her pace towards the station. Her train back to Totnes left at two-fifty and the next one would not be along for another hour. It was good to be back in Barnmouth, but she could do without a further hour on a draughty station platform.

Her route took her past Arthur's old office and waves of nostalgia swept through her. From childhood sweethearts to that fateful stray bomb, they had rarely been parted, even working together in the business. Friends had said that it would never work. But it had. Early on, there had been an occasion when he had been dictating a letter to her and she had queried his use of a particular word. He had made it quite clear that, in such a situation, he was the boss. From that moment on, it had, indeed, worked.

She had learnt so much from him, particularly about organization. His training and financial discipline had certainly helped after his death. She had even introduced his beloved filing system into her home life. It was as though his presence was still with her. If she had a problem at home, she still asked his advice. What would others say, if they heard her? But it gave her such comfort.

The road curved to the left and began to run alongside the railway track. As Doris walked, her thoughts moved on to Alison, then to Hank and their subsequent life in New York. What a blessing the young had been, splendidly filling the void left by Arthur.

As the train station came into view, her mind drifted back to her childhood. Such happy times. Schooldays were particularly joyous – apart from one lasting blemish at primary school. Nearly seventy years later, she still felt the indignity of being on the receiving end of the headmistress's slipper. It was not the form of punishment that had offended her, nor the pain, which was minimal. No, it was the sheer injustice of being punished for having her eyes open in prayers. Even as a six-year-old, she could perceive that a teacher's eyes must also have been open to have seen her.

Despite then living through two world wars and the Depression of the thirties, life had continued to be far from unhappy. Arthur, until his untimely death, had mainly accounted for that. After that, it had been Alison. And her love of jazz had always provided a lift when it was most needed. It had been good talking to Trevor Smith and recalling her first love of Louis Armstrong. The music of Benny Goodman and Glenn Miller had then entered her life. Then, moving to New York, she had grown to love the clubs. She had even seen Trevor Smith's idol, Sonny Rollins. It was at the Village Vanguard, a basement club in downtown Manhattan. But she did not have the heart to confess this to the cashier. That would have been out of order. It might well have hurt the boy whose likely chances of realizing his dream were slim – in the short-term, at least.

Reminiscences. It was as though her whole life was being played out before her. It certainly put in perspective her frustration at not getting her bank statement. But what did that really matter? It was only a piece of paper confirming the few thousand pounds she had on the account. But she needed the bank's confirmation before passing the bulk of it on to Alison and Hank. Far better for them to have it now than waiting until she had passed on. She could sort this out tomorrow when she received the statement and could see the actual balance on the account.

A shrill whistle pierced the air and interrupted her thoughts. But she breathed in relief as she heard the clickety-clack coming from the west, to her right. An express train sped through the station on its way to Exeter and then, no doubt, on to London. The fireman must have been shovelling coal into the engine's furnace. Acrid black smoke belched from the locomotive's funnel and trailed in the train's wake, drifting down to the adjacent beach.

The noise and activity had certainly broken her train of thought. As she approached the station, she returned to the question of how Mr Goodhart could be in two places at once. On the other hand, that was not her problem; getting her train was now her only concern.

Passing through the booking office, she was glad to have already bought her return ticket; the foyer was overflowing with school-children and accompanying adults. They must have been on some outing or another; it was too early for normal school-leaving time. She had to force her way through the throng and up the metal stairway to the platform. It was already crowded with fellow passengers. What was going on? Perhaps previous trains had been cancelled.

Would she now get a seat? It was only a local stopping train from Exeter to Plymouth, probably with just a half-a-dozen carriages. The last thing she wanted was to have to stand; she had already been on her feet for most of the day.

The platform was getting even more crowded as the school party made its way from the booking hall. The excited babble of the children matched their eagerness to reach the edge of the platform. It took all of her determination to keep them behind her. She could see the likelihood of her getting a seat receding. On the other hand, once on the train, one of the boys might take pity on her and give up his seat. If not, the bulk of the passengers might get off at Newton Abbot, allowing her some comfort for the onward journey to Totnes.

Hearing a distant whistle, she turned to see a plume of smoke in the distance. It was the cue for more jostling on the platform and she splayed her elbows to try and give herself more room. The red signal at the end of the platform clanged down to authorize the train's onward progress. As it approached the station, Doris saw that it was headed by a Prairie 2-6-2 tank engine. Arthur would have been really proud of her. He had been a train buff to his core and had done his best to educate her on the wide range of GWR engines.

As the train entered the station and approached where she was standing, Doris could see it had only two carriages. This caused even more consternation on the platform. But this did not stop her seeing the engine's number on the front of its boiler.

5185.

It was the last thing she noticed. As the crowd jostled behind her, a push in her back made her realize why her life had flashed before her on the way to the station.

The sharp push sent her headlong into the path of the oncoming train.

# CHAPTER 8

David heard about the accident just as he was about to leave for home. It had been a quiet afternoon. There had been few distractions, giving him ample time to ponder on his visit to the police station. He had then told Jane to take advantage of the lull in work and go home early. He would have to mention this to Trevor; even with the manager in situ, it could be possible for staff to leave before five.

But within minutes, Jane had returned. She now sat, ashen-faced, putting him in the picture.

Her route home took her past the railway station, but the way had been blocked by a posse of ambulances, police cars and fire engines. It was patently clear that a major incident had taken place. Bystanders had told her that someone had fallen under a train. All train services had been cancelled and she had returned to the branch to forewarn the other staff. In particular, ledger clerks Jilly and Daphne both used the train to get them home to Newton Abbot.

"Did anyone know how it happened?" David asked, immediately realizing that Jane was unlikely to be privy to such information.

She shook her head. "No. And I'm so sorry... that I'm feeling a bit queasy. It's just the thought of someone having such an accident. It's too awful for words."

"Let's get you a glass of water," David said, getting up. He was not at all surprised at Jane's discomfort. He had spent his war years as a fireman in the RAF. Although major incidents had been infrequent on his station, there had certainly been times when his equilibrium had been upset. The sight of blood could be a particular problem. He well remembered an incident after his demob. He had encountered a major traffic accident outside Exeter. Two cars had overturned and bodies lay by the kerb. Although he had not been involved, simply driving by on the opposite side of the road had turned his stomach. It had made him go weak at the knees and he had been thankful to have been sitting down.

Yes, he could quite understand Jane's reaction. And he would get two glasses of water. The likely outcome of the accident was also making him feel out of sorts.

When he returned to his room, he found some colour had returned to Jane's cheeks. She sipped her water and then seemed eager to re-start their conversation.

"I wonder if it was anyone we know," she said, wiping her moist lips with her handkerchief.

"Unlikely," he replied. As opposed to Torquay, Barnmouth was not a large town, but the chances of knowing the person were slim. A train passenger could also be a visitor. Although the holiday season was not yet underway, day trippers frequented the town throughout the year. One of Barnmouth's popular features was the haven of wildlife in its centre, a meandering stream attracting a wide variety of birds. Specific sanctuaries had also been set up to encourage ducks and wild geese to share the habitat of the resort's famous black swans. But the area's tranquillity would now be shattered by what had occurred just up the road at the station.

"We'll probably know tomorrow," David added. "It's bound to be in the evening's Herald Express. If it turns out to be a customer, we might even know earlier."

"I certainly hope it's not a customer," Jane said, screwing up her face. "That would be horrible."

David nodded. Last year's tragic death of butcher customer, George Broadman, had been bad enough for him – and the town.

With that thought whirling round his mind, he soon sent Jane on her way again and he was thankful that he had his car at the bank to get him home. He was hardly in the mood to cycle.

The road alongside the station was still cordoned off and he had to take an alternative route. It took him through the middle of the town and then around its outskirts.

Passing the black swans as they elegantly cruised along their stretch of water, he had to force himself not to draw haematic connotations from their bright red beaks. There was likely to be much blood and gore at the station. How could those in the emergency services cope with that? As a conscript, he might have had to confront such spectacles, but the people at the station had specifically chosen occupations where they could encounter such sights throughout their working lives. Thank goodness he had gone into banking.

As soon as he was through the front door, the aroma assaulted his nostrils. Assaulted? Caressed, more likely. It could only be leek and potato soup – leeks which Sarah must have lifted from his vegetable patch that morning. She might be a dab hand with the flower beds – castigating him for his alleged lack of selectivity in weeding – but growing vegetables was his domain. He nurtured his leeks through the winter months; then Arran Pilot earlies; followed by runner beans – always Scarlet Emperors. Being well into April, Sarah must have dug up the last of the leeks and he must turn over the ground this weekend, ready for his seed potatoes. They had been in their trays for about six weeks and, with shoots having reached half-an-inch or so, they were ready for planting.

Now, as David closed the front door behind him, he could almost taste the exquisite texture of Sarah's home-made soup. He only hoped this would be followed by his favourite main course – Lancashire Hot-pot.

"I'm home," he called out, as he took off his coat. "Sarah?"

There was no response.

"Sarah?"

At once, all thoughts of soup and vegetables evaporated. In an instant, the whiff of leeks turned into one of fear. He felt weak at the knees, as though he had witnessed another road fatality. Involuntarily, he raised a moist open palm to his mouth. Sarah? Mark? They had to be here.

"Sarah?" he called again, making for the kitchen, only to find it empty.

His worst fears started to envelope him, but he then heard a movement upstairs.

"Hello, darling," Sarah suddenly called out from the landing, then making her way downstairs to greet him with a hug.

Was this what it was going to be like? Every time he came home? Wondering if that note had been a genuine threat? Was the man – yes, Sarah's instinct must be correct; it had to be a man – was he an out-and-out villain? A kidnapper? A paedophile, even?

"Darling?" Sarah said, drawing back from him. She must have felt his vibes. He could not hide his relief to have her in his arms.

"Where's Mark?" he asked, but with things clearly being well, he had no real need for her answer. Easter was only just over a week away; United had three games in four days. Mark must be in his bedroom – checking the statistics; working out the chances of the team getting promoted to the 2nd Division.

"In his bedroom," Sarah duly confirmed. "He's getting so excited about Easter."

But not about the religious festival.

"I was really scared just then," David said, easing Sarah towards their kitchen/breakfast room and the source of that enticing aroma. "I can't wait for Easter, either... the school holidays, I mean. I'll be so glad when Mark's at home with you."

Sarah's clerical job did not include school holidays; otherwise she would not have taken it on. Mark was due to break up tomorrow. Surely, the threat to his welfare must then reduce?

"It was when you didn't answer," David continued, "When I called out. I really feared the worst."

"I'm so sorry, darling," Sarah said, squeezing his hand, as they sat down at their Formica-topped table. "That was my fault. I never thought. I heard you come in, but I just wanted to put the last of the clothes away. I've been ironing ever since I got home."

"Lucky you!" David replied, thankful he had not had to do the ironing. Having said that, he was a dab hand at pressing trousers. It went back to his RAF days. Whether it was by way of brown paper or a damp cloth, he had the knack of achieving knife-edge creases. So much so that Sarah had delegated him to press her own slacks.

"What happened with the police?" Sarah then asked. "What are they going to do?"

"That's the disturbing thing," he answered, knowing he could not give her the comfort she was seeking. "They were very pleasant and it was Inspector Hopkins again – though he's now Chief Inspector. They listened, all right. But as for help?"

"But they've got to help."

"And I'm sure they will – in due course. It's just that… put it this way, I got the impression they hoped the problem would go away."

"But that's crazy."

David nodded. "I know. On the other hand, they probably don't want to put all their resources into something which might be a one-off."

Sarah's eyes flashed. "A one-off? It might be only one thing to them. How do they think we're feeling? I suppose Mark's got to come to some harm before they do anything."

David put his arm around her. He had already wrestled with

that one. He had dwelled on it in his office after his visit to the police station. "We won't let it come to that. But let's first think about it ourselves. Maybe we can work out what's going on."

Sarah's jaw opened in astonishment. "Us?" she cried out, though her eyes had softened.

"Why not? Just think about it. Let's put our heads together and see what we come up with. Is the threat to Mark linked to the warning at the bank? We haven't really thought that one through. Who could do such a thing? Who'd want to do such a thing? And if it's a real threat, what can we do to stop it happening? I've got all sorts of security measures in place at the bank; should we be taking specific precautions here? Never mind on the way to and from school. Once we've done our thinking, we might have some answers… to put to the police… to give them something to work on."

"You think we'll find some answers?" Sarah asked, not hiding her scepticism.

"Perhaps not, but we can try. Incidentally, you know how things are supposed to go in threes…"

Sarah made to interrupt, a 'what now?' query darkening her countenance.

"Don't worry," David added hastily, to stop her in her tracks. "The third thing isn't to do with us. But after our two threats, there's now been a terrible accident at the station. Someone's fallen under a train."

Sarah clasped a hand to her mouth in horror.

"No-one seems to know who it was, or how it actually happened. But the place is chock-a-block with emergency vehicles."

"I'm not surprised. How awful! That's probably why your Dad's not back yet with his paper. He might know more when he gets in."

"I doubt it. I don't think we'll learn any more until tomorrow's Herald Express. And it's unlikely to make the nationals. On the other hand…"

He stopped as Sarah suddenly rose from her chair.

"Sarah?"

"I think we need some respite from all this," she said, smiling for the first time since he got in. "Fancy a stiff drink?"

Perfect. " But I know what I'm also looking forward to."

"You can smell the soup."

"Of course. And to follow? Hot-pot?"

"You'd have hot-pot every meal if you had your way. No, It's sausages tonight."

Well, that was something. Especially with lashings of fried onions. Good heavens, he was starting to think like Julian and Dick in Mark's *Famous Five* books. Next, he'd be hankering to wash it down with a glass of ginger beer.

But there were more serious matters to think about. Perhaps the drink and a meal would help. But would they be able to come up with any answers?

# CHAPTER 9

At this time of year, Friday was always the busiest day of the week. As the clock crept agonizingly slowly towards closing time of three o'clock, Trevor Smith felt almost out on his feet.

It seemed as if all the citizens of Barnmouth had been in to withdraw their weekend requirements. At least, it meant he could keep a tidy till. How different from Mondays – particularly in the summer. The paying-in of weekend takings could turn into a nightmare, notes and coin spilling – sometimes literally – over the counter. Every compartment of his till would be crammed to capacity, notes higgledy-piggledy, all having to be re-counted once the bank had closed. The sheer volume of cash made it virtually impossible to keep his till in any semblance of order.

That was not the case today, but after all his exertions, he could really do with a pick-me-up. It appeared to have arrived when he heard a 'psst' behind him and he turned to see Katie Tibbs.

What was it about this girl that made his heart pound? The only other time it had happened to him had been at Chagford. Apart from the raid, his only other abiding memory from that branch had been the attractive brunette from Lloyds. Each day, the town's banks exchanged cheques under the local cheque clearing arrangement and he had decided to drum up the courage to ask the girl out – even though he did not yet know her name. The raid then put a stop to that and he had not seen her since.

But instead of providing his pick-me-up, he soon found that Katie was there to give him some shattering news.

She had clearly been waiting behind the low wooden screen which separated the back office from the counter run – waiting for a lull in customers at his till before catching his ear with the news.

"Mr Goodhart has asked me to tell you," she said, hardly able to get the words out, tears welling up in eyes which Trevor had only seen sparkle. How he had always envied her sheer vitality, ever-conscious of his own inhibition whenever he was in her presence. At twenty-one, he was a couple of years older than Katie and should have coped easily in her company, yet it was never the case. But here she was, displaying rare vulnerability. He was thankful to have the partition between them, otherwise he might have embarrassed them both by instinctively putting an arm around her shoulder.

"Tell me what?" he asked, encouraging Katie to continue, any ensuing words appearing to be stuck in her throat. Thank goodness, the next customer had gone to Bernard's till. Katie did not need to be inhibited still further by someone waiting to be served by himself.

"I feel so upset for you," Katie then said, as though getting a second wind. "I didn't meet her myself. But Mr Goodhart said you did. He said you got on so well with her. He asked me to apologise to you. He wanted to tell you himself. But an important call came through to him from Regional Office. He said he might be some time and he wanted you to know straight away and..."

This torrent of words was more like the normal Katie, but breaking off to wipe a tear from her cheek was totally alien to her. What was it all about?

"It was her who fell under the train," Katie managed to continue, apparently not realizing that wiping away the tear had left a smudge on her cheek.

"Her? Who, Katie?" She was such a lovely girl, but could be so exasperating. Her mind always seemed to be one step ahead of what she was saying. She knew exactly what she intended. But as for others...

"Mrs Martingale. The lady you saw yesterday. Mr Goodhart said you seemed to really like her. Barbara told me she was having problems with her bank statements. She gave me her latest one yesterday afternoon to post to her. Barbara said she was staying with her sister in Totnes. And now she won't get it. I can't believe I sent something to someone who's now dead. I feel so terrible about it."

And at that, further tears rolled down her cheeks, her eyes craving some form of support. "But it must be worse for you, Trevor," she was able to add. "You actually met her!"

Trevor was stunned by the news. He stared open-mouthed at Katie as she blurted out the story. It was extraordinary that one moment he had been building such a good rapport with such a lovely old lady and within what must have been less than an hour yesterday afternoon, she had died. The whole office had been agog with the news when Jane had returned from the station to tell everyone about the accident. But the thought of actually having known the person had never crossed his mind.

"Ahem."

Trevor turned from Katie to find Mr Sargeant, a partner in next door's solicitors, Ducksworth Sargeant, standing at his till. Katie immediately turned tail and headed for the cloakroom.

"I'm so sorry," Trevor said, hardly able to speak from the shock of what he had just heard. "I hope you've not been standing there long."

"No, no," Mr Sargeant said, smiling kindly. "But I did overhear some of what that young lady was saying. What a tragedy to happen... and to have it occur right here in Barnmouth."

"I...I really can't believe it," Trevor replied. Thank goodness it was almost closing time. Concentration on the job would now be nigh impossible.

"In fact, that's why I've come in," Mr Sargeant said. "I need to see Mr Goodhart. I gather Mrs Martingale was a customer and it looks as though we're going to be acting for her estate."

That was not surprising, Mr Sargeant being the senior partner of the largest solicitors in town. On the other hand, Mrs Martingale lived in the States. Would she not have someone over there? An attorney... was that what they called them? But that was not his problem and he asked the solicitor to sit down while he tried to get hold of Katie for her to tell Mr Goodhart.

Get hold of? Chance would be a fine thing. Not that he could even contemplate such an encounter in the present circumstances. He would much rather have Mrs Martingale standing in front of him – alive and well. What must her family be thinking? Her sister lived in Totnes, but did she have any relatives in the States? If so, no doubt they would be coming over straight away. There would be so much needed to be done and he was thankful the banking side of things would be handled by Mr Goodhart.

He managed to catch the eye of Jilly Sheffield who had just finished machining a list of cheques in the back of the main office and she hurried away to get Katie. When they both returned, Trevor was relieved that Katie had clearly freshened herself up in the rest room and he told her that Mr Sargeant wanted to see the manager.

# CHAPTER 10

Solicitors, and not forgetting accountants, were often the wellspring of new banking business and David was not displeased with the excellent relationship he had developed with Ducksworth Sargeant – formerly Ducksworth, Sargeant and Brown, until the enforced leave of Stuart Brown at Her Majesty's pleasure.

'The Brown Affair' had proved to be the biggest scandal in Barnmouth for many years and the integrity of the town's most prominent solicitors had taken a battering. No-one could believe that such an affluent man as Stuart Brown had become embroiled with a criminal gang which specialized in robbing banks and post offices; though this now seemed to pinpoint the source of his acquired wealth.

It had been to the credit of Oliver Sargeant that the firm was recovering its reputation. The ageing and increasingly-infirm Charles Ducksworth had not recovered from the affair and was in no fit state to take the place of Stuart Brown as senior partner. This left Oliver to take the helm.

He had immediately launched a charm offensive on the town, visiting businesses, holding meetings and giving talks to local organizations. He wrote articles for the press and trade magazines and had told David that he would have taken paid advertisements in periodicals if it had been allowed. His basic message was that the state and future of the firm was as sound as it had ever been. It should not be judged on how one man had usurped his position to curry personal gain from his own criminal activities.

The miracle of Oliver's exercise was that, in such a short time, it had apparently succeeded. He had recently confided to David that clients were now at a record level.

"Many thanks for seeing me without an appointment," he

said, as David ushered him into his room. "What a bad business this is."

David groaned inwardly. Not another problem?

"At the station... last night," Oliver added hastily, as if realizing that David had not been told the reason for his visit. "Mrs Martingale."

"Yes... yes, of course," David acknowledged. He had only been told of the identification half an hour earlier by Chief Inspector Hopkins. The policeman had ostensibly rung to enquire about the well-being of the Goodhart household. Could it be that the Chief Inspector was not immune to what they were going through? He had taken the apparent opportunity of saying he was investigating the accident. It was only after putting down the telephone that David had dwelt on why a chief inspector of police should be getting involved in such an incident.

"I just wondered if Mrs Martingale still had an account with you," the solicitor said. "We're acting on behalf of her estate."

"So soon?"

"Yes, it is a bit quick, isn't it? I had a call this afternoon from her sister in Totnes – Mrs Silverstone. You might imagine she wasn't totally coherent."

"I'm not surprised," David said. "I felt bad enough and I hadn't met the lady."

"So, she's not a customer now?"

"Oh, yes. But she lives in the States. I didn't know of her until yesterday afternoon. She was leaving the branch just as I returned from the police station,"

"The police station?"

Damn his slip of the tongue. "About another matter," he simply said.

"So, when she left here... she probably went straight to the railway station?"

"To get back to her sister's, I suppose."

"Yes. Mrs Silverstone said she expected her back late afternoon. When she didn't arrive by mid-evening, she contacted the police. They immediately treated Mrs Martingale as a missing person. They couldn't identify the victim of the accident straight away – as you might imagine."

"But why did Mrs Silverstone call you?"

"We act for her; have done for many years."

David did not hide his surprise. Why would somebody in Totnes use a solicitor in Barnmouth?

"It goes back to Mr Martingale," Oliver added. "He appointed our firm when he set up his accountancy business. You might not know, but it was here in Barnmouth. I personally got involved when he was killed by a bomb – in the war. I handled the winding up of his estate. Since then, we've looked after his widow. We dealt with the sale of her house when she went to live in the States. And before she left, she very kindly recommended her sister to us."

Oliver paused to blow his nose on a voluminous handkerchief which he extracted from the sleeve of his jacket. Although the solicitor had certain aristocratic tendencies – he also favoured cravats and sometimes sported a monocle – David had always found him to be a down-to-earth man and was not surprised that his leadership had overcome the firm's recent business turbulence.

"When did Mrs Silverstone know that it was her sister who had been killed?"

"This afternoon. A couple of hours ago. The police rang her."

"She had to wait that long? She must have been going spare."

Oliver shook his head in sympathy for his client. "The police eventually recovered Mrs Martingale's handbag. That clearly identified her and they were already treating her as a missing person. I don't want to even try and imagine how Mrs Silverstone took the news. To have something like that happen to such a close relative…"

His words tailed off and David could only agree with such sentiments. He immediately thought of Mark. How would he and Sarah cope if something dreadful happened to their darling son?

His thoughts turned to the police and to Chief Inspector Hopkins, in particular. "Who actually phoned Mrs Silverstone from the police," he asked, unsure of why he should pose such a question, but not expecting to be surprised by Oliver's answer.

"A Chief Inspector Hopkins."

Of course. "He was the one who told me."

"That's not surprising – if he's in charge of the case."

"But would someone of that rank get involved with such an accident?"

"Don't forget Mrs Martingale was being treated as a missing person."

That was logical enough. But Oliver was not to know about Hopkins's involvement in the threats against the bank and Mark. Would it be wise to divulge this to him? No, that would be indiscreet. Although there was no question as to the solicitor's integrity and discretion, these matters must be kept under wraps. In any case, there could be no connection with Mrs Martingale's death.

"The problem I have now," Oliver continued, "is getting the death certificate. I don't know how long the inquest will be. So, at this stage, I can't give you any documentation."

"We'll block the account, anyway," David said. He could not allow further transactions on an account once a customer had died. Any cheques which might be subsequently presented would have to be returned, marked 'drawer deceased'. The payees would then have to make claims against the customer's estate. "We've certainly had effective notice of death. There can't be any doubt about that."

Oliver was clearly pleased at his response.

"When we get the death certificate," David continued, "we can then open a personal representative's account." He paused and then added, "I hope Mrs Martingale made a will."

He had experienced problems when a person had died intestate – without making a will. Such a person could cause their surviving loved ones all manner of problems. He was always amazed how long-lost relations could turn up when there was a whiff of inheritance in the air. Only the making of a will could adequately clarify the intentions of the deceased. He had stressed so often to customers that there was one essential thing that everyone must do before dying: make a will.

"Yes, she has," Oliver replied. "We drew it up before she went to the States. We hold it ourselves… in our office."

"I imagine Mrs Silverstone's the executor?"

"Yes, jointly with me."

"In due course, then, we'll get you both to sign the mandate for the personal reps' account. The executors' account can then take its place when probate's been granted. In the meantime, we'll stop any transactions going through Mrs Martingale's account."

"Good," Oliver said, looking satisfied. "I doubt if the account is very active, anyway… with her living abroad, I mean. And the will's very simple. Her principal asset's likely to be cash – in her bank account. That's where she put the proceeds from the sale of her house. And she also sold all the shares she inherited from her husband. She didn't want anything to do with our stock market while she was abroad."

That was sensible. Her attitude seemed to fit in with Trevor's high opinion of her. And how was the boy taking the news? What a pity Katie had to tell him, rather than David himself.

"I don't blame her for that. With the market being so volatile, long-distance trading could have been a nightmare."

Oliver nodded. "And the will's simplified by her daughter,

Alison, being the sole beneficiary. She was the reason her mother went to the States. Alison met a GI and, after the war, they set up home in New York."

"That must have been a big step for Mrs Martingale."

"Yes. But I gather it worked out well for them all."

"Until now."

Oliver grimaced. "Such a bad business. Now, if you don't mind, I must be on my way."

"I'll hear from you in due course, then," David said, as Oliver rose to leave. Apart from blocking the account, which he would get Jane to do straight away, there was nothing more to be done until after the inquest and receipt of the death certificate. He was only thankful he was not the coroner – and especially not the pathologist. What grim jobs some people did have.

Four hours later, he was dwelling on this as, with eager anticipation, he contemplated sinking his lips into the fine head which adorned his newly-drawn pint of Watney's Red Barrel. Coombe Cellars Inn boasted a host of fine ales and Red Barrel was tonight's choice, mainly because it was Greville's favourite tipple.

Most Fridays they had a convivial pint or two and Sarah had pooh-poohed his protestations that, on this occasion, he should be at home with her. This afternoon, the talk of Mrs Martingale's death – distressing as it was – had actually taken his mind off their own problem of what might or might not happen to Mark.

Yet now?

It was bad enough imagining what Mrs Silverstone was going through, but if Sarah and he were to lose their only child…

But Sarah had been adamant.

She and Mark would be together – behind locked doors. What possible harm could come to them? Nevertheless, she almost had to lever him out of their semi, stressing that this week of all weeks was the one to have a jar and a chat with his very best friend.

She even suggested they ought to draw Greville into their confidence. After all, he was a great friend to her, as well. He had been particularly good, by keeping a close eye on her, when David had attended his five-week pre-management residential training course in Surrey. And now, he worked in the same office as Sarah. It made him ideally placed to keep a further eye on her, should the perpetrator of the note again intend to get to Mark through her.

But it was not a suggestion which met with David's approval.

No, as he awaited Greville's arrival, he knew there were enough other topics they would cover this evening: train accidents; coroners; pathologists; the threat of a bank raid; even whether United would win at Southend tomorrow. His own family problems were not ones to feature tonight.

But where was Greville? It was not like him to be late. That first pint of Red Barrel was almost gone by the time his friend eventually showed up, anxiety etching his face.

For one moment, David feared the worst, but then remembered that Greville often appeared anxious. It was part of his make-up, like his general demeanour, which screamed out the words 'bank clerk'.

Not all bank clerks were small, thin and scrawny. Nor did they all have short-back-and-sides and wear horn-rimmed spectacles. But Greville was exactly the public's perception of how a bank clerk – or any clerk, for that matter – should look.

So often, it was the depiction put out in films. David and Sarah had recently been to the Regal in Torquay to see *The Lavender Hill Mob*. That really was a case in point. Alec Guinness played a seemingly mousy cashier, against Stanley Holloway's larger-than-life entrepreneur. In the film world it could never be the other way round; a larger-than-life bank cashier?

And, unwittingly, Greville compounded the problem; he was a boffin, through and through. He had completed his banking diploma in four years, when it took David (and many others) ten. He knew banking law backwards and was even studying for a law degree in his spare time. After finally getting his own banking diploma, David had vowed never to take another exam again.

But at least Greville enjoyed a pint or two of Red Barrel.

"I'm so sorry I'm late," he gasped, as though he had sprinted from the pub's large adjacent car park. Pushing his horn-rimmed glasses back to the bridge of his perspiring nose only enhanced this perception. "We've got the inspectors."

David smiled in relief. Was that all?

"As usual... ten-past-three... the dreaded ring at the front door!"

"Was the security chain used?" David asked, ordering a couple of pints from the barman. When the inspectors descended on Barnmouth last November, poor Roger Singleton committed the cardinal sin of throwing the front door open with the alacrity of a stage illusionist. The inspectors immediately clocked up their first black mark of the inspection.

"Fortunately, yes. But then we forgot to ask for their identification. Get one thing right and then..."

"No matter how much you drum it into everyone" David said, picking up the pints and leading Greville to a table by the long window which overlooked the River Barn, "when the time comes, someone always seems to drop a clanger."

Greville nodded, now looking less stressed as he took his first gulp of beer.

"Who's the inspector?" David asked.

"Parker – the one you had last year."

"Is he still wearing that crumpled suit and stained tie?"

David had never met such an unkempt person. The irony was that part of the inspector's task was to assess, not just the efficiency, but also the suitability of all members of staff – including their appearance.

"The very same," Greville replied, his own three-piece suit

and stiff-collared shirt being in sharp contrast to the inspector's normal attire.

"But he's a good man."

"You didn't think that on the day he arrived."

That was true. Parker could not have been more intimidating. It was only later in the inspection that David had learnt that the inspector had another agenda – apart from carrying out the usual clerical inspection. Head Office had an inkling that something was seriously amiss in Barnmouth and this then led to 'The Brown Affair'. But, initially, everyone in the office, including himself, had been treated with some suspicion.

"But once things started to come out into the open, he was most supportive. We were definitely on the same side."

"That's because you're a manager."

"Not at all. He was the same with all of us."

Such rapport was not always apparent during branch inspections. There was often a feeling of 'them and us'. Inspectors were deemed to be spies – preying on staff and almost willing them to carry out misdemeanours. It did not encourage an easy relationship.

"Time will tell whether that applies to us," Greville said. "He's bound to have a go at my securities section."

He drained his glass and got up to order refills. David smiled. Greville might be clerkish, but he certainly liked his beer.

"Anyway," Greville said, when he returned to the table, "I don't even want to think about inspections, never mind talk about them; nor work for that matter. What's news with you?"

Where to begin?

"Sure you don't want to talk about work?"

Greville let his eyelids drop in feigned resignation – though maybe not feigned? "Go on, then," he said, wearily.

"How about the threat of a raid?" David said and he

recounted all that had happened on Wednesday. Despite Greville's wish to keep banking off the agenda, he listened, wide-eyed. He had also not yet heard of yesterday's drama at the station. David had already read the comprehensive report in tonight's Herald Express, but Greville's copy, which he had brought into the pub, lay on the table still folded and unopened.

"And this Mrs Martingale," he asked, "was she a customer?"

David nodded, now feeling queasy about what happened at the station. Perhaps he needed a whisky to steady his nerves. But the beer was certainly loosening his tongue, because, on an impulse, he decided to take up Sarah's suggestion and involve Greville with their personal problem.

"And that's not all that's happened this week," he said. Suddenly, he had to unburden himself; share his anxiety. His normal stiff upper lip was beginning to wilt. Sarah and he always shared problems with each other, but he now had an urge for Greville's support. He felt his eyes smarting as he thought of Mark, sleeping in his bed, no doubt dreaming of the fortunes of Torquay United.

"Greville," he continued, trying to compose himself against the distraction of the gulls which, even in the dark, were causing a commotion over the river, just outside the window, "there's something else. We've got a problem... at home."

"You and Sarah?"

"And Mark."

"Health-wise?"

"Not really. Promise to keep this to yourself?"

"Of course, but..."

"We've had a threatening letter... an anonymous one. It was sent to Sarah, to be precise."

"Threatening her?"

" No, Mark. It said we must keep a close eye on him if he's

not to come to any harm."

Greville's eyes widened in alarm. "That's dreadful. Where did it come from? Was there a postmark on the envelope?"

David took a swig of beer, thankful he had decided to recount events which he could still not believe were happening to them. "It wasn't posted. Someone handed it in at your branch. It appeared on Sarah's desk just before lunch – on Wednesday."

"The day your raid was planned."

David nodded and stared into his glass.

"Is that just a coincidence?"

"I don't know. But it was certainly a double blow."

"You've seen the police?"

"The note said Sarah mustn't tell anyone – not me or the police. But, yes, we had to. They probably think it's a hoax. Though they did ring me today – to see if we were all right."

Greville removed his glasses and frowned as he polished the lenses with his handkerchief. "You poor things," he simply said, before leaning forward, intently. "Is there anything I can do to help? I can certainly keep an eye on Sarah at work."

Good man. That would be just the job – just the support Sarah needed. It would be such a blessing for her to turn to Greville immediately – should the unthinkable happen, like another threat.

"You deserve another pint for that," David said, gathering their tankards to go to the bar. "That's exactly what I'd like you to do. Just keeping a surreptitious eye on her. Being there should she need you. That'd be perfect."

He now felt even more affection for his old friend and knew that Sarah would relish the news when he got home. Such an arrangement hardly lifted the burden from their shoulders, but sharing the problem with Greville was certainly a step forward.

# CHAPTER 11

Edith Whytechapel gazed around the sitting room in despair. What had things come to?

As usual, in the window corner, a badly-tuned wireless blared out words and music. It was incessant. Throughout the week, *Workers' Playtime*, *Family Favourites* and *Dick Barton* took turns to battle with senses which had long ago ceased to function properly. This afternoon, it was the turn of *Mrs Dale's Diary*. The poor lady could do worse than to let her good doctor-husband loose on this lot.

Edith focussed her eyes on the chairs which nestled against all four walls. There were twenty four in total – all but two being occupied. It had been a full complement yesterday. The place seemed to reek of death – or of its anticipation.

How depressing was that?

Take old Mrs Blackstone – now well into her nineties. She always occupied the chair by the window, next to the wireless. Yet, heaven knows, she was oblivious to all sights and sounds. With her chin tucked permanently into her chest, she had no hope of seeing the daffodils and multi-coloured tulips on the other side of the glass. What a difference they could make in lifting her humdrum existence. But it would never be. Nor would her doubled-up posture ever allow her to handle the afternoon's cup of tea which was now being served.

Mrs Armstrong had no such problem. Sitting diametrically opposite Mrs Blackstone, she supped her tea with the gusto of an African wildebeest suddenly encountering a rare waterhole. With the tea swishing around her dentures, her slurping resonated across the whole room. Yet, other than by Edith, the noise, apparently, went unheard by the other residents.

Miss Bassenthwaite certainly did not hear. She was too busy pouring the tea from her own cup into its saucer, then raising the saucer to her lips. In an uncharacteristic lucid moment, she had once explained to Edith that the operation was to test the correct temperature of the beverage.

It was so depressing.

"Come along, Mrs Whytechapel. Time for your cup of tea."

Edith turned to face Mrs Flintshire, the nursing home's senior carer. Could that be what she was really called? Custodian or guard might be more appropriate. She was a fulsome woman, rolls of fat striving to escape through the bulging seams of her official blue overall. Her physique matched her indubitable dominance. Not only was she in charge, but she had to be seen to be in charge.

"Come along... here... take it," Mrs Flintshire commanded, her dislike of Edith mirrored in her flashing black eyes which seemed to pierce everything in their path.

The ill-feeling was mutual. Being virtually the only resident with any control over her limbs and bodily functions, Edith should have been Mrs Flintshire's ally. Instead, the carer apparently saw her as a threat; someone who might – and certainly did – question her motives. It seemed that it was not enough for the woman only to dominate and bully those who could not put up any self-defence.

Edith held out her hand and took hold of the cup and saucer, relieved that Mrs Flintshire immediately turned back to her trolley to administer her draconian attention on the next unsuspecting resident.

How had it come to this? If only Albert was still alive – living with her in their little seaside bungalow. Life had been idyllic then – despite her arthritic bones. Albert had been her bedrock – always had been – caring for her, seeing to her every need, showing compassion that had meant so much. Mrs Flintshire should take note!

Then he had died – six years ago. Edith had tried to cope on her own, but even in the normally-manageable bungalow, it had soon proved impossible. And she hated being a burden to friends and neighbours. With no children of their own – and no relations, even – there was only one possible solution – a nursing home.

At least it had been financially feasible; Albert had seen to that. As he lay dying, he had set up a trust fund – specifically to pay her nursing home fees. Even then, he had known she would not be able to cope alone. Edith smiled, recalling how he had tied up all the loose ends. Normally, his assets would have been transferred to her automatically, but she had always been a spendthrift. What she could have done with all that money! So, he had been wise, putting it in trust, specifically to ensure that she would be properly cared for throughout the rest of her life.

But she had lived longer than either of them might have expected and Albert had not foreseen the spiralling costs of nursing care. The trust funds had now nearly whittled away. Thank goodness she still had the monies from the sale of the bungalow – safely ensconced in her bank account. That would keep her going for a few more years and she had just instructed the bank to set up a standing order to cover the nursing home's fees.

*Mrs Dale's Diary* had now finished and it would soon be time for supper. Edith had now been a resident of The Riverside Nursing Home for five years and could still not get used to her evening meal being served between five and five-thirty – too early, even, for a prior glass of sherry. Not that a Marmite sandwich and a limp piece of lettuce would do justice to an aperitif of any kind.

Edith knew that she could escape such fare – and also Mrs Flintshire – by moving to another nursing home. But would it be any better? And at ninety, she did not have the energy, let alone the inclination, to make such a move. The company might be better – snoring was already echoing round the sitting room and it was not yet five – though, in a way, she would miss Mrs Blackstone and the others.

And she had a large bedroom here; it was big enough to house most of her cherished personal mementos. Her photographs, in particular, reminded her of the many good times she had shared with Albert.

The room also provided respite from the suffocation of the downstairs living room, but being packed off to bed by seven-thirty was like being treated as a child. On the other hand, she was still cognisant enough to appreciate that nearly all the other residents deserved to be considered as children. She only had to cast her eye around the sitting room to know that.

It was just that, unlike the others, she still had the mental capacity to think for herself. She had no need for the strictures adopted by Mrs Flintshire. After all, but for the arthritis, she would not be here in the first place.

Having consumed her sandwich – potted meat today – she eased herself out of her armchair to make her way upstairs to her bedroom. Mrs Flintshire would be in the kitchen for another half-hour until about seven and making a move now would avoid that woman's strong arm tactics.

By the time she reached her room, Edith was all but flaked out, but it had been worth it. Lying down on top of her bed to recover, she closed her eyes and tried not to think about Mrs Flintshire's likely annoyance that she had made her own way up here, independent of the woman's ungracious help.

She had no idea how long she had snoozed, but the opening of her door woke her up with a start.

"What are you doing in here?" Edith managed to gasp, trying to rise from her bed, only to be pushed back hard, her pillow being wrenched from under her head.

Edith attempted to struggle free, but it was no use. She simply did not have the strength to resist the pillow being forced down over her face, and in no time at all, any sign of life had been extinguished from her frail body.

## CHAPTER 12

It was ten-thirty by the time David left Coombe Cellars. He only had to drive about three miles to reach home and he knew the road well. High hedgerows on either side made its width seem even narrower in the dark, but his Hillman Minx had effective lights. They were far better than the single faint beam he had endured with the old BSA Bantam he owned before graduating to four wheels.

He also felt safer driving along these winding country lanes after nightfall. The presence of oncoming vehicles would be flagged up by their headlights when they approached a corner. In daylight, he had experienced several near misses when coming face-to-face with cars which had been hidden from view until the very last moment. Sarah did not like driving in the dark; she claimed to get dazzled by the other lights. But he found it just as comfortable driving at night.

Except that, tonight, he was feeling a little intoxicated.

He was certainly not drunk, but his driving warranted extra caution – especially as anxiety about his home life was not aiding his concentration.

But along this lane from the pub, other traffic was non-existent and the first car he met was on the road bridge which spanned the River Barn. As he made the crossing, he glanced up and down the river. Not surprisingly, there was no activity at this late hour. Even the squawking gulls appeared to have laid down their heads for the night.

He exited the bridge and made a few back-doubles to take the shortest route to their house. Most of the houses he passed were dormant, but outside one, a man was actually cleaning his car. At this time of night? Just as well he was not their own next-door-neighbour.

He soon entered his own road and turned the Minx into the short driveway in front of their pebble-dashed detached garage. The first thing he noticed about the house was a light on in the front sitting room. That was unusual. Sarah had normally turned in at this hour on a Friday night, simply leaving a light on for him in the hall.

After getting out of the car, David quickly made for the front door and was soon inside the house.

Silence.

There was something wrong. Had his earlier apprehension about going out been justified?

The sitting room's door was ajar, allowing the room's electric illumination to flood the hall. But there was no sound; no automatic greeting from Sarah at his arrival.

He quickly stepped through the doorway and immediately saw her slumped in one of the armchairs at the side of the fireplace, an unopened book in her lap. Even though he had not been quiet, his presence had failed to stir her into life. His heart missed a beat. For one dreadful moment, he feared the worst. Then, he saw the whisky glass on the adjacent coffee table and noticed Sarah's arm hanging over the side of the chair, as if she had just put down the glass.

Relief! Sarah rarely drank Scotch, but whenever she did, only a tot would send her to sleep. As if to prove the point, she suddenly lifted her eyelids and smiled at him. "Hello, darling. Had a good time? I was so engrossed in my book, I didn't hear you."

Oh, yes?

He moved to the chair, pushing her back as she attempted to rise, and gave her a kiss. "What are you reading? What intriguing tale could have possibly distracted your attention away from the arrival of your dear husband?"

Sarah looked sheepish, now apparently realizing that the book on her lap was closed. "All right, then. I fell asleep. It must be catching."

David grinned. It was true that he had been known to nod off in the evening – particularly after one of Sarah's hearty meals.

"And what's this, then," he asked, pointing to the glass.

Sarah actually blushed. A secret drinker? No, she never drank on her own.

"I thought it might help."

"Help?"

"Aha. To take my mind off things. No, that's not true. I need to keep thinking – as to what to do. I thought the drink might calm me down – or at least give me inspiration."

"We both need to keep thinking," he corrected her. "As to what we should do."

"I know, darling, but you were out… I felt alone."

Apart from Dad and the lad upstairs. "How's Mark?"

"He's well down to it – sleeping the sleep of the innocent. Thank goodness he doesn't know what's going on."

"We must keep it that way. But I shouldn't have gone out tonight."

"Why ever not? You had to go. I'm glad you did. You needed the break. And how was Greville?"

"He was fine," David replied, getting up and moving to the drinks' cabinet. "I'm going to join you – if there's anything left in the bottle." Perhaps he had already had enough tonight, but his relief that all was well with Sarah had sobered him up.

Sarah smiled. "I only had a small one, honest. And you know it always sends me to sleep."

"Now you're being really honest."

David poured himself a measure and sat on the chair opposite Sarah. He only hoped the drink would not make his own eyelids feel like dropping – especially after three pints of Red Barrel. Or was it four?

"Anyway," he continued, taking a sip and feeling the liquor's harshness in the back of his throat, "I decided to tell Greville."

"Thank goodness for that."

"I did the right thing?"

"Remember? I suggested it before you went out."

David nodded. "I didn't think it right then. But talking to him... I suddenly felt it would be good for you to have some support at work – should you need it."

"I'm glad. Another shoulder to lean on."

"Not literally, I hope." Sarah might have known Greville almost as long as he, but...

"David!"

"Anyway, should something else arise, you must speak to him. He won't say anything, otherwise. And he knows it's just between the three of us."

"Did he have any thoughts?" Sarah asked, tasting her drink and pulling a face. "Heaven knows why I poured myself one of these. I can't stand the taste."

That sounded like good news. All the more for him. "No... even though I also told him about the threat of a raid. But there must be a link. The person who handed in the note could also have written the threat on the blotting paper. It could easily be the same customer."

"Someone seeking revenge?"

David nodded. But this was the stuff of fiction – of films. How could he and Sarah possibly be drawn into such an intrigue? Here, in Barnmouth?

"But I can't believe any customer would do this," he said, eyeing Sarah closely. "Can you?"

Before she had a chance to reply, he already knew her answer.

"John English," she duly obliged. "He's just such a person."

English was probably the one person in Barnmouth whom Sarah positively loathed. It went back a year or so when she and her friends started having morning coffee at the Esplanade Hotel. English had owned the establishment for many years and seemed to think this entitled him to take possession, or share some of the attributes, of his customers – the female variety. One or two of her friends had appalled her by actually welcoming his attention and it made her question the strength of their marriages. But for her, his unctuousness and overt pawing had been revolting.

All this had become known to David when, last November, English had asked him to take over the hotel's bank account from the District Bank. It was ostensibly because the manager there was not able to handle – in English's view – such a significant business account. That kind of reasoning always signalled danger and, sure enough, David soon established that English had in mind other ulterior motives. Before he was able to give any advice, English had thrown a wobbly and stormed out of the bank making disparaging comments about banking in general and David in particular. It was after this that Sarah had told him of her coffee mornings and he was thankful he had not taken over the hotel's banking business.

Yes, English was certainly a man to bear a grudge. But would he take revenge? Maybe.

"It's a possibility," he replied to Sarah's question which he now realized had been posed some while ago, "but not while the police are keeping tabs on him. Stuart Brown might be a better bet."

"But he's in prison."

"Don't forget, for murder and being involved in bank raids."

"But he's still in prison."

"With friends outside."

"Including John English."

That was true. David had not been able to get to the bottom of the friendship between the two men. A question of opposites, possibly. But the police seemed to think there was a link between

English and Brown's gang – without this being supported by concrete evidence. Hence their keeping an eye on English.

"It just seems a bit co-incidental," he said. "Perhaps too obvious. But we still probably can't discount these two."

"So, which customers have you upset?"

"Hang on a minute. I hope that's the drink talking."

"You know what I mean. What about lending propositions you've turned down?"

"The police asked me that. I've certainly been thinking about it. But it seems so unlikely. Having said that, Charlie Hicklemaker isn't too pleased with me."

"Charlie who?"

David grinned. "Hicklemaker."

"And what does he do? How did you fall out with him?"

"He dabbles in property – commercial and residential. He wanted me to finance a new housing development on the way to Newton Abbot."

"So?"

"So, he wanted me to put up all the money and he would take all the profit. And his thinking was that if it all crashed around him, the bank would take all the loss."

"Heads he wins: tails the bank loses."

"Exactly. When I said it was a commercial risk the bank would never undertake, he suggested I should take note of that last word – with an 'r' at its end."

"He what? That's enough of a threat to put him on the top of our list."

"Not really. He's all talk and no action. But he is a bit of a rough diamond."

"You never told me any of this."

"Only because it wasn't a real threat – just hot air."

"Well, he's down on my list, anyway. Who else haven't you

told me about?"

David was relieved to catch a smidgen of a twinkle in Sarah's eye. The whisky was certainly not sending her off to sleep again. If the possible repercussions of what they were discussing had not been so serious, it was almost as if she was relishing this inquisition. But with midnight approaching, it was time they made for bed. It might be Saturday tomorrow, but he still had to work in the morning. He alternated Saturday duties with Norman Charlton, but it was his own turn tomorrow.

"Come on, Sarah, it's time we hit the sack."

She shook her head. "No, not before you've racked your brain completely. This is far too serious. Now we've started…"

"It might surprise you," he interrupted, "that I don't go around upsetting many customers – not to my knowledge, anyway. All I want to do is to satisfy their needs – customer care, they call it…"

Sarah looked at him sharply as his words tailed off. She knew him so well… that his train of thought had triggered something else that was deep down in his mind.

"David?"

"There's one other possibility," he eventually said. "Michael Farthinshawe – he owns the Riverside Nursing Home – not far from the bridge."

"So, what happened with him?"

"He came to see me a couple of months ago. The account's not been much of a problem – until recently. It used to go in and out of credit and never exceeded its overdraft limit. But in recent months, the credit balances have disappeared altogether and the overdraft is nearly always at its limit – or even over it."

"Has the home fallen on hard times?"

"No. On the contrary, it's nearly always full. When someone eventually dies, a new resident steps in almost immediately. They always have a waiting list."

"Perhaps the fees are too low?"

"No, that's not a problem If anything, they're on the high side. Farthinshawe can justify this because the home's in such good condition."

"So, what's the problem?"

"I don't know, but I think something underhand's going on. In a tactful way, I broached the subject at the interview, but he went wild – way over the top. He accused me of questioning the integrity of him and his staff. I certainly wasn't doing that. But it's patently clear that something's going wrong – probably tied up with income and cash. It's just not covering the overheads. Yet those overheads are in line with his size of business."

"You think someone's putting a hand in the till?"

"I wouldn't be surprised. Yet Farthinshawe didn't want to know. It's all very strange."

"But that's not enough to put him on our list. He hasn't threatened you with anything?"

"No, he hasn't. But there's definitely something dodgy going on. And he most definitely didn't like my suggesting it."

## CHAPTER 13

As he left the house on Saturday morning to walk to work, David rued the fact that it was past one before Sarah and he had got to bed last night.

Through lack of sleep – surely because of nothing else? – he was feeling a little woozy and he chose to walk, rather than cycle or use the car. He enjoyed walking, especially with the scented cherry blossom still caressing the air. His route also took him along the seafront which he always found bracing and, this morning, the ozone could only do him a power of good. The added bonus in the morning was the scarcity of other pedestrians; even during the summer months, holidaymakers would still be tucking into their full English breakfasts. The nearest he ever got to such a feast was through the aroma of sizzling bacon which wafted from the adjacent hotels and boarding houses.

As he reached the promenade, an express train thundered past and he had to steady himself against the turbulence created by the locomotive and its twelve attendant carriages. He felt slightly annoyed that the train had approached from behind, on its way up to London. He had not been able to catch the engine's number. It was certainly a King-class monster, but Mark would subsequently chide him for his oversight – should he admit it to the boy.

The two of them occasionally went train-spotting together and he had to admit he enjoyed the thrill of spotting a previously-unseen locomotive. Mark's favourite venue was an embankment at one end of Newton Abbot's station and, along with other similarly-inclined youngsters, he would spend hours with his Ian Allan reference book, underlining the numbers once the appropriate engines had been seen.

Both of them were, in fact, aiming to go there this afternoon. For the last year or so, Sarah and he had allowed Mark to stay there with his friends, having taken him and arranged to pick him up later in the afternoon. That would certainly not be the case today. In the present circumstances, there would be no time – away from school – when they would allow him to be out of their presence. On this occasion, it was an arrangement which David was quietly pleased about. Rumour had it among the train-spotters that the famous Bulldog-class City of Truro would be in the area this weekend.

But train-spotting was only on the agenda today because there was no football; Torquay United were playing away at Southend. Otherwise, he and Mark would be taking their places on the terraces at Plainmoor.

In his first season of supporting United, Mark had revelled in enjoying numerous victories – and handsome ones at that. It was proving to be a season and a half for the team – far better that anything David had seen before. Not that the side were constant strugglers in the lowly 3rd Division (South); middle of the road was more like it. The season before war broke out, United had actually come second and, this season, there was a distinct possibility that this position might even be bettered.

But, today, any excitement which the team might generate would be restricted to news of their result on the wireless at five o'clock.

David also enjoyed his golf, sometimes on a Saturday afternoon, although Sunday mornings were when most competitions were held. But the game was time-consuming. Five hours could be taken out of a weekend and he was not prepared to leave Mark alone with Sarah for that length of time. It was not fair on her. She had enough responsibility keeping an eye on him during the week. For the moment, golf must go on the back burner. He shook his head. That might not be such a bad thing; his recent form had been appalling.

As he continued his walk, the sea lapping the sand to his right and with the railway line on his left, he approached the station from which a tank engine with just two carriages was drawing out. It must be a local train, probably going on to Totnes and Plymouth after its next stop at Newton Abbot. It was a stark reminder of the dreadful accident on Thursday. How was Mrs Martingale's sister coping with such a trauma? No doubt, the daughter and husband would be coming over from New York, but with an inquest to be held, it could be some time before funeral arrangements might be able to be made. Some people did so suffer.

But what about themselves?

Were they really at risk of Mark coming to some harm? If that were the case, the police, surely, would have become more actively involved. Did their experience lead them to believe it was a harmless hoax? If only. But his nervous system, not to mention Sarah's, dictated otherwise.

He reached the bank, never failing to admire its imposing York-stone structure at the bottom corner of the High Street. He also checked the flag pole above the front door. Whenever possible, he liked to fly an appropriate flag, including one he had acquired from Torquay United to recognise significant achievements by the team. This standard-bearing seemed to have gone down well with customers of a branch he had been particularly proud of getting for his first managerial appointment.

He rang the front door bell and prayed that whoever answered would use the security chain before throwing the door open. Thankfully, Roger Singleton duly obliged. He had not always done so.

After entering his room – and it was so good having his own room, at last, rather than having to work with everyone else in the general office – he sat down at his desk and opened his diary to check on this morning's appointments. He liked to keep interviews to the minimum on Saturdays. That way, he could help out the others with their clerical work. He shared the objective of all the staff: to get out as soon as possible after the bank closed its doors at noon – especially if United were playing at home.

There was only one problem with his interviews: one of his appointments was with Charlie Hicklemaker.

"How did that happen?" he asked, when he rang through to Katie.

"He phoned yesterday afternoon," Katie said, "just after you'd left. I checked your diary and your only appointment was with Mrs James – at ten. I know you try to keep your interviews with her as short as possible. Well, she does go on and you always say she only comes in for a chat. Of course, she must be ever so lonely now – since Mr James passed on and…"

"Katie!"

"Oh, sorry, sir. Anyway, Mr Hicklemaker said he wanted to come in at ten-thirty, so I said I was sure that'd be all right. I was going to tell you first thing this morning, but you beat me to it. I told Mr Hicklemaker I'd ring him if it wasn't okay. Do you want me to phone him, sir? I'm sorry, but I thought I was doing the right thing, but…"

"No, that's fine, Katie. Ten-thirty is fine."

He put the phone down and shook his head. Katie was incorrigible. But there was no-one better.

As for Charlie Hicklemaker…

Why would he want to come in and see him again? He could not have been more aware that the bank would not support his proposed new housing development. But was it a softening-up move? Could it be something to do with this week's threats? Surely not. People making such threats would need to retain their anonymity – otherwise they would feel the full force of the law. On the other hand, Hicklemaker might be curious as to how he and Sarah were coping. If he saw obvious signs of torment, he could be encouraged to increase the pressure on them.

But this was nonsense. It was like living in a dream. In the middle of night, this type of thinking – irrational experiences – was so vivid, so real. And, upon awakening, they were still there – but only for a few seconds. Reality soon stepped in, throwing such outrageous images into oblivion.

He must do this now. Hicklemaker was a builder – as simple as that. He had been, all his working life. And in Barnmouth, at that. This man could not possibly be a… a child abductor? No, that was the stuff of fantasy. It was impossible.

Or was it?

He must cast such thoughts to the back of his mind. Before Mrs James's interview, there was much to be done. His staff had already opened the incoming mail and had deposited a small pile of letters on his desk.

It proved to be the normal fare: applications for overdrafts; requests to open new accounts; a notice of death of an elderly customer; and numerous returns needed to be completed for Head Office.

He would also have to deal with a number of cheques presented in this morning's clearing. Most such cheques would be processed to customers' accounts with no questions asked. Some, though, would be drawn by customers when there were insufficient funds to cover them.

To pay or not to pay: that was the question.

One thing was, however, categorical: the indubitable opinion of customers whose cheques were bounced was that it was always the bank's fault and in no way were they, themselves, to blame.

Such is life.

Ten o'clock and Katie was right; Mrs James had come in just for a chat. She tried to cover her intentions by asking for some investment advice, but there was only one thing she was seeking: a chat.

The talk between them was so inconsequential that he could not help his mind switching forward to ten-thirty. He knew there would be nothing meaningless about his next interview.

Charlie Hicklemaker actually smiled when he greeted him in the banking hall, before David guided him into his room. Or was it a grimace?

Whatever, David had never been so apprehensive at the start of an interview and when Hicklemaker was sitting opposite, he looked full of menace. He was thick-set and no more than five-feet-six tall. Muscles bulged beneath his jacket, making it appear two sizes too small. His ruddy weather-beaten face clearly identified him as an outdoor worker, while ingrained grime on his leathered skin and around his fingernails proved that he was not afraid of getting his hands dirty. But just by way of his building work?

It was not a promising start.

"How to get my own back." It was a statement, not a question.

"I beg your pardon?"

Hicklemaker scowled. It had clearly not been a smile back there in the banking hall. "That's all I could think of – when I last left your room."

So, it was him. He was already making himself patently clear. But why an admission so soon?

"I had my job to do," David said. If only it were that simple.

Hicklemaker's eyes narrowed. "Your job is to lend money – especially to long-time clients."

It was not the time to point out that solicitors had clients, while banks had customers. "Not if it means the bank takes all the risk. Our shareholders would soon object to that."

"Shareholders!"

The man actually spat out the word. No wonder he was still

a one-man-band. He would not be one to tolerate shareholders breathing down his neck.

David made sure he maintained eye contact. "Would you lend money to someone on a wing and a prayer?"

"That's not the point. It's not up to me to lend money. That's your job. Horses for courses."

"And I'm not a builder. So, I don't tell you how to build your houses. Why should you tell me how I should lend the bank's money? And, remember, it's the bank's money, not mine – entrusted to us by our depositors. At some time, they will want it back. They certainly wouldn't want us to put it into high-risk schemes."

That may well be true, but it was unlikely to have any impact on Hicklemaker. He would be too one-tracked to see such a different point of view.

"Anyway," David continued, forcing himself to remain positive, "what did you mean by getting your own back?" He had to get this into the open. It was not the sort of thing any customer would say. They might think it, but actually say it?

Hicklemaker suddenly sank back in his chair. He seemed visibly deflated – as if all his bombast had been pricked out of him by a pin.

"Me and my big mouth," he eventually said. "I'm sorry."

An apology?

"I've done a couple of things I should never have…"

His words tailed off, as though he could not bear to admit what he had done. David could not believe what he was hearing. Even without the sentence being completed, was it a confession? If so, it would bring their torment to an end. But what about the police? With an admission of guilt, they would have to take action – more so than they appeared to be doing now.

"When you turned me down," Hicklemaker eventually continued, "I reckoned it was a class thing – you in your three-piece suit and grammar school tie…"

"You can't be serious."

"I've been a worker since I left school."

"And so have I."

"A worker – with my hands. And I reckon I've done all right. I build good houses. But when you turned me down…"

David sighed. "I'm not saying you don't build good houses. I know you're a great builder. You might, even, be the best builder in the world, but if you over-extend yourself with borrowing…"

"But it would have been the most profitable development I've ever done. You'd be at no risk at all."

David had heard that one before. So often, would-be borrowers could be blinkered by the prospect of future profits. Yet profitable businesses can go bust, simply because ultimate profits do not equate to cash in hand – during the course of the project. If cash is unavailable to cover regular outgoings, such as the weekly wages, the end of the project – and subsequent profits – may never materialize. Turning Hicklemaker down was probably the best decision he could ever have made for the builder.

He spent the next five minutes explaining the dangers of overtrading – taking on too much new work in relation to the cash resources available to the business. If only he had been able to do this at the previous interview. Instead, Hicklemaker had walked out on him before he had the chance to give him such good advice.

"I can only apologise again," Hicklemaker eventually responded, having given David his full attention. "Taking retribution was not the answer. I'm sorry for even thinking about it. And I can tell you now… the site actually proved unsuitable. Anyway, next time… let's just say I'll know what you're looking for."

After that, there was little more to be said and he left, leaving David sitting at his desk, wondering what to do.

Hicklemaker had all but confessed to making the threats against the bank and Mark. Or had he? At the beginning of the interview, he had admitted to thinking about getting his own back and, just then, had actually used the word 'retribution'. But that did not mean he had actually taken it. He had said he had done a couple of things he should not have, but such action could have been unrelated to the actual threats.

David's initial hopes that this would now be the end of their problems were now looking less sure. And the police would, no doubt, think the same – unless they wrung a confession out of the builder. But from what was said this morning, he had no case to report to the police. The banker/customer relationship was a confidential one and, without having concrete proof against Hicklemaker, reporting to the police was not an option.

In other words, despite his initial hopes, he and Sarah looked like being no further forward.

When he got home, Sarah agreed with that and he reflected on her reaction when he and Mark later took the road to Newton Abbot railway station.

It was not surprising that lunch had been a little fraught. Sarah's initial high hopes had turned to despair by the time he had finished his account of the interview with Hicklemaker.

She had agreed that they could not divulge to the police what the builder had said. But she was not prepared to discount him entirely from being the perpetrator.

"Try and dig around a bit more," she had urged. "There might be something more to link him with the threats."

That was all very well. But where to look? As Mark and he made their way to Newton Abbot, they actually drove past Hicklemaker's proposed building site and the builder had certainly been right; it did not seem at all suitable. Pools of water lay all around, despite not much recent rain. There could well be a drainage problem – even underground springs – in which case, the building of new homes would be foolhardy.

He pressed on with the journey. The road to Newton Abbot ran parallel with the railway line and followed the contours of the river which ran all the way down from Dartmoor. The old Great Western Railway had used this stretch of line for some of its advertising material and it certainly depicted a picturesque way of taking a journey. Perhaps the waterlogged building site was related to its proximity to the river, but there had never been any evidence of subsidence on the adjacent railway line or road.

David left most of the afternoon's train spotting to Mark; his mind was too busy on other things. It was now three days since receipt of the threats to the bank and Mark. It was still too soon to take comfort from the lack of any follow-up threats. These might come at any time and the only sure way of stopping them was to discover the author. But how to do that?

He was no further forward by the time they were heading home, their estimated time of arrival being just before five o'clock – ready to re-tune the wireless for the football results. Dad was bound to have been listening to another wavelength during the afternoon.

Mark was feeling pleased to have logged up a couple of new Castles, a Manor and a Grange. GWR's choice of classes for their locomotives certainly had a hint of national heritage about them. But there had been no sign of the *City of Truro*.

They then ran into a snag. Their progress was halted just outside Barnmouth, a long queue of cars threatening their getting home in time for the football results. The cars eventually inched their way forward and David then saw a uniformed policeman directing traffic in the distance.

As they approached, he noticed three police cars parked on his side of the road, effectively stopping the normal two-way traffic. With vehicles piling out of the rugby ground on the other side of the obstruction, the police cars had created an untimely log-jam.

It was now clear that he and Mark would have to await the later second reading of the football results. Then, he could not believe his eyes. If only he could stop to find out what was happening. A hive of police activity concentrated on the large property adjacent to their cars and he was astonished to see Chief Inspector Hopkins coming out of the Riverside Nursing Home.

## CHAPTER 14

Trevor Smith closed his eyes against the glare of the spotlight and placed the mouthpiece of his saxophone between his lips. The pianist had eased himself into the introductory bars of 'Autumn in New York' and Trevor immersed himself in the mood of a tune which was so apposite. All right, it was spring, rather than autumn, but, this week, he had embraced the images of New York City like never before.

Thank you, so much, Mrs Martingale.

Yet now the lady who had inspired him to cross the water, to follow her footsteps into the clubs of his dreams, was gone. How could someone like her be no longer with them?

The poignancy of the tune he was about to play stung his eyes, the lid of his left eye failing to stem a tear which now tumbled slowly down his cheek. It did not embarrass him at all. Music was all about emotion and he knew that each note he was about to play would come straight from his heart. It would be his tribute to a grand old lady. How he hoped the audience would share his mood, even if it was unaware of its inspiration.

And where better to express his homage than at the Walnut Grove Club? It was a most unlikely jazz venue, tucked away in the Torquay suburb of Chelston and nestling at the bottom of a parade of shops. Its position probably reflected the populace's antipathy to jazz. Why else would the town's only jazz club be so hard to find? It was as if it were an embarrassment to the genteel folk of Torquay. Yet these people had, more than likely, never listened to the music, preferring to blaspheme it, unheard. It was their loss. They might never know that most jazz encompassed the lyricism and invention of the likes of Gershwin, Porter and Rogers and Hart. Only classical musical snobs could deny the genius of such distinguished composers.

If only Mrs Martingale could have been here. Instead, there was someone else – someone special – sitting at the back of the club and waiting to hear him play for the very first time.

He could not see her; his smarting eyes, even when open, saw to that. But he felt her presence and he would play, as it were, just for her. That was never a bad thing. Good music was about feeling – personal interplay – and he never forgot the advice of his spiritual mentor – Frank Sinatra. If only it had been given to him personally. The great man had stressed that musicians should always heed a tune's lyrics; listen to what the composer had to say. That way, the music would transcend its intended purpose. Trevor would put that lesson to the test tonight – especially with the ballads he intended to play.

He never got over the thrill of being on a bandstand. Friends could not understand how a bank cashier by day could become a jazz musician at night. But why not? Both jobs were about communication – whether with customers at the bank or with an audience in a club. And his music was always a release from the rigours at the bank – the only problem being that late nights could create additional pressure the following day.

But tonight, it was Saturday – with no work tomorrow. There was only one problem: living at home. Not that he would want to live elsewhere – not yet, anyway – but his parents could get anxious about his lying-in on Sunday mornings. It was not as if such late rising was caused by a hangover, because he never drank. But the concentration of playing – interpreting the composers' lyrics – was mentally taxing and not conducive to getting up bright and early the next day. For this reason, he liked to restrict his club appearances to Saturday nights.

Fifty minutes later, he ended the set to rapturous applause. He knew he had played well, not that this was always readily appreciated by audiences. So often, conversations at tables would seem to be more important than listening to the musicians they had paid to hear. On one occasion, he had been tempted to stop playing in the middle of a number and apologise for breaking into the conversation of an especially noisy table. But most of the time, he was able to shut out extraneous noise and concentrate on his playing.

This particular evening, the audience had chosen to share his feelings by giving him its complete attention. He only hoped that this also applied to a certain young lady at the back of the club.

After packing his saxophone into its case – he was only playing one set tonight – he searched out the audience and saw her making her way towards him, grinning broadly. He could still not believe that Katie had accepted his invitation for a date. He only prayed that the rest of the evening would not turn into an unmitigated disaster.

They were like chalk and cheese. He might well be older than her, but she was the confident one – the life and soul of any situation. National Service had certainly brought him out, but he only felt really in control when his saxophone was between his lips. Of course, last year's bank raid had not helped, as far as his day job was concerned.

"Trevor!" Katie almost shrieked, as she reached the bandstand. "That was great."

"I wasn't really sure you liked jazz."

"Trevor! I love it. Mind you, until now, it's always been traditional jazz: Acker Bilk, Chris Barber – and I love Lonnie Donegan. Can you play skiffle? I adore it. And did you know, Mr Goodhart likes jazz. He told me last year; that time us girls took Jane to see Chris Barber. Remember? It was the first time she'd been anywhere. Can you believe that? That's when she got going with John. You know, from the golf club? She's been dating him for about five months now. Isn't that amazing? Do you think they'll marry? They make such a lovely couple, don't they? Anyway, Mr Goodhart told me he used to play the banjo. Did you know that? He could have been another Lonnie Donegan. Does he know you play the saxophone?"

Katie paused for breath and of all the questions she had just asked, it would seem she only expected him to answer this last one. He felt almost exhausted after her burst of excited babble. Was going out with her really going to work?

"Yes," he replied. "He's seen me here."

"Really?"

For once, Katie seemed to be stumped for words.

"He told me he couldn't believe it when I walked out on to the bandstand. He had no idea I played the saxophone."

Katie grinned mischievously. "Did he ask you for your autograph?"

"No – and nor have you."

"I will, I will," Katie trilled. "Here," she added, pulling a biro out of her handbag, "do it here, on my forehead."

"Katie!" How was he going to be able to cope with this?

"Go on, go on."

"No, that's daft."

"Well, on the back of my hand, then. And I'll promise never to wash it again."

She was teasing him now. But why not do as she asked? It was a ready-made excuse to take her hand in his. He would never have the nerve to make such a move, otherwise.

And it did feel good.

It was an intimacy which he feared Katie was not sharing. She could hardly contain herself as he scrawled his signature on the back of her hand. Surely, she'll wash it off before work on Monday morning?

Then, the moment was gone.

Other people came up to pat him on the back – metaphorically. The only physical contact was with Katie, as he ushered her away towards the bar. This was the next challenge. He already knew she did not smoke – thank goodness – but was she a devotee of gin, Cinzano or Dubonnet? No, she asked for orange juice and he made that two.

Half an hour later, they made their way to the railway station for their train back to Barnmouth. Trevor could not have been more pleased that Katie had enjoyed the music and he could hardly believe she also seemed to like his company. They were getting on so well. But having held her hand once that evening… As they strolled to the station, he simply could not summon up the courage to do it again.

But he had no need to.

As they chatted about this and that – he had never been really good at small talk, but this seemed different – she slipped her hand in his, as though it was the most natural thing for her to do.

And her action coincided with her suddenly becoming serious. It was like a character transplant. Was her seemingly natural ebullience her true self? Whatever, it made her seem even more fascinating.

"Do you think there's something wrong at work?" she asked, an unlikely frown creasing her pretty features. "I'm getting really worried – about Mr Goodhart."

"You mean the threat of a raid?"

"Yes, certainly that. But I think there's something else."

Her words accompanied a squeezing of his hand. It was not an affectionate squeeze, more like a need for some form of support. "It's Mr Goodhart," she continued. "He seems ever so worried."

"Wouldn't you? If your branch is threatened with a raid?"

"No, no," Katie said, squeezing his hand still further. If only it was through affection. "I don't think it's just that. I'm sure there's something else."

"What sort of thing?"

"That's the point. I don't know. But he was so worried when he knew Mr Hicklemaker was coming in to see him."

"I'm not surprised. I can't stand the man."

Hicklemaker was a typical self-made man. He had no airs or graces – not that that was such a bad thing – but he was coarse and arrogant. He always seemed to have a gigantic chip on his shoulder. On one occasion, he had even poured scorn on bank staff for wearing suits and ties. What did he expect? Open necked shirts and sandals? After all, Barnmouth was a seaside town. People like him made Trevor sick.

"I don't think any of us like him," Katie said, staying serious as they neared the station, "but Mr Goodhart seemed… he seemed even scared… certainly very apprehensive."

Trevor had never seen Katie so serious. It was a side of her which must have encouraged the manager to select her as his secretary. His decision had surprised everyone, but they all now acknowledged that he had got it right. He was extremely perceptive, our Mr Goodhart. After all, he loved jazz saxophone, so he must be all right.

"So, you think there's more to it than a possible raid?"

"I don't know," Katie replied, actually drawing him close to her. Whatever was causing her concern, he certainly appreciated her proximity. "But I am worried. There's certainly something else troubling him."

They had now reached the station and made their way to the 'up' line. Trevor cast his eye up and down the platform. The last thing he needed was for someone from work to be catching the same train. In recent times, he had encountered Bernard… and Jane. It had not been a problem, because he had been on his own, but tonight? No, he did not want the rumour mill to start turning

– not yet, anyway.

Their expected train from Paignton was already signalled and there was now quite a crowd to get on it, no doubt heading home to Newton Abbot, Barnmouth or, even, Exeter.

Katie suddenly tugged his arm. "Look," she hissed, in her best stage whisper. "Up the platform… there… by the waiting room…"

With some foreboding, Trevor followed her gaze, but nothing registered.

"There," Katie urged. "Under that sign."

Oh, no. This time it was Barbara Bolton.

"Come on," he said, "let's move back to the end of the platform."

"All right, then, but see? She's with a man."

"So?"

"So, her husband's in Spain, isn't he?"

Perhaps it was Katie's youth, but was Barbara Bolton meant to be handcuffed, manacled and not let out of her house, simply because her husband was out in Spain? No doubt, he was out and about, enjoying himself, so why not Barbara? She might, even, have been at the Walnut Grove, though he hoped not.

"But that's not a sin," he said. "People do have friends. It might even be her brother."

"I suppose so," Katie acknowledged, visibly disappointed that her imagined intrigue had been rebuffed.

"Anyway," Trevor said, "keep your head down. Don't let her see us." The last thing he wanted was for people in the office to believe that something was going on between him and Katie. He might well have designs on her – who wouldn't? – but an apparent office romance could be the kiss of death. And he certainly did not want that to happen just yet.

But was Katie the sort of person to keep this date to herself?

# CHAPTER 15

David was relieved to get to work on Monday morning.

It had not been a good weekend.

Yesterday, it had poured all day. Even if he had wanted to play golf, the course would have been closed; not from the rain – the sandy terrain was able to soak up copious amounts of water – but from the low cloud which wrapped itself around the high moorland, as if protecting it from other climatic threats. So often, the course would be closed when, down below, the town and beaches would be bathed in sunshine. It could be so frustrating.

But golf had never been on his agenda; this weekend he had to be available for Mark and Sarah. Not that Mark seemed to appreciate their apparent desire to keep him in sight at all times. Despite the rain, he wanted to knock a football around outside. Certainly not. Then, why not let him go to Newton Abbot? His quest was still to spot the *City of Truro*. You must be joking. Instead, he contented himself on his bedroom floor, taking charge of the GWR by way of his Hornby 'Dublo' model railway.

On his hands and knees, David took the opportunity of joining him on the carpet – well, it was better than getting involved in housework, or helping to prepare the lunch.

As he connected sections of the rails together, he marvelled at the detail of the trains which would soon be running on this model permanent way. Engines – especially the Duchess of Montrose, on loan from the LMS for Mark's West Country Line – carriages and trucks, all splendidly replicated the real things. Though this was not the case with the track itself.

Clockwork trains had now been consigned to the past and the electrically-operated 'Dublo' system had to make use of a third 'conductor' rail, set in the middle of the track. Yet, who had seen such a thing in real life? Electric trains on the Southern Region certainly used a third rail, though this was positioned outside one of the others. But Mark and he were intent on operating the Great Western. One day, someone might invent a two-rail electrical system, but, for the time being, they would have to settle for three.

Not that Mark seemed to mind. As the designated engine driver, he was clearly in charge. He was oblivious of the niceties of the track. That could be left to dear old Dad – along with menial duties, such as points changing and signalling. Not that David minded. He spent his working life being the boss. A change was supposed to be as good as a rest and when better to achieve this than at weekends?

But this weekend could never really become restful. Perhaps they should let Mark know what was going on? After all, he was a mature boy – more than might be expected for his nine years.

"No," Sarah had said, clearly thinking the idea was crazy. "If we're frightened, how would he react? It simply wouldn't be fair."

"Just a thought," David muttered. If he were in Mark's shoes, how would he have reacted? With great excitement, more than likely. It would be like playing a starring role in a special episode of *Dick Barton – Special Agent*. The kudos at school would also be second to none. David smiled at the thought – careful not to let Sarah see. In fact, if everyone knew about the threat – everyone at school, at work, throughout Barnmouth, if necessary – would that not effectively mean that Mark was the safest person in town? Would not the perpetrator of whatever harm was intended for the boy be frightened off completely?

"You're barmy," Sarah said, when he put this theory to her. "You really would put your son at such a risk? Remember what it said in the note? Don't tell anyone. Yet you want the whole world to know?"

It got worse in the evening, after Mark had been packed off to bed.

"I think we should keep him off school," Sarah had blurted out, interrupting a long period of untypical silence. She must have been chewing over all the options available to them.

"We can't do that."

"Why not?"

"Because he'll be just as safe at school. He'll have so many other people around him. The teachers will provide just as much protection as we can."

"How can you say that?" Sarah's eyes flashed alarmingly. "He's our child; he doesn't belong to them."

"I know that, darling, but let's be sensible…"

"I am being sensible. You're the one who doesn't seem to care."

How could she say that? He had hardly left Mark's side for 48 hours – getting out of Sarah's hair by overseeing the railway system at Newton Abbot yesterday and then spending hours upstairs, today, on his hands and knees, helping to operate a more efficient operation in Mark's bedroom. Yet he didn't care? Count to ten; it was not a time for a hasty – and probably ill-judged – riposte.

He rose from his chair and made some pretence at tidying-up the Sunday papers. They lay strewn around the room, dog-eared at being read and re-read throughout the day – in between, of course, his looking after Mark. What else had there been to do? As he did this, he felt Sarah's blazing eyes boring into his back. When he turned to face her, the disconsolate look on his face must have made her realize she had gone too far.

"I'm sorry, darling," she said, beckoning him to sit down again beside her, "but I'm so worried. This thing's never going to go away."

Now, sitting at his desk this Monday morning, he could only reflect that it had not been a good weekend – compounded by

United losing 2-0 at Southend. But what lay ahead?

At least, he had some light relief as he dictated his letters to Katie. From her shining eyes and her natural ebullience, it was clear she had enjoyed a great couple of days.

"And how was your weekend?" he asked, in between dictating answers to requests for a bridging loan and for a worldwide letter of credit for someone lucky enough to be embarking on a tour of Europe. The nearest he had got to going abroad was his honeymoon on the Isle of Wight.

"Have you heard, sir?" she answered, putting a hand to her lips.

"Heard? What do you mean, heard?"

"So, you haven't?"

"Katie, I have no idea of what you're talking about."

"Oh, that's all right, then, sir."

This must be the first staccato-like conversation he had ever had with Katie. There must be something wrong.

"Katie, you're dangling me on a piece of string. What's going on?"

"I'm sorry, sir, but we agreed we wouldn't tell anyone. I just wanted to make sure."

"We?"

"Please, sir, don't make me say anything. I promised."

Katie keeping a secret?

"But there's nothing wrong? There's no problem?"

"No, no, no. Quite the opposite. I'm so excited."

What was new? The girl was always excited. And as he continued his dictation, she could hardly keep a smile off her face. Her mood certainly lifted his spirits, even though she was clearly determined not to let him in on her secret.

Before he could consider whether to press her further, there was a knock on his door and, at his shouted "come in", Jane entered the room.

"There's someone wants to see you, sir. It's that Inspector

Hopkins – you know, the policeman ? Last November?"

Was this foresight on Sarah's part? Last night, when equilibrium had been restored, she had suggested they sought the advice of Hopkins – let him know of their increasing concerns. Yet, with the police seemingly taking a low profile, they had decided to delay making contact. But with Hopkins now wanting to see him?

"He's Chief Inspector, now," he replied, then asking Katie to get on with her typing; he would continue his dictation later. "I wonder what he wants?"

"It's got to be about the raid," Jane suggested.

David nodded, though not inclined to agree. Jane was not aware of anything else. "I'll come out and get him. But do you need me at all?"

"Not yet, sir. I'm still dealing with my post and the clearings."

"I'll see you a bit later then," he said, and went out into the banking hall.

Hopkins could not have looked more serious when he had sat down across the desk in David's room. He chose not to remove his raincoat, even though it was damp from what must be a light drizzle outside. Did this mean he expected his visit to be brief? No matter, his demeanour did not encourage small talk and David waited for him to get the conversation rolling.

"Until now, I've never really believed in coincidences," Hopkins said, without preamble. He opened a file he had taken from a document case which he now deposited on the floor. "After your visit on Thursday, I really couldn't see the threat of a raid – here in your bank – being linked to the note your wife received. I was even more sure that I wanted to have the handwriting analysed…"

And? Was the man's inordinate pause as he looked at his file made simply for dramatic effect?

"And I wasn't surprised at the result," Hopkins eventually said. "Our expert's almost certain the two hands are different."

"Almost certain?"

"Ninety-nine percent sure. I'm certainly satisfied we're dealing with two people."

"And have you come up with anything yet?" David scrutinized Hopkins; his answer would probably dictate whether he would let him know exactly how they were feeling at home.

Hopkins shook his head. "No, but there's been a development – two, in fact."

He paused again. Were the police always so intent on such delaying tactics? It was as if information had to be dragged out of them; not unlike with Katie this morning. This time, though, any enjoyment from the exchange was non-existent.

"This is where coincidences come in," Hopkins continued, at last. "And they all relate to National Counties. First, you had your threat of a raid, here in Barnmouth; secondly your wife received her own threat – at her branch in Newton Abbot; and now, we're investigating two deaths and treating them both as murder."

"Murder?" What was he talking about?

Hopkins did not reply, as if letting the news sink in before elaborating.

Jane was wide of the mark in thinking his visit would be just about the threat of a raid. But murder? It was less than six months since George Broadman's murder – the first in Barnmouth in living memory. And now, two more? Two more he had not even heard about? And this coincidence business? Did Hopkins mean these murders were linked to the bank? How could that be so?

Hopkins continued, as if in anticipation of David's unspoken question. "These deaths are only a tenuous link with the bank – at this stage, anyway. But both victims were customers of yours."

David could not stop his jaw dropping and he gaped at

Hopkins. This was astonishing. It was impossible. If a customer of his was murdered, he would have known about it by now. How could such a thing not have come to his attention? The grapevine in Barnmouth would have been working overtime.

"You wouldn't have known about them yet," Hopkins continued. "One only happened at the weekend and, for all intents and purposes, the other appeared to have been a tragic accident."

Oh, no. Surely not? "Not Mrs Martingale?" David gasped. There had been no other tragic accident in Barnmouth. But how could it not have been an accident?

"I'm afraid so," Hopkins replied, running a finger over one of the pages in his file. "According to witnesses, there must have been a hundred or so people on the platform – all rushing to position themselves to get on the train. As it approached the station, they could see it only had two carriages – not the usual six. Apparently, there was quite a melee on the platform. As the train came in, Mrs Martingale fell in front of it."

"That's what we heard at the time. And Oliver Sargeant – he's the senior solicitor next door with Ducksworth Sargeant – he came and told me personally. He's acting for the estate. But he said it was an accident. The whole town believes that."

"And so did we – until two separate witnesses came forward on Friday. We would have been sceptical if it had been just one, but with two… They both said Mrs Martingale had been deliberately pushed."

David felt himself turn ashen. It was bad enough for the old lady to have fallen to her death, but he did not bear thinking of her actually being pushed. "So, who did it?" he finally managed to ask.

"We still don't know," Hopkins said, sighing audibly. "Neither witness saw the actual person."

"So, how can they be reliable witnesses?"

"They didn't see who actually did it. There were too many

people on the platform. But they are both adamant they saw an arm deliberately shoving Mrs Martingale on to the track."

Not for the first time these last few days, David felt himself living in a film. It was unreal. Yet, so often, there could be truth in the saying that life can be stranger than fiction.

"But just because she banked here..." his words tailed off; he was still not able to grasp the enormity of her violent death.

"On its own," Hopkins said, "that wouldn't signify anything. But I said there were two murders."

David had been so overcome with the news about Mrs Martingale that he had already cast the other death to one side.

"And Mrs Whytechapel," Hopkins added, "also banks with you."

"Mrs Whytechapel? That's not a name I know."

"I'm not surprised. For a number of years, she's been a resident of the Riverside Nursing Home."

So, that was what it had all been about on Saturday.

"I can hardly believe this," he said. "We saw you... my son and I... we were coming home from Newton Abbot. There was such a jam – caused by your police cars. Then, I saw you. I can't believe you were investigating something which might involve the bank."

"It might not, of course. And that aspect will not be in the report in tonight's Herald. We were called on Saturday afternoon – alerted by the ambulance crew. They smelt something suspicious. The nursing home staff found her dead in her bed in the morning. They thought she had died in her sleep. It was certainly not the first time a resident had done that. But the ambulance chief didn't like the look of her. He reckoned she'd been dead for some time – probably since early Friday evening. To him, that didn't sound like dying in her sleep."

"But how do you know it's murder?"

"We managed to get a post mortem done yesterday. We

stressed the urgency – because of Mrs Martingale's death. Two suspicious deaths in such a short space of time seemed decidedly odd. And it turns out that Mrs Whytechapel definitely died of unnatural causes."

David was stumped for words. He had never met the lady and, although he had briefly seen Mrs Martingale, he certainly did not know her, either. He was getting extremely uncomfortable about these unfolding events.

"It seems there's a serial killer in Barnmouth," Hopkins said, confirming David's worst fears, "and I'm desperately worried. As for that question of coincidences… we've had two deaths and two threats, though, admittedly, not death threats. But in each instance, there's a link to your bank – no matter how tenuous. Certainly, the link of the murders is flimsy. Both ladies kept diaries. We recovered Mrs Martingale's from her handbag and Mrs Whytechapel's was in her room. And each diary had a recent reference to making contact with your bank."

"That was certainly the case with Mrs Martingale," David replied. "She came to see us the afternoon she was…"

"That's interesting," Hopkins said, as David struggled to finish his sentence. "We'll need to follow that one up. What about Mrs Whytechapel?"

"As I said, I know nothing about her. But if she was in a nursing home, she'd hardly be able to come and see us."

"But has she been in contact?"

"I've really no idea. But I'll ask around."

"Good," Hopkins replied. "It's just that I have this gut feeling."

And such feelings should never be discounted. David had experienced enough of them when considering lending propositions to know that it could be perilous to ignore them. In this respect, a bank manager's instincts were not dissimilar to those of a policeman.

But how did all this leave his family? If there was a serial killer at large, anyone might be vulnerable – except that not everyone had already received a warning letter. Had Mrs Martingale and Mrs Whytechapel been given prior warnings?

"I don't know," Hopkins said, when he posed this question, "but I doubt it. One thing's for certain: we're now treating your own two threats extremely seriously."

Thank goodness for that. At least, he now had good, as well as bad, news for Sarah.

"We're going to keep the bank under surveillance and we also want to do the same for that son of yours. Mark, isn't it?"

David nodded. This was getting even more disturbing.

"Don't worry, we'll be as inconspicuous as possible, but we'll be there – at all times. We want your wife to act normally – as normally as she can – when she takes Mark to and from school. Also, when she goes to work. But we'll have someone following, just for the journeys. We must also tell the school – in strictest confidence – but we don't want Mark to know. He doesn't already, does he?"

"No." At least they had got that right. "We decided that'd be wrong."

"Good. Anyway, we hope this will only be a temporary measure. Every spare hand I have is now being assigned to the case. If there's a serial killer about, he needs to be caught pretty damn quickly."

"And we'll make sure we're all on full alert at the bank," David said, knowing this was already the case.

"Yes, be on your guard at all times. And I need to know all I can about Mrs Martingale and Mrs Whytechapel. I'd like you to look at their accounts – dig out any facts that could be relevant. Then, let me know anything you discover. It could be vital."

The digging around would not be a problem; he would get Jane started on that straight away. He would also quiz Trevor and Barbara about their discussions with Mrs Martingale. But this was now getting out of his hands. There were strict laws about customer confidentiality and he needed the advice of the Chief Inspector's Department before passing anything over to Hopkins.

And he knew he would not simply get advice from the Chief. He was also sure to receive a knock on his door by a visiting inspector.

# CHAPTER 16

Wednesday again already. Early closing day. How portentous was that?

How the week had flown by. At least, today would be different – no interviews. He had blocked out his diary completely.

It had not been a popular move.

Customers knew he was not away on holiday, yet they were being foisted on Norman Charlton. They were not happy. Nor was Norman.

A chief clerk's lot was not always a comfortable one. He might not have the manager's overall responsibility for the branch, but he was number two and managerial thinking came firmly within his domain. Yet he was ostensibly still a clerk – evidenced by his title. David hoped that, one day, the bank would better recognize a chief clerk's status. To start with, his title could be re-named as assistant manager or deputy manager. As it was, his present designation could mean that Norman's allegiances might lean heavily towards his colleagues in the general office. Such staff did not always appreciate the reasoning behind managerial decisions – did not necessarily recognise the broad picture involved in running the branch.

Norman's difficulty was to maintain an equilibrium between the beliefs held by these staff and those of their manager. In this, he was not always successful.

Six months ago, David had needed to question his handling of a tricky manager-versus-staff situation. Norman had confessed that he had much preferred his previous solitary wartime role in the cockpit of his Spitfire, pitching and rolling his plane, high in the luminous skies above the Garden of England. The obvious dangers had not, apparently, entered into his reckoning. But there must have been some sort of psychological backlash. How else would he have eschewed the excitement of the RAF for what some might think were the South Devon backwaters of humdrum banking.

But there would be nothing tedious about his travails today. Half-a-dozen interviews on top of his normal duties would see to that.

Meanwhile, David knew he had enough on his own plate, without being hampered by interviews.

His desk bore proof that banking was a paper-generating business. Jane had actually needed a trolley to bring into his room the ledgers and documents she had accrued from her dormant account investigations.

Yet such extensive probing had not, at first, been intended.

After his meeting with Chief Inspector Hopkins David had asked Jane to look into the accounts of Mrs Martingale and Mrs Whytechapel, but it had not, apparently, taken the girl long to decide to expand her field of research.

"Have a look at Mrs Martingale's account first," she said, passing the customer's latest ledger sheet across his desk.

David could hardly avert his eyes from Jane's face to the ledger sheet which he took into his hand without looking. Her serious expression could not shield an intensity in her eyes. He had seen it before when she had carried out a particularly demanding exercise. It was as if it were visible evidence of the adrenalin pumping through her. It also enhanced her attractiveness. No wonder John had taken such a shine to her. And it was clear in the golf club's shop that the feeling was mutual. The young assistant professional exuded bonhomie which most of the members put down to an attractive young girl being in the background – without knowing the relationship was with Jane.

David forced his eyes to the sheet in his hand, still having to adjust to the introduction of machine-produced ledger sheets. Until recently, smaller branches such as his had up-dated customers' accounts by hand, inscribing entries into huge tomes – bound ledgers, almost too heavy to carry. Senior staff were entrusted with this task, their years of experience in using best copperplate effectively creating what some might consider to be works of art.

It had not been the same for statements and passbooks.

These copies of the bank's records had been completed for customers by junior staff. David had often felt the compilers of ledgers and statements might have been better reversed. The standard of the youngsters' handwriting bore no comparison with that of their elders. Many a time, customers must have puzzled over entries on their statements. Now, following mechanization, cheques were identified by their printed numbers, rather than by the specific names of the payees, no doubt much to the relief of all.

Mrs Martingale's ledger sheet looked perfectly normal. The opening balance, carried forward from the previous bound ledger, stood at exactly £11,000. This related back to last October, the time when mechanization was introduced. Since then, there had been six withdrawals of £1,000.

"Not a very active account," he said, glancing up a Jane. "But she seems to be getting through her money."

Jane nodded but said nothing, as if waiting for him to utter pearls of wisdom.

"But no credits," he added.

Jane shook her head.

"But that's presumably because she's been living abroad?"

Jane smiled, as if satisfied at his perceptiveness. "And she was retired, sir. So she wouldn't have been getting any salary or wages."

"What about a pension?"

"No sign of one coming through here. It might have gone

direct to the States."

That was possible. If, of course, she had been entitled to a pension. Oliver said she used to work for her husband, but that was some time ago. And the job might not have warranted a pension. As for a state pension... who knows? "She'd certainly have to live on something. Is that what these withdrawals were about?"

"I don't know, sir," Jane replied. "As you can see, they've just got TFR against them."

David sighed. This new-found mechanization might be the way forward, but the entries were now less informative. It was now all about symbols: TFR for transfer; SO for standing order; and three-figure numbers to identify cheques. In the old-style ledgers, the beneficiaries of transfers, standing orders and cheques would be specified in full. This information would paint a comprehensive picture of what was taking place on a customer's account. Now? You just had to be satisfied with symbols. Progress they call it.

"So, they could be transfers to New York?"

"Yes, but I'll need to check the actual vouchers to make sure."

David frowned. "You've not done that yet?"

"No," Jane replied, looking a little askance. "I really haven't had time. It's been bad enough getting this lot out."

All right, he had been a little sharp with her, but these new systems could be so frustrating. "I'm sorry, Jane," he said, smiling. He needed to keep her spirits up and thinking positively. "It's just that I've come to think of you as some kind of superwoman."

Jane visibly relaxed and actually blushed. Only six months ago, she had reddened at every opportunity. It said much for her growing maturity that such overt embarrassment was almost a thing of the past.

"Anyway," David continued, "perhaps you'd do that next. It

should then tell us what we want to know."

"But have a look at this," Jane then said, heaving open one of their old-style handwritten ledgers which, with some difficulty, she had previously put on his desk.

She leafed through the folios until she came to Mrs Martingale's account and then turned the ledger round to face David.

The only entries on the page were ten years ago – all credits to the account which then led to a balance of £11,000. This was the figure which was subsequently transferred to the new mechanized sheet.

"I know what these credits are," David said. "Mr Sargeant told me about them. The first one was the proceeds of the sale of her house. He dealt with the sale before she went to New York. The others were from shares she sold. Her husband had left them to her."

"But why would she leave all that money on a current account? Wouldn't she want to put it on deposit and earn some interest?"

Financially-sophisticated customers would do just that, but David knew that many never gave such consideration a thought. Knowing the money was sitting safely on an account was enough for them.

"You and I would do that," he replied, "but Mrs Martingale? Who knows? She might have thought the deposit interest rate didn't make it worthwhile."

Deposit rate was always set at 2% below bank rate which, in recent times, had been around 3% and 5%. Most people would consider such a return to be better than nothing, but Mrs Martingale?

"She could have invested it," Jane then suggested, "or, at least, some of it."

"Mr Sargeant said she didn't want to take the risk. That's why she sold the shares. She didn't trust the stock market so soon after the war."

"But that was over ten years ago."

"Yes, but living in the States…"

Jane nodded, as if acknowledging the potential difficulties, though not necessarily accepting them.

"Maybe," she said, "these latest £1,000 transfers were some form of investment."

"It's possible. That's why we need to see the actual vouchers. But it's strange the payments have only started going out this last year."

"That's what I wanted to point out," Jane said, her eyes shining. "Until this year, her account was dormant. She's one of the reasons why we haven't got so many dormant accounts."

David had a sudden thought – and he was almost afraid to express it. "You're not going to tell me it's the same with Mrs Whytechapel?"

"Not exactly, sir," Jane replied.

David raised his eyebrows.

"For one thing, Mrs Whytechapel also has a deposit account."

"But what about her current account?"

"It's a bit like Mrs Martingale's, sir. Except that Mrs Whytechapel's withdrawals were all cheques – either £300 or £500. They all went out of the account over the last six months. At this stage I don't know who the payees were."

"You need to dig out the cheques, then. And the deposit account?"

"Cash withdrawals, according to the ledger."

Jane moved Mrs Martingale's ledger to one side of the desk and replaced it with a similar-sized tome, bound in a dark red cover and emblazoned with the words 'Deposit Accounts'. She turned the pages to reach the back of the ledger and turned it towards David so he could clearly see the page for Mrs Whytechapel.

Not unlike Mrs Martingale, she had a five-figure balance – £10,548 to be exact, ignoring shillings and pence. The account was certainly not dormant. Apart from half-yearly amounts of interest being credited to it, there had been regular withdrawals in recent months. These also amounted to £300 or £500.

"So," he said, "apart from interest payments, this account had been dormant before these withdrawals." Was this whole question of dormant accounts about to blow up in his face? Why did he feel this way?

"Yes – until six months ago," Jane replied. Was she confirming his fears? "It was a joint account with her husband until he died. That was in 1951. Until then, it was really active. It became dormant after he died."

"When Mrs Whytechapel went into the nursing home?"

"I'm not sure, sir."

"Well, she wouldn't have many outgoings at the home."

"Apart from the fees."

That was true. And they would have gone up annually. "That could be the reason for all the withdrawals in the last year."

Jane leaned back in her chair and looked at him pensively, her glasses almost magnifying the compassion which radiated from her eyes. "I still can't believe these two old ladies have been murdered," she said.

He could only share her disquiet.

What was Barnmouth coming to? And National Counties, for that matter. Most towns would never encounter a murder, yet Barnmouth had now chalked up three in six months. Most banks and their managers would have occasional involvement with the police and the law courts, but usually by way of providing evidence against fraudulent customers. Yet, here in Barnmouth, his encounters with the police were about violent crime.

Could it have been a case of Mrs Martingale and Mrs Whytechapel being in the wrong place at the wrong time? They were hardly the most likely murder victims. And it was ironic that Mrs Whytechapel had been in a nursing home for her protection, yet she had apparently been murdered in her bed. It was so unjust.

"Anyway," he said, "remember on Monday, I told you the police had said that Mrs Whytechapel had recently been in touch with us. Have you found anything out about this?"

"No, sir. I've checked the correspondence files, but there was nothing there. So, I asked Katie and Barbara, but they'd never heard of Mrs Whytechapel. Neither had I, for that matter."

"Nor me," David said. There was no way in which he would know all his customers, especially those living in a nursing home. But, as far as Mrs Martingale and Mrs Whytechapel were concerned, he was starting to learn a great deal about them now. And was there more to come with other customers? There were still items on his desk to which Jane had not yet referred.

"But I'll keep searching," she said. "And I'll also dig out the vouchers for all those withdrawals. I'm sorry, sir, as I just said, I really haven't had the time yet."

Of course not. It was a miracle she had done so much in such a short period. "Don't worry, Jane," he said, giving her what he hoped was a comforting smile. "You've done brilliantly already, But what else have you got here?"

Jane returned his smile, as if in relief. "Not a lot actually. I've generated plenty of paper...as you can see... but the rest is to do with the dormant account question. I might be wrong, but a trend seems to have been developing – of accounts having been re-activated."

"But that could be good news. I said that to you last week."

"I know, sir, and I hope you're right. I just need a bit more time. I've only been through the A-F section, so far, and six accounts have been re-activated. If that rate continues, there'll be twenty to thirty in all."

"That's impossible," David replied. Even if they had mounted a drive to contact customers with dormant accounts, they would never have had such success. There had to be another reason. "Have you checked the names on your list with the PM cards?"

Each customer had a Private Memorandum card on which any piece of salient information was recorded. After each interview, David would dictate a note to Katie, so that anyone subsequently wanting to know something about a customer had the full history available in one place. This was particularly useful to others, particularly Norman, when deputizing at holiday times, and also to bank inspectors. The inspector who would shortly descend on the branch would certainly make full use of the PM cards.

"Yes, but none of them had any recent entries."

"What about the vouchers?"

"I still haven't managed to locate them."

"Well, that's your next task. We need to see them – and those for Mrs Martingale and Mrs Whytechapel – before the inspector arrives. I'm surprised he hasn't come already. What's the position with your other work?"

Jane frowned. "I've quite a bit on my desk."

"I'll get Norman to help out."

Jane's furrows grew deeper. "I don't think he'd appreciate that."

No, not with all those interviews of his. "What about Katie and Barbara? They could help. I'll have a word with them."

"It would certainly be better coming from you, sir."

She was right. Jane had become so adept at her job that he kept forgetting she was still only just twenty-two. In banking terms, she was extremely young to be doing her present job. She would have no problem in getting Katie's assistance, but with Barbara being so much more senior, it was not fair to expect her to seek out the supervisor's help.

After sending Jane on her way, telling her to leave the heavy ledgers behind for the time being, he sat back to contemplate his next move. But within minutes, Katie had put her head round his door to say the bank's inspector had arrived.

# CHAPTER 17

The inspectors were at Newton Abbot – just down the road – and GG had said the boss man was Parker. In the circumstances, David could not imagine anyone else knocking on his door.

He was not disappointed.

Not disappointed? Did that mean he welcomed the man? He was distinctly uneasy about that. Admittedly, Parker's inspection of the branch last November had ended satisfactorily, but it had been a decidedly fraught beginning. The inspector had been irascible and aggressive. He had gone out of his way to make David's hackles rise. In this, he had patently succeeded.

Would this be his strategy today?

Yet Parker was here to advise, not cajole; to provide support, not resistance; to give comfort, not disquiet. Was he capable of this?

His appearance had remained unchanged. Sitting opposite, David could not believe someone in National Counties had reached such a senior post despite his appearance. Prior to any managerial appointment, stringent assessments were made at the bank's Staff Training College. A gruelling five-week course covered all aspects of banking practice. But personal qualities were assessed even higher than technical expertise. This must be the major reason why GG had still to step on the first rung of the managerial ladder.

Good manners, personality, general intelligence and, yes, appearance were pre-requisites for managerial advancement. Yet Parker sat there looking like an unmade bed. Not only was he dishevelled, but his shirt, tie and suit all bore evidence of meals gone-by.

It had been the same last year. David had assumed he was unmarried, but then learnt there was a wife in the background.

How sad must she be? Sarah might be prone to making minute adjustments to his tie and insisting on a fresh shirt each day – never mind clean underwear – but any niggles he might feel at the time were always tempered by the knowledge that she cared. There was nothing like having someone to care for you. So, what was Mrs Parker up to?

But the intensity radiating from Parker's steel-blue eyes overrode any shortcomings in his general appearance. This was not a man to underrate. Perhaps his unkempt appearance was part of his ploy; it might encourage his adversaries – branch managers? – to under-estimate the man with whom they were dealing.

"You've got yourself into a bit of a mess here," Parker said, as though this was something of David's own making.

"I'm not sure I…"

"I wouldn't be here, otherwise," Parker interjected, apparently not wanting to hear any possible rejoinder.

It did not augur well. Yet Parker must have been properly briefed. Was this really a time for hostilities?

"Let me get the basic facts right," Parker continued, not having to turn to any papers from in his briefcase which remained planted on the floor next to his chair. "First, you had advance warning of a possible raid. Secondly, you received… or, to be precise, your wife received… a threat against your son. Then, two of your customers have apparently been murdered. It all happens in Barnmouth, doesn't it?"

"And don't forget last year's murder," David interjected, his hackles already rising. Why not remind Parker that life at Barnmouth branch had previously conspired to make banking different from how it had been depicted at the Staff Training College.

"Ah, yes. How could I forget?"

"You probably don't know, but the police inspector... Hopkins... got promoted after that particular case."

Parker's eyes narrowed. "So?"

"Just thought you'd like to know. No doubt you'll come across him again, this time. It's Chief Inspector now."

An imperceptible movement of his head indicated Parker's thoughts about promotions in other organizations. Was it professional jealousy on his part?

"I suppose I'll have to call him 'sir'."

Which side of the bed did he get out of today?

"Anyway," Parker continued, "apart from the two deaths – which might or might not have anything to do with the bank – nothing has actually happened."

Oh, no? Apart from having an armed policeman in the branch; a cashier effectively re-living a previous raid; a wife at home going spare about the safety of her only son; and he, himself, bearing the responsibility for ensuring the safety of his staff and family. No, nothing really had actually happened.

Parker must have read his thoughts. He actually apologized.

"I'm sorry. The fact is I'm peeved at having to be here. I'm on a tight schedule at Newton Abbot and now this has come up."

It was difficult to feel sorry for the man. His job was hardly front-line stuff. Being in the firing line was what pressure was all about.

David's silence must have spoken volumes.

"Let me start again," Parker said, clearly re-marshalling his thoughts. "We need to work together – like before, eh?"

Yes, indeed. And because of that, last year's murderer got caught. Teamwork had paid off – even if only one promotion had subsequently materialized.

And Parker's unexpected humility had the desired effect. David felt the tension of the previous minutes ebbing from him. This was more like it. He could work with this particular side of Parker.

"So, where to begin?" he asked, reaching across to his telephone. "Coffee? Tea?"

"Coffee, please," Parker said. "Black, no sugar."

Sweet enough as he was? Hardly, but this was not the moment to air such thoughts. Katie took the coffee order over the telephone and he awaited Parker's response to his first question.

"I imagine you've had a comprehensive session with the police," Parker said, now visibly relaxed, though his eyes retained their previous intensity. "So, just give me the gist of what they thought of the two threats. I'd then like to get our heads together about the two old ladies. I must say... at this stage... it's difficult to see how their deaths could be linked to the bank."

David described the events of the last week, starting with the note having been found on the blotting paper and the subsequent presence in the branch of DC Pound. He made particular mention of Trevor Smith's involvement and how the lad had been subjected to a previous raid. He then explained how Sarah had received the note which threatened Mark's safety and how he had subsequently sought the advice of Chief Inspector Hopkins at Torquay police station, getting a response which he had found less than satisfactory.

"It sounds as though the police weren't convinced the threats were real," Parker said, frowning.

"That's the impression I got – to start with, anyway."

"And now? Are they now thinking differently?"

"Yes, because of the murders. Hopkins now seems particularly concerned about Mark. He says the school's got to be told and he's getting his people to keep an eye on our house. They'll also follow Sarah when she takes Mark to and from school. But that particular part won't start yet; he's just broken up for Easter."

"Of course, I'd forgotten. Easter's this coming weekend."

David nodded. Even more than usual, he was looking forward to a four-day break. For Mark and him, the holiday period would be dominated by football. United had home matches on Good Friday and on Saturday – against Southampton and Newport County. It would give him a heaven-sent opportunity of relieving Sarah of having to keep Mark in close attendance. He would also be able to yell and shout – something he had to refrain from doing in the office and at home. Being able to let off steam in the company of many like-minded people was great therapy in countering other stresses.

"But before we get round to the old ladies," Parker continued, "do you think there's a connection between the two threats?"

It was a question which David kept asking himself – without getting a conclusive answer.

"I just don't know," he replied, shaking his head. "On the one hand, I feel there must be. Yet Hopkins got the handwriting analysed and he says the notes were written by different people."

"The handwriting could have been disguised."

"That's what I said, but…"

Parker pursed his lips. "So, more than one person could be involved."

"But it doesn't seem likely if the two threats are connected. One person might bear a grudge, but…"

He was interrupted by a knock on the door and, at his behest, Katie entered the room, a round metal tray balanced on the palm of her left hand. She closed the door with her free hand, which was then immediately needed to prevent the contents of the tray – two pale-blue Poole Pottery cups and saucers – from sliding off the now skew-whiff tray. The cups were full to their brims with steaming black coffee and David could only look on with horror as the drinks were about to cascade over Parker's back. Just in time, Katie's remedial action righted the tray, the only consequence being that some of the coffee was deposited in the saucers.

"That was a close one, sir," Katie exclaimed, grinning broadly at Parker. "What a welcome back that would have been."

David was unsure whether the inspector shared Katie's spirited greeting, but Parker actually smiled.

"I had a feeling it wouldn't be long before we met again," he said, helping himself to one of the coffees and placing the cup and saucer on the desk in front of him. "But before anything else, I must congratulate you on your promotion."

Katie positively beamed and, for one moment, David believed the compliment had left her speechless.

"Thank you, sir... so much," she then said, quickly recovering from any inhibition. "I was so nervous when it happened... that's about four months ago now. Time flies, doesn't it, sir? But Mr Goodhart's been really good to me. My shorthand wasn't half as good as Miss Harding's, but I'm getting quicker now. Mind you, I still make mistakes. My spelling was never any good at school. I still have trouble with their and there, if you know what I mean. I'm not very good at commas, either. Of course, I'm talking about typing now, not shorthand, but..."

David gently tapped the end of a pencil on his desk. It had become his signal when Katie's chatter became non-ending and she grinned at him, pressing her lips together as if they were sealed with glue.

"That'll be all for now, Katie," he said. "Many thanks for the coffee, but you'd better get on with your other work."

The girl skipped out of the room and when the door was closed behind her, Parker seemed almost exhilarated from her presence. "She's incorrigible, isn't she?" he enthused, taking a sip of coffee, apparently not noticing the pool lying in the saucer. David watched a succession of drips deposit themselves on the lapel of the inspector's jacket. No wonder his apparel was in such a forlorn state.

"You might imagine the difference between her and Miss Harding," he said, recalling, not with any relish, the formidable spinster who had been secretary to various managers since before the war. "She's like a breath of fresh air. And although she berated her shorthand and typing, she's actually very good – especially as she's not yet twenty."

"Anyway," Parker said, "back to your threats. You think it's down to a grudge factor?"

What else could it be? " Put it this way, I've gone off any idea that it might be someone playing a prank."

"So, who might bear you a grudge?"

David sighed. "I'd like to think no-one." He was into his third year at the branch and he knew he had not always pleased. It went with the job. Satisfying some aspiring borrowers would be downright reckless. But would such declines lead to a grudge? And such an extreme one, at that? "But not everyone has agreed with my decisions."

"I know the feeling," Parker acknowledged.

David could well believe that. A bank inspector's job must be far from easy. In essence, he was an auditor – scrutinizing branches' books for the ultimate benefit of the bank's shareholders. Accounts had to be properly signed off, as for any limited company. But Parker and his inspectorial colleagues also had other agendas: checking on the quality of managers' lending; reviewing the adequacy of security requirements; and assessing the ability of the staff, especially with regard to their possible future promotion. Such a wide-ranging brief was unlikely to endear inspectors to all.

"I've been racking my brains," David said, moving on, "about possible perpetrators, but I can't believe any of them would take such drastic action."

"You've got some names, then?"

He certainly had. But should he share them with Parker? It was all very well throwing some names at Sarah – not least John English – but Parker would expect personal feelings to be backed up with substance.

"John English?" He was safe with this one. Parker knew all about the hotelier from last year.

"Are the police still keeping an eye on him?"

"As far as I know."

"He'd be a fool, then, to do something like this."

Parker was now echoing Hopkins.

"And he's certainly no fool," David said. This was the trouble with dealing with two inspectors; their similar trains of thought demanded some repetition on his part.

"He might still have a link with Stuart Brown," Parker said. "That man's certainly one to bear a grudge."

David smiled. In fiction, an incarcerated Brown would be a prime suspect. But in real life? "He might have a grudge, but would he have the wherewithal to carry it out?"

Parker nodded. "You're probably right. He's a non-starter – like English."

Two down, how many more to go?

But should he now mention Charlie Hicklemaker? The man might make a more credible suspect with a different name. In any case, Saturday's interview shed new light on the man. He was, surely, just a working man with a huge chip on his shoulder. Yet he had made threats; there was no question about that. But he had also apologized. No, at this stage, Hicklemaker could take a back seat. But what about Michael Farthinshawe?

"There is someone else," he said, his words making Parker look at him sharply. "And it really brings us on to the two old ladies – specifically Mrs Whytechapel."

"Go on."

"It's the owner of the Riverside Nursing Home – Michael Farthinshawe"

"That sounds ominous. Is this the link between the ladies and the bank… never mind the threats?"

"It might be in the case of Mrs Whytechapel. She was a resident at the nursing home. But apart from that, I don't think so. It's just that I saw Farthinshawe a couple of months ago. He's been a customer for years, but this was my latest meeting."

"You see him regularly?"

"Yes, a couple of times a year to review his facilities… and, sometimes, socially."

"Is his account a problem?"

"No… not exactly. But I don't like the trend we're now seeing."

Parker raised his eyebrows and the resultant furrows seemed to stretch across the whole of his bald head. When the inspector first came to the branch last year, David compared his head to a mature conker and he saw no reason to change this impression now.

"We used to see a fully swinging account – in and out of credit – but, now, credit balances have disappeared. He's usually hard up against his overdraft limit."

"Sounds like overtrading."

"Yes," David agreed, "but he didn't like it when I started asking questions. I tried to establish what was going wrong with his cash flow and he went wild. He accused me of questioning his integrity – and that of his staff."

"How many people does he employ?"

"Probably about ten altogether. On the nursing side, he has a senior carer and the rest are mainly part-timers. Others do cleaning and catering – again, mostly part-timers."

"Does Farthinshawe, himself, get involved in the day-to-day

running of the business?"

"He used to, but he's more behind the scenes, these days. I think he leaves most of the running to the senior carer."

"That could be the problem. Taking his eye off things."

David nodded. It could easily happen.

"Who's this carer?" Parker asked.

"It's a Mrs Flintshire. She's been there for years. I don't have any dealings with her; all my interviews are with Farthinshawe."

"Does she sign on the account?"

"Not to my knowledge."

Parker frowned. "Even so, she has a feel of Miss Harding about her."

Parker had a point. A long-standing member of staff could effectively become part of the furniture, the hub of everything going on in the business. That could be a great asset, but should that person develop less than honourable tendencies... Miss Harding had sheltered under an umbrella of total respectability, yet, unbeknown to anyone, she had been milking her own mother's account. Could Mrs Flintshire be doing the same sort of thing with Farthinshawe's business?

"Yes," he agreed. "And, as I said, Farthinshawe was certainly put out when I queried the possible integrity of his staff."

"Did you specifically mention this Flintshire woman?"

"No... no, I didn't. I was extremely tactful. But of all the staff – if there was any wrongdoing going on – she would have the most opportunity."

"Even so, if things are going awry in the nursing home, why should that lead to Farthinshawe being a suspect here?"

"No reason at all," David replied. It was certainly sounding like a thin case against the man. "It was just his extreme reaction at the interview. He was so angry."

"Angry enough to bear a grudge?"

David shrugged. "Perhaps I'm just grasping at straws." The case against Farthinshawe was certainly no worse than the one against Hicklemaker. Maybe, after all, he should tell Parker about the builder. But, after doing so, the inspector said he was inclined to add him to his list of non-starters.

"I just feel this nursing home is the link." Parker said, having mulled over all they had discussed.

"But what about Mrs Martingale? She had no link with the home – not to my knowledge, anyway."

Parker leaned back in his chair, displaying his well-stained suit in all its glory. "Perhaps, there are clues in the bank accounts," he mused.

"I've got Jane looking into those – alongside our annual check on dormant accounts. Can you give me a couple of days?"

Parker nodded. "I must get back to Newton Abbot. I'm already well behind. I'll come back after the bank holiday – on Tuesday. But if anything crops up before then, let me know and I'll be back straight away."

After Parker's departure, David sat back and reflected that they only had this afternoon and Thursday to establish what might have been happening on the bank accounts – if anything significant at all. He only hoped that this would provide sufficient time, without having to impinge on the forthcoming Easter break.

# CHAPTER 18

With contrasting emotions, Trevor contemplated his cheese sandwich as he watched the waves gently lapping the shore.

Wednesday lunchtime.

This time last week, he had not been able to eat a thing. Fear; apprehension; sheer anxiety – the gamut of such emotions had flowed through him as he had reflected on the possibility of a raid. But it had not happened.

Could its non-occurrence have been deliberate? Could the raid, instead, take place today?

As he nibbled at the corner of the sandwich, the sharpness of the strong Cheddar tingeing his tongue, he tried to get into the mind of a possible raider. One thing for certain, he, himself, would not have given prior warning by way of that threat on the blotting paper. Unless… unless it had been a deliberate red herring; a ruse to put everyone on full alert – adrenaline pumping. The eventual relief of the staff would be manifested in smiles, nervous jokes and, even, words of bravado – though now based on hindsight. But a perceptive raider might calculate that such relief, in time, might lead to complacency.

So, if his plan was only being delayed…

This Wednesday – early closing day again, the shops shut down at one for further business – would be the perfect time. Few customers, if any, would be in the branch. And the quiet town and its streets would facilitate a speedy getaway. Trevor could also see similarities between Barnmouth and Chagford. The towns, themselves, could not be more different; a seaside holiday resort, against the hub of a moorland farming community. But each town's access and, thereby, exit presented no insuperable difficulties. Admittedly, Barnmouth was bordered on one side by the sea, and no raider could possibly contemplate escape by boat. But the main roads, north and south, and several minor roads inland, provided multiple options for getaway vehicles. It was the same at Chagford, where a maze of country lanes could spirit a car away from possible pursuers. The topography there must have helped last year; the raider had still not been caught.

But the possibility of a raid in Barnmouth did not occupy his undivided attention. Other strong emotions were coursing through him.

Was he being melodramatic in choosing this place to meet? The end of a kaleidoscopic line of beach huts certainly provided perfect seclusion. These bastions of a typical English seaside town backed on to the embankment of the railway line. It meant that access could only be achieved along the narrow promenade which separated the beach huts from the beach. At their end, where he was waiting, the cliff face immediately rose above him. It ensured that no-one could approach from that direction.

Yes, it was a good place for an assignation. At this time of the year, the beach huts were unoccupied and the whole area was deserted. Only someone with a specific mission would come to this spot. He could only hope that Katie would keep her promise to join him here.

Office romances were effectively taboo in the bank – not that he could really contemplate such a relationship with Katie. Not yet, anyhow. Husbands and wives were never allowed to work in the same office and Trevor even knew of one couple who, on becoming engaged, were split up, the girl being transferred to another branch. Goodness knows what the bank thought such conjoining couples would get up to during office hours. So, it was far better to try and keep any possible relationship clandestine. Trevor could imagine the ribbing he would get from Bernard, Barbara and Jane – never mind Mr Goodhart – if even the thought of his dating Katie ever got out.

The only problem was Katie.

Not whether she would consider going out with him again, though this was extremely questionable. But, if she did, whether she could keep quiet about it. First things first, though. At least she had agreed to meet him here. He was not sure why. The more he thought about it, the more his reason for getting together – the reason he had given her – seemed so weak.

"Do you think we could meet up one lunchtime – away from the branch?" he had asked her on Monday. "I've got this problem. I simply can't get over Mrs Martingale's death. I just want to talk to someone about it."

That was what he had said. And Katie had agreed – with alacrity. And the compassion in those lovely eyes had made him feel guilty. It was true he really was disturbed about Mrs Martingale, but it was the aftermath of his date with Katie on Saturday night which was now all-consuming. He could not get her out of his mind. Yet, in the branch, he was not able to summon up the courage to ask her out again. In any case, someone might overhear. Far better to get Katie somewhere on her own.

But what would be her reaction? She had made no subsequent reference to Saturday night, yet she seemed to have enjoyed herself. But she would enjoy herself anywhere – and, probably, with anyone. No, his thoughts were simply fanciful.

Although… she had taken hold of his hand and…

"There you are," Katie suddenly exclaimed, her head peering round the last beach hut. "Isn't this exciting?"

Trevor grinned. Her bonhomie was infectious. "By hiding behind a beach hut?"

"No. The intrigue. It's like being in a film."

"Everything going on at the branch is like a film. How could two of our customers have been murdered?"

Katie simply shook her head, her exhilaration now replaced by unaccustomed gravity.

"That's why I asked you to come here," Trevor continued. "Mainly because of Mrs Martingale. I suppose it's because I actually met her. I never knew Mrs Whytechapel – I'd never even heard of her. But Mrs Martingale…"

"Let's sit down," Katie said, motioning him to a narrow ledge on the adjacent rock face.

"I suppose it's because we seemed to strike up an immediate affinity," Trevor added, quietly pleased that the ledge was only just wide enough to accommodate them both. "And it wasn't just because she liked jazz. It was as if there was no age difference between us. She seemed to have the knack of…"

"I don't think age difference means anything at all," Katie interrupted. "It's the actual person that counts."

That certainly sounded encouraging. The three years difference in their ages might not be significant. "You really think that?"

Katie nodded, opening a paper bag she had brought with her and taking out a steaming Cornish pasty.

"Lucky you," Trevor said, sniffing in appreciation. "That puts my cheese sandwich in the shade."

"You can have a bite."

Trevor grinned, but shook his head.

"Look at me and Miss Harding," Katie then said, scrunching into the pasty, her full mouth giving Trevor time to contemplate the difference between Katie and her predecessor. Sorry, Miss Harding – no contest.

"Miss Harding," Katie continued, having emptied her mouth and licking her shiny lips, "must be over thirty years older than me. Yet, Mr Goodhart chose me to take her place."

"He's a man, isn't he?"

"What do you mean?"

"Just think about it."

"Don't be silly, Trevor. Be serious. Anyway, I know I'm not as good at the job as Miss Harding was, but I'm still doing it after four months. So, I can't be doing too badly. But you see? It didn't matter to Mr Goodhart how old I was – so long as I did the job properly."

Age doesn't matter? That's my girl. Except that she wasn't his girl. Not yet, anyway.

"But you know what?" Katie continued, her eyes having regained their usual animation, "Jane's doing a big investigation – into the accounts of Mrs Martingale and Mrs Whytechapel."

Extraordinary. "How do you know that?"

"Mr Goodhart asked me to help her out with her other work. He needs to know what she finds out by tomorrow. I think it's tied up with the inspector. Mr Parker's been with the manager all morning."

"But the murders couldn't be linked to the bank."

"It's because both women banked here. And Mr Goodhart also asked me if Mrs Whytechapel had recently been in touch with us."

"But she was in a nursing home."

"Yes, the Riverside. And they also bank with us."

"So, why would Mrs Whytechapel contact us. And how?"

"That's what Mr Goodhart wanted to know. He thinks she might have written to us. I have a feeling he got that from the police."

"Well, if she's written in – that should be easy enough to find out."

"I know. But I haven't found any letter and no-one else has. Me and Barbara have spent ages looking. If she wrote about her account, one of us two would have seen it. I think it's a wild goose chase."

"What about Jane? Has she found anything out yet?"

Katie shook her head and, having finished her pasty, brushed some stray crumbs off her chest. How could such an innocent action distract him so? "No," she said. "She's having trouble in finding some of the vouchers. She wants me to help out this afternoon. It's all a bit of a mystery – and ever so exciting. But, you know what? I don't think you wanted me to come here to talk about the bank."

"Why ever not?" And why had he started to blush?

"We could have done that at the branch."

Was it his imagination, or had Katie edged a little closer? "I told you – I was bothered about Mrs Martingale. I wanted to talk to someone – away from the branch."

"But why me? You know what I think?"

Whatever she thought, he knew that Katie would not be shy in letting him know. She was so up front – and in more ways than one.

"I think," she said, not giving him time to answer and, now, she had definitely moved closer, "I think you were going to ask me out again."

What should he do now? Had it been that obvious? His normal inhibition with girls urged him to deny her claim. Yet, it was true. Why not take a leaf out of Katie's book and bluntly admit it?

His ongoing silence had effectively confirmed Katie's theory. "I knew it," she cried out, now taking his hand in her own. "And the answer's yes – yes, please."

Why had he made it so difficult for himself? Why could he not have been more open? But that was the power of hindsight. He knew her answer now. Before, it had only been a figment of his imagination. "I'm a dolt, aren't I?" he said, finding the courage to squeeze her hand.

"You're lovely," she simply replied. "But where are you going to take me?"

The next problem. "How about football?"

"You men! Torquay United, I suppose."

Trevor nodded. "They're playing on Friday and Saturday."

"You mean we've got two dates?"

Trevor shook his head and grinned at her sense of fun. "No – just Saturday. And after the match we could go down to the Strand and have a drink or something. I don't have a gig this Saturday."

It was with a lightness in his heart and head that he made his separate way back to the branch. Katie had promised to keep their going out together secret, though how long she – and, for that matter, he – could keep that up was another thing. But he now had a problem. He had lost track of time and it was already ten-past-one. Bernard would be going bananas. His wife, Celia, hated his getting home late for lunch.

As he approached the branch, Barbara Bolton hurried down the front steps, cradling her large shopping basket in her arms.

"Where have you been?" She was clearly not in a good temper.

"I'm sorry. I got delayed."

"Well, I've had to help out on the counter and now I'm late for my shopping. As for Bernard. You know what Celia's like – when Bernard's not on time for lunch."

Trevor could not care a jot for Celia's cottage pie, or whatever else might be getting cold on the table, but he was sorry not to have been back by one to relieve Bernard. It was never fair when those on the twelve-until-one lunch hour were dilatory in returning.

And when he got to the counter to take over, the first cashier was certainly white-faced. But not from anger.

"We've just been raided," Bernard gasped, sitting down on his stool and putting his head in his hands.

# CHAPTER 19

Trevor could not believe what he had just heard.

The shock of being castigated in the street by Barbara had been bad enough, but what had been going on in the branch? How could it have possibly been raided?

What was Bernard talking about? For goodness' sake, Barbara had just gone out shopping. After the branch had been raided?

Bernard remained seated on his stool, his head still buried in his hands. "We've just been raided," he repeated, as if by rote, his words almost inaudible.

This was madness. "What do you mean, Bernard? We can't have been raided. Nothing's happened. It's all too quiet."

It was a far cry from the torment of Chagford. There, once the raider had fled, utter confusion had prevailed. It had been a living nightmare. The strident alarm bell had vied for attention with screaming customers and the heart-rending sobbing of the young girls behind the counter. They were already traumatised by the unexpected and unexplained assault on their cherished place of work. But their shock was nothing compared to what Trevor, himself, the prime victim, had been going through.

Yet here? Bernard sat immobile, admittedly white-faced, with his head in his hands and… and Barbara had gone out shopping.

It was unreal.

"Bernard!" Trevor pleaded, placing an arm around the first cashier's shoulders, but resisting the not unreasonable temptation of urging him to pull himself together. "What do you mean, raided?"

At last, Bernard released his head from his hands and looked him in the eye. "Raided? Robbed? What's the difference?"

His acting and talking like this made it difficult to believe that

Bernard must be thirty years older than himself. The difference in their maturity should be immense. Yet, it was he who had been tempted to tell the other to pull himself together. But Bernard's confusion over words now made more sense. Robbery could certainly differ from a raid. It might occur surreptitiously, quite contrary to a raid. Trevor had once had his wallet stolen and it had been a while before he had discovered it to be missing. Could it be a similar case here?

"You mean we've been robbed?" he asked. It was as well there were no customers in the branch. Bernard was in no fit state to serve them and Trevor had not yet had the opportunity of opening up his own till. In fact, the only person in the vicinity was Roger Singleton. The junior was behind the counter, struggling to list a pile of cheques on a manual adding machine which he had clearly not yet mastered. There was no doubting he was unaware of anything untoward having happened in the branch.

Bernard nodded disconsolately. "The money was here... on my till... and when I got back, it was gone."

"When you got back?" What had the man been up to?

The first cashier now looked sheepish. Bernard? Looking sheepish?

Unbelievable.

"I had to go back there," he answered, flicking his head towards the back of the office, fire now burning in his eyes. "Some idiot had taken the open credit box off the counter. It had been left by the deposit account ledgers. I had to mark off Mrs Mottram-Smythe's withdrawal."

"And the money was on your till? You mean, it was on the till – not in it? On the actual counter?"

Bernard nodded again, the fire in his eyes immediately doused.

"How much are we talking about?"

The first cashier remained silent.

"Bernard? How much?"

There was a continuing pause until he eventually muttered, "£2,500."

Trevor could only gaze at Bernard, appalled. Any carelessness in banking was frowned upon – even in the completion of vouchers or book entries. Accuracy was a byword. Clerks would be castigated for making even rare mistakes, each one having to be crossed out with a horizontal red ink line. Trevor still went hot and cold when recalling how he had entered a whole list of debits in the credits' column of the revered General Ledger, causing Mr Goodhart's predecessor a chronic attack of apoplexy.

Yet, as first cashier, Bernard should be setting an exemplary standard of correct cashiering, leading his junior colleagues by example. He had, nonetheless, left his till open and unattended when he went to the back of the office. He had also left bundles of notes on the counter within easy reach of customers. It would have been bad enough if protective screens were in place between customers and cashiers. After the raid in Chagford, Trevor had actually made that suggestion to Mr Goodhart, who had put it forward to Head Office. But without such screens, a customer would not have had to be long in the arm to help himself to notes which Bernard had so generously left unattended.

But it was clear from Bernard's whole demeanour that he was well aware of his shortcomings. His reply had been racked with guilt. And no wonder. Any control over his cash had vanished once he had left his till unattended. It was the cardinal sin of any bank cashier. Even if no money had been taken, he would have been for the high jump if he had been found out. As it was, it would seem that the not inconsiderable sum of £2,500 had walked out of the branch.

But when did this happen? Certainly before one-fifteen. In

which case, Barbara must, surely, have been there. Had she really left to do her shopping, oblivious of the fact that the branch had been robbed?

"She didn't know," Bernard answered, after Trevor had posed the question. "She'd been making such a song and dance about you being back late. I just told her to get out of my hair. And, at that stage, I wasn't really sure I'd been robbed. I thought my mind was playing tricks. But when she'd gone, I realized the money had disappeared."

"But who took it? Didn't you see anyone in the banking hall?"

"Yes, I did!" Bernard exclaimed, immediately perking up, as though he had found the answer to his prayers. "He was sitting at the table over there – nearest the door."

"He? Who's he?"

"How the hell do I know?" Bernard snapped. "If I did, I wouldn't need to put up with this interrogation of yours."

Trevor sighed. So much for trying to help and provide some comfort. Goodness knows, Bernard would need all the support and comfort he could get once Mr Goodhart knew what had happened. And the sooner the manager found out, the better. The problem was not simply going to disappear. To delay telling the manager would only make matters worse. As it was, after all Mr Goodhart's recent directives for everyone to be on full security alert, he was likely to be apoplectic at Bernard's blatant disregard of his instructions.

"I'm sorry you feel like that," Trevor simply answered, taking his keys from his pocket and opening up his till, "but if you'll allow me to say anything else, I suggest you go and report what's happened to the manager straight away. You might well think I've been interrogating you, but just you wait until…"

He deliberately let his words tail off. He would not normally have dared to sound so impertinent, but, whichever way he put it, he would probably be wrong. Yet, it was the best advice he could give Bernard. Seeing the manager immediately was the only option available to him. He was only thankful that he, himself, would not be on the end of Mr Goodhart's wrath.

# CHAPTER 20

"Raided? You think? You think we've been raided?"

David glared across the desk at Bernard Groves, now slumped in his chair, chin buried in his chest. Having waived his break for lunch to catch up on his work, David could see his plans totally disintegrating – if what he had just heard was true.

Bernard remained silent, avoiding any eye contact. When he eventually looked up, he seemed wracked with guilt. Guilt? It was not the likely reaction of someone on the receiving end of an attack.

"Bernard. What actually happened? How can you just think we've been raided? We either have or we haven't. But there's been no commotion. I haven't heard a thing. No-one else has said anything. What on earth are you talking about?"

Three minutes had now elapsed since the cashier had come into the room and he still sat mute on the other side of the desk. How frustrating was that?

Three minutes and there was still no further explanation of the cashier's initial confession. Confession? That was certainly how it had come across. "I'm sorry, sir," he had said, on entering the room, "but I think we've just been raided."

Now, he sat opposite, looking shell-shocked, still remaining silent. Just before the drama had arisen, David had made himself a cup of tea and this still sat, untouched, on his desk. He pushed it across to Bernard who grasped it with both hands, slurping the contents noisily. It had been a good move. Colour immediately started to return to the cashier's face.

"Well?" Perhaps nudging Bernard into saying something might work better than repeated questioning.

"Thank you," Bernard eventually said, pushing the cup and

saucer away from him. "I needed that."

"And I need you to tell me exactly what's happened. You think there's been a raid? How can you simply think such a thing?"

"I don't know," Bernard replied, now looking shamefaced. "That's all I could think had actually happened."

This was such a different Bernard from only six months ago. Shamefaced? David could never have previously thought it of the man. He had been so arrogant. He and his wife, Celia, had lorded it around the town as if they owned the place. They seemed to think that wealth equated to status. From where their wealth arose was not known. It certainly did not stem from Bernard's salary; bank cashiers did not command high earnings. It was generally assumed that Celia was the source of their affluence – presumably through inheritance.

"I think you'd better start at the beginning," David said, hoping he might now get somewhere with this exasperating man. He was also less troubled by the cashier's belief that the branch had been raided. Everything was too calm out there. If there was even a sniff of a raid, Trevor, for one, would be at his wit's end.

"We'd had a very busy lunch period," Bernard began, at last making eye contact, "particularly between twelve and half-past. Trevor was out at lunch and I had to call on Barbara."

That was fair enough. Prior to closing their shops at one, many traders paid in their takings beforehand. They needed to get surplus cash off their premises. Even though Barbara had enough to do in the back office, she would need to open her relief till at busy times. David had instructed Bernard to call upon her whenever there was any risk of queuing in the banking hall. Lunch times were a case in point. Customers abhorred queuing then. And it was never a valid excuse to claim that cashiers also had to eat. Far better to find a relief cashier to avert possible complaints.

"Anyway," Bernard continued, drawing the cup and saucer

back towards him, as if he needed further sustenance to carry on, "at about half-twelve, there was a lull, but I asked Barbara to stay. I needed to bundle up the stacks of notes I'd accumulated. I could then get them into the safe – out of the way. You know you always insist on this."

That was true. Fewer notes in the tills would lessen any loss should – heaven forbid – a raid actually take place. And bearing in mind they had received that warning last Wednesday...

"I'd soon sorted out £2,500 in £1 notes – five bundles of £500. I'd got them on the top of my till to put bands round – ready to take into the safe. Then... at about five to one... Mrs Mottram-Smythe came in."

David frowned. It was not someone he knew.

"She's an open-credit customer – a pensioner," Bernard explained, acknowledging his manager's apparent unfamiliarity with the name. "She banks at Plymouth branch and has a cashing arrangement here."

Oh, my my. This was now getting ominous. David had a foreboding of what was to come. Not the actual detail, but the general scenario was making him go hot and cold. He had no concern about Mrs Mottram-Smythe, but why had Bernard specifically pointed out that the bundles of £1 notes were on top of his till – and not tucked away inside.

"I paid out her money," Bernard continued, "and when she left, I went to record the entry on her card."

"But you should have done that before you paid her out – to check it was within the authorized arrangement."

"I didn't need to do that. I know her well. She comes in every week. £25 a week, she's allowed. She never takes more."

This was the problem last year – being lulled into a false sense of security. Bernard had been duped by George Broadman's friendship and apparent respectability. Unwittingly, he had aided and abetted the butcher's manipulation of the banks' cheque clearing system, simply by failing to carry out normal banking procedures. At first, it was thought he may have been a conspirator to the fraud. But nothing could be proved and he simply suffered a severe reprimand.

Now, it seemed, he was at it again. Would he never learn?

"But when I went to mark off her card," Bernard continued, "the open credit box wasn't there. Then, I saw it on a desk behind the counter. I suppose someone had been up-dating the cards and hadn't put it back. Anyway, I left the cashier's run... it would only take a tick... but Mrs Mottram-Smythe's card wasn't in the right place. Some clot had filed it under M, rather than S. But this all took longer than I expected."

It was now looking abundantly clear and David started to seethe. After all his lectures on security requirements... And, for God's sake, the last one had only been last week – after an actual warning of a raid.

"Are you about to tell me," he said, enunciating his words through gritted teeth, "that you left your till open and unlocked when you left the counter?"

Bernard's Adam's apple rose and fell in his throat.

David took a deep breath. "And the £2,500 was sitting on the counter on top of your till?"

The cashier closed his eyes, as if in disbelief at what he had done.

"And the cash was in grasping distance from the customers' side of the counter?"

"But Barbara was there," Bernard blurted out. "No-one would have tried anything with another cashier there."

How naïve could a person be?

"So," David pressed, "the money was still there when you got back to the counter." He posed his words as a statement, not a question, but he already knew the outcome. This was duly confirmed by Bernard's doleful shake of his head.

"And what did Barbara say?" David asked, finding it increasingly difficult to maintain any sense of equilibrium. But never mind his own outrage; it would be nothing compared to Parker's, when he was told.

"She was serving a customer. And then she locked her till and rushed off before I could tell her what had happened."

"You mean to say you didn't stop her? You're the one supposed to be in charge of what goes on on the counter."

The cashier nodded forlornly. "But you know what Barbara's like. She said she was late to do her shopping – and she was off."

Shopping. It was difficult to know whether to shout and scream at the man, or simply accept the inevitability of a huge black mark against himself. That could well come from Parker, but what would Spattan say? This lapse would hardly endear himself to the Regional Manager.

Yet, this could not be a raid. Raids are pre-planned. No would-be raider could have anticipated Bernard's stupidity. This sounded much more like an opportunistic snatch.

He looked hard at the cashier. "Why on earth did you say we'd been raided – or, should I say, you thought we'd been raided?"

Bernard immediately perked up at the question, as if this was his chance for a get out. "There was a man in the banking hall – at one of the tables. He'd been there for a while. It must have been him. I reckon he'd been planning it."

This was cloud cuckoo land. "How could he have planned it? He didn't know you were going to sort out your notes. He couldn't have known you would then be so stupid as to leave them within his reach – especially leaving them unattended when you then went behind the counter. This wasn't a planned raid. It was a one-off smash and grab – without the man having to do the smash bit."

It was so infuriating. As for Bernard, he must be abundantly aware that, after his last reprimand, he was now in the deepest trouble. And he was not the only one. But how could it have been possible to legislate for such ineptitude?

"So, this man in the banking hall – you got a good look at him? You'd recognize him again?"

"I said he'd been there a while."

"So, you can give the police a good description?"

"The police?"

"Of course. This is robbery. And not only the police. Don't forget the inspectors. I can't believe what Mr Parker's going to say. He left me this morning to go back to Newton Abbot to get on with his backlog there. Now, he's going to have to come straight back here."

David could not suppress an exasperated sigh. There was only going to be one person to tell the inspector of this latest development. But could there be a chink of light?

"Before you do anything else," he said, "I want you to go out there and close down. I want you to balance your till and then…"

A ring of his telephone interrupted him. He listened for a few minutes, his blood pressure rising.

"Just tell her," he said to Katie at the other end, while looking pointedly at Bernard, "that her husband won't be coming home to lunch today."

The last thing he needed was for Celia Groves to be bleating about the absence of her husband for lunch.

"So, Bernard," he said, having replaced the telephone in its cradle, "get Trevor to serve all this afternoon's customers. It's early closing day, so that shouldn't be a problem. Balance your till and come straight back in here when you've done it. It's just possible you're confused and those notes are there all the time."

It was the longest of all possible long shots, but before he contacted Parker and the police, he must be sure of his facts. He would look as stupid as Bernard if he reported now, only for Bernard then to admit that he had forgotten he had put the £2,500 into the back of his till. It should take the cashier no longer than half an hour and, if necessary, he would then ring Parker.

He was, however, sure it would, indeed, be necessary.

# CHAPTER 21

Parker and his two assistants arrived at ten past three. And what a relief it was to hear that Roger Singleton had duly made use of the spy-hole and door chain when he let them into the branch. There had been no need for him to demand production of identification; Parker was fast becoming part of the furniture.

The inspector now sat opposite David, unkempt, as usual, and adopting his normal sprawled posture. David could hardly believe he had only got shot of the man three hours earlier. The feeling might well be mutual; Parker was clearly not enamoured at being back so soon.

"How do you expect me to finish my inspection at Newton Abbot?" he growled, into his chin

But this was not David's problem. If Parker had a complaint, he should pose it to his boss, the Chief Inspector. But he would never do that. He knew the system. The inspector working nearest to the branch which suddenly encounters a problem would be the person to attend. If that should mean spending longer on his normal branch inspection, so be it. No, Parker was simply carping for effect; attempting to put David at a psychological disadvantage. That may have worked last year, but it would not happen again. David had got to know the inspector too well to fall for such a well-tried ploy.

"Anyway," Parker continued, his glare matching his growl, "in addition to all your other problems, there's now a little matter of a missing £2,500."

David nodded, suppressing a wince at the undisguised criticism. It had taken the expected half-hour for Bernard to report back with the bad news. The cashier's till should then have been independently checked, along with those of Trevor Smith and Barbara Bolton, but this task needed to be left until after closing time. Following Parker's arrival, his two assistants were now hard at it.

"You better tell me what you know about it," Parker said, slumping still further in his chair. David recounted all that Bernard Groves had told him and, at one stage, Parker gave a good impression of someone checking the backs of his eyelids. But this was a man who would be never less than on full alert. And that was how David wanted it. He needed all the help the inspector could provide. One way or another, this particular crime had to be solved... and quickly.

"We need to call the police," Parker said, when David had finished. "They'll want to know all about that man in the banking hall."

"Groves was rather vague about him," David said. Bernard would have to rack his brains to come up with a meaningful description.

"Well, he'll just have to get his thinking cap on," Parker said, echoing the thought. "Who else might have seen the man?"

"Barbara Bolton did. She was on the counter at the time. But when I tried to get a description out of her, she was as vague as Groves."

"Anyone else?"

"Possibly. Trevor Smith was out at lunch, as was Norman Charlton, but Jane Church was around. She's doing the investigation into the accounts of the murdered ladies. But she probably spent most of the lunch hour in the back office. The only other possibility would be Roger Singleton. He knows he has to stay in the main office if no-one other than the cashiers is there. But whether he'd notice anyone specifically in the banking hall is another matter."

"We'll need to interview them all – as will the police when they arrive. We ought to get on to them now. I think I should do it – even if only to prove you've drawn me into the investigation. We need to speak to Hopkins – or his DC. What was his name?"

"Pound," David replied, pushing the telephone across the desk to Parker who was already looking the number up in his diary. A police station's number would not necessarily feature in a bank inspector's diary, but Parker and Hopkins had been in frequent touch last year.

"It'll be DC Pound," Parker said, when he eventually finished the call. "Hopkins is out on another case. Pound said he'd get here by five."

"That gives us the time to interview the staff first," David said, "provided your assistants get a move on with the till checks."

Did Parker bridle at that? He certainly visibly stiffened. "My lads don't hang about – provided the tills are in good order."

*Touché.*

"I imagine you'll want to do the interviews," David said, moving on quickly.

Parker frowned and pursed his lips. "No," he said, "I don't think so. We'll do it together. I think you should play the lead with the questioning; I'll take down the notes. Your staff will probably be more relaxed if you do the questioning."

Behind his gruff exterior, there was actually a sensitive side to Parker. It had been in evidence last year and it was pleasing that it was manifesting itself again now. David would certainly prefer to take the lead with the interviews, if only because it was, after all, his branch. His position might be seen to be demeaned if Parker overtly took charge. On the other hand, it would not be easy with Parker sitting in the wings. And the inspector would not hesitate to take over, if he disapproved of the line of questioning. This could be a separate trial in itself.

"While the cash is still being counted," David suggested, "we could start with the others – with the back-office staff. What do you think?"

Parker nodded. "At this stage, I think we can discount your machinists – and your secretary, for that matter. They wouldn't normally see what might be going on in the banking hall. We can draw them in later, if necessary."

"The only one of those who might see something out there would be Katie, but she was out at lunch between twelve and one."

"So, that leaves Jane and..."

"Roger... Roger Singleton."

"And your deputy was also at lunch?"

"Yes. But I think we should include him. Norman might have heard the others talking. They might have said something to him... something they might prefer to keep quiet about in here."

"We'll leave him till last, then," Parker said, heaving himself out of his chair and pushing it to one side of the desk. He then positioned the other chair on his side centrally to face David directly. He had done all this before David could step round from his side of the desk to do the job himself, but Parker did not seem to mind playing the part of furniture remover. In fact, his general grouchiness seemed to have deserted him. That was a good thing, unless his change of mood was tactics on his part.

"Ah, Jane," David said, a few minutes later when his assistant came into the room and sat down opposite him. Parker now occupied his own chair which he had positioned against the wall away from the door into the room. For once, he sat upright in his seat, appearing to be giving his full attention to a notebook which he clasped in both hands. "You'll appreciate, Jane," David added, "that we appear to have been robbed. Clearly, we need to speak to everyone about this... as will the police. They're arriving later."

Jane gave him her full attention as he spoke and appeared close to tears. It made her slight physique seem even more vulnerable than usual. The self-assurance which she had developed in recent months seemed to have deserted her. But why should that be? Was she aware of something significant?

"In the light of last week's warning," David continued, "this business is even more serious than it would normally be. Goodness knows, any robbery is alarming, but the two things could be linked. So, we need all the help we can get from everyone. Did you see anything... anything at all... that might have a bearing on what's happened?"

A single tear actually tumbled down Jane's cheek as she listened. "I'm sorry, sir," she said, stifling a sob, "but I'm so upset. What's happened is all because of me."

From the corner of his eye, David saw Parker look up sharply.

"It's all my fault," Jane then blurted out.

"Your fault?" What was she talking about? "How could it have been your fault?"

The girl could not hold his gaze and looked down at her hands, her fingers twisting nervously in her lap.

"How could it have been your fault, Jane?"

"I hadn't done my job properly," she eventually said, looking up at him, some composure returning. "Remember? Last week? You asked me to keep an eye on what was going on out there. And I'd started... honestly, I had. I know you could tell I wasn't very happy about it, but I was determined to do as you asked. I'd already seen Roger leave his postage drawer open and unattended. He had gone into the machine room. I had a word with him and he promised not to do it again. But that was Roger. It was easy with him... with me being much more senior. But with Bernard..."

Her words petered out and David could only speculate on what was to come. But he had no need to prompt her.

"Earlier in the morning," Jane continued, "Bernard left his till open..."

Again, she cut off her sentence, concentrating once more on

her fingers.

"Go on, Jane."

She looked up again. "Bernard will go mad if he finds out I'm telling you about this."

This was starting to sound like misplaced loyalties. "Remember, Jane, we're dealing with a robbery here."

Yet, he had some sympathy for her. It was not easy for youngsters to go behind the backs of their colleagues, particularly their seniors. Especially, someone with such arrogant – even bullying – traits as Bernard Groves.

"You've no need to worry," Parker butt in, speaking for the first time and giving Jane an encouraging smile. "Whatever's happened, everything will eventually come out into the open."

It was a good intervention, not the sort David had feared might happen. But this was with one of the youngsters; someone who could not possibly be involved. Parker was hardly likely to act so kindly with someone like Bernard Groves. Yet, Jane had said it was all her fault.

"Thank you, sir," the girl said, glancing sheepishly at Parker, before returning her attention to David. "He actually did it twice... left his till open... when he came off the counter. Each time, it was only very briefly, but I didn't say anything. I was too scared to. You know how Bernard can be. But if I'd said something, he probably wouldn't have done it this last time... and that man wouldn't have been able to steal the money."

"That man?"

"The one in the banking hall at the time. Bernard has told us about him. The man was sitting at one of the tables. He'd been there for some time. But it seems he never went to the counter to cash a cheque – or do anything."

Except snatch the £2,500?

"So, you didn't actually see this man?"

"No, sir. Most of the first lunch hour, I was in the back room – looking into the accounts of Mrs Martingale and Mrs Whytechapel."

That was that, then. Jane was unlikely to be able to shed any light on anything. It was all hearsay about this man in the banking hall. With Bernard, probably, having given everyone his version of the would-be thief, the other staff were likely to be in the same position as Jane. But what she had categorically done was to expose Bernard's blatant flouting of the basic rules of security – so soon after last week's specific instructions. It was maddening – especially with Parker in close attendance.

"She's a good girl," Parker said, after David had assured Jane she had been most helpful and sent her off to continue her investigations. "But there's one huge question mark over your Mr Groves."

There was no doubting that. Even if the £2,500 turned up, which was now extremely unlikely, Bernard's total disregard of the rules put him in deep trouble. And with his disciplinary warning from last year still in place, he would now be lucky to keep his job. After Miss Harding's dismissal, that would be two sackings of senior staff in only a few months. What had he done to deserve that?

David simply shook his head in complete acknowledgement of Parker's assessment. "We'd better get on," he said, conscious of time marching forward. "I'll get Roger Singleton in."

But the office junior was no further help. Between twelve and one, he had certainly spent all his time in the outer office behind the counter. The only thing he could confirm was that Bernard had, indeed, left his position to search out the open credit box. He did not know whether the till had been left open, but he remembered the incident vividly. Bernard had sworn viciously when he had discovered Mrs Mottram-Smythe's card had been misfiled.

After dismissing the boy to get on with his other duties, it was a relief to hear from Parker's assistants that all the branch's cash had been counted. Apart from the missing £2,500, all was present and correct. The tills of Trevor Smith and Barbara Bolton had balanced to the penny. It meant that the main players in this sad and sorry business could now be interviewed. David could only hope that something tangible would arise from this.

## CHAPTER 22

An hour and a half earlier, shortly after two, Bernard had returned from the manager's room, clearly mortified. "I've got to shut down my till and balance it right away," he said. "You'll need to hold the fort. Call on Barbara, if necessary. But we shouldn't have many customers this afternoon."

Trevor simply nodded, not inclined to enquire what else might have been discussed. They would all know soon enough. No doubt, everyone would suffer the repercussions from what had happened. For the moment, it all still seemed rather vague and nebulous. And when Barbara had returned from lunch, she had been astonished that the branch had been robbed.

"The manager's pinning his hopes on my till being correct," Bernard added. "He thinks I might be confused; the money's in the till without me realizing it. That's why I've got to do a full check now – before he contacts the inspectors and the police. But it's wishful thinking on his part. I know the money's gone."

Wishful thinking? That was simply not Mr Goodhart's style. Without doubt, he must be absolutely certain the money had been stolen. It would have been interesting to have been a fly on the wall in the manager's room. Bernard's matter-of-fact view of what was said must be way off beam.

"What did the manager say about the man in the banking hall?" he asked.

"Just that I've got to come up with a full description."

"Can you do that?"

Bernard bit his lower lip. "I've got to, haven't I?"

That was all very well, but if Bernard had not taken particular notice of the man...

"He was short and stocky," Bernard volunteered, opening

up his till and starting to sort his notes, ready for counting. "I'm pretty sure he had short dark hair... almost black. He was wearing a jacket... Harris Tweed, it looked like. And cavalry twill trousers."

"Sounds too smart for him to be a bank robber."

Bernard turned to glare at him. "What do you know about such things?"

How insensitive was that? How could the man deserve any sympathy when he was as crass as that? These last few months, Bernard may well have been friendlier and less arrogant; after his last rocket, he had to be. But after that tactless remark, had he really changed? Yet, it was best not to rise to the bait. Far better to ignore his hurtful words.

"Do you think Barbara saw him?" he simply asked.

"Good thinking. She must have," Bernard replied, turning round to Roger Singleton who was working immediately behind him. "Roger, be a good chap and go and get Barbara. She'll be in the machine room."

Trevor was serving a customer when the supervisor came out, but he had no trouble hearing Bernard explain to her what was happening. Yes, she had certainly seen the man at one of the desks in the banking hall.

"Do you agree he looked short and stocky? With black hair?" Bernard then asked.

"Yes, I'm sure he was," Barbara replied, frowning, as if plumbing the depths of her memory.

"And what was he wearing?"

"I'm not sure."

"Oh, come on, Barbara. This is important. I reckon he was wearing a Harris Tweed jacket. What do you think?"

"I don't know, Bernard. I can't remember."

"But you must," Bernard cried out, his tone striking Trevor

as one of desperation.

"I'll try and think about it," Barbara replied, looking peeved, when Trevor glanced at her. "If I remember anything, I'll let you know."

"Well, do it soon," Bernard snapped. "The inspectors will want to know. And the police."

"What?"

"The inspectors and the police. If the money's gone, they'll be here soon enough. They'll want to grill everyone."

"Today?"

"I imagine so."

"What time will we get away then?"

"I've simply no idea," Bernard said, irritably, getting stuck into his counting. Barbara could be in no doubt it was the end of their conversation.

As she made her way back to the machine room, Trevor heard her muttering about the stupid man causing such trouble and inconvenience. At least, he himself was not now the only one to have incurred her wrath.

And talking about wrath, how would Celia Groves be feeling? He could not help but smile. It was clear that Bernard was not going to be home for lunch at all today, never mind being late after one o'clock. It was as if a little light had been lit among all this doom and gloom.

Within half an hour, Bernard had established that exactly £2,500 was missing from his till. He immediately went to see Mr Goodhart. On his return, he said the manager was contacting the inspectors and the police.

At ten past three precisely, the front door bell rang.

Roger Singleton rose to answer it and Trevor hastily warned him it could be the inspectors. On no account must he omit to use the door chain.

Like everyone else, Trevor viewed the arrival of bank

inspectors with trepidation, especially as these visitors turned up unexpectedly and unannounced. This time the feeling was no different – even though the staff had been forewarned of their arrival. Normally, they would be seeking out possible misdemeanours; this time, thanks to Bernard, one was right there, sitting on a plate.

At least, it turned out to be Mr Parker making a return visit. He could be an irascible man, but because of the threatened raid, he might have some in-built sympathy for them all. He probably also had a high regard for the branch and the manager, in particular. Last year's problems had all been resolved satisfactorily. But that was all in the past. His opinion could change in an instant and probably would – thanks to Bernard.

Parker was accompanied by his two assistants from before, Richard Allen and John Fisher. They were soon involved in counting all the cash. Last year, the girls in the office – much to Trevor's envy – had vied with each other in seeking the attentions of these apparently eligible young men. This time, such impressionable feelings would probably not get near to being on the agenda.

Mr Parker himself was immediately closeted with Mr Goodhart in his room and word soon came out that the two men would be interviewing each member of staff.

As Richard Allen was busy checking his cash, Trevor noticed an extremely-nervous-looking Jane Church being the first to enter the manager's room and he was a little disconcerted she was in there for some time.

When she eventually came out, she still looked considerably ill-at-ease. Roger Singleton was next to go in, but he was in there for no more than a few minutes. Could that augur well for the rest of them?

It was a relief when Richard Allen declared his till had

balanced to the penny, but the feeling was short-lived. Within minutes, Katie came up to him to say the manager and Mr Parker now wanted to see him.

## CHAPTER 23

"Who's next?" Parker asked, now that all the cash had been counted by his assistants.

"I think we'd better leave Groves till last," David replied, not relishing the prospect. From what the cashier had told him already, there would appear to be no excuse for his gross negligence. Parker might well have taken a back seat in the interviews with Jane and Roger, but this was hardly likely with Groves. Nor should it be. The man deserved to be on the end of full salvos from them both.

Parker nodded. He was certainly being amenable.

"So," David added, "it's either Trevor Smith or Barbara Bolton. Trevor, I think. Like the two we've just seen, he's a peripheral figure. He wasn't there when the cash was actually stolen."

"Just as well," Parker said, "after his experience at Chagford."

David pursed his lips. "It's extraordinary, isn't it? Bank robberies are so rare, yet Trevor's been involved with two. It's enough to make him lose his nerve completely."

"Is there a chance of that?"

"I don't think so. He's such a level-headed lad. He did suffer after Chagford, but I really think it made him stronger. I've got a lot of time for the boy."

"Let's have him in, then," Parker said and David picked up the telephone to ask Katie to get Trevor to come into his room.

David had never seen the cashier blush before, but that was the reaction when he opened the questioning by asking why he had been late back from lunch.

Trevor looked down at his hands (was Jane's habit catching?) as if stalling for an answer.

"Bernard told me," David persisted, "you were ten to fifteen minutes late. I gather it caused a kerfuffle with Barbara, never mind Bernard not getting off to lunch on time."

"I'm sorry, sir," Trevor eventually said. "I just lost track of time. It won't happen again."

What a lame excuse from someone he had just extolled to Parker. Was the inspector thinking the same?

"Anyway," he said, unable to shake that answer from his mind, "this missing money – what can you tell us about that?"

Trevor's version turned out to be little different from what he had previously learned from Bernard Groves. The boy tried his best not to denigrate his first cashier's blatant disregard of cash control requirements, but this was hardly the time for misplaced loyalty.

"What about the man in the banking hall," David then asked. "I realize he wasn't there when you got back from lunch, but outside the branch? Did you see anyone coming out? Did you pass anyone in the street – someone who might have looked suspicious?"

Trevor shook his head. "I had my eyes down. And I was hurrying – because I knew I was late. The only person I saw was Barbara. She castigated me for being late. Apart from delaying her shopping, she said Bernard would be in trouble from Celia."

Celia again.

"But when I got to the counter," Trevor continued, "there was no question of Bernard thinking about lunch. He seemed shell-shocked. And then he told me what had happened."

"Do you think it's feasible for the man in the banking hall to have taken the money?"

"Of course, sir. If it was lying on the counter, anyone could have stretched across for it."

There was no doubting that and it was extraordinary that a cashier as experienced as Bernard Groves should have left himself so vulnerable. It was more than extraordinary; it was outrageous –

especially when they had already been threatened with a raid. David's anger had not diminished. It was a miracle he had managed to keep relatively cool when Groves had been sitting in front of him.

"What do you think?" he asked Parker, having dismissed Trevor from the room. Once again, the inspector had refrained from contributing to the interview, but he had taken down copious notes.

"You said you have a high regard for young Mr Smith?" Parker replied, turning a page in his notebook.

David frowned. "You think that might be misplaced?" Surely not. But the inspector's question did seem to be laced with scepticism.

Parker pursed his lips. "Just trying to look at all the angles. As you said, yourself, it's extraordinary how he's been around at two separate robberies."

What was the man implying? "You're not suggesting that..."

"I've been long enough in this game not to take anything at face value."

"I understand that, but..."

"Were you satisfied with his answer about being late back from lunch? And the way he coloured up? From a lad you think so highly of?"

No, it was not satisfactory, at all. The weak excuse had been most disappointing and it was not surprising Parker had latched on to it.

"He was certainly keeping something back," David replied. "But he can't possibly be involved."

"Why not?"

The starkness of the question almost rocked him back in his chair.

"Who," Parker added, the chill now reaching into his eyes, "discovered that warning on the blotting paper last week?"

"Trevor did, but..."

"And who was conveniently not around... I repeat, not

around... when the branch was robbed today?"

"You're thinking the two things are connected?"

"I don't see why not."

"And Trevor Smith's involved?"

"It's possible."

"But that's inconceivable!"

"Just think about it. The bank was robbed sometime around one o'clock... maybe a little later. Trevor Smith should have been there, but wasn't. And why not? Because he'd lost track of time in his lunch hour. Really? Sounds very thin to me."

"But no thief could have expected Groves to leave the cash unattended on the counter."

"Unless Groves was also involved."

Hang on a minute. This was madness. Parker was letting his imagination run riot.

But then the inspector actually smiled, a grim smile, admittedly. "All right, all right," he said, "keep your hair on. But the point I'm trying to make is to keep an open mind. Anything's possible. Until last week, you'd never have envisaged being given a written warning about a raid. Until today, you'd never have believed your first cashier would have left £2,500 unattended on the counter. Why not consider other possibilities – things you might never dream of happening?"

Parker was right, of course. This was a man talking from years of inspectorial experience. A branch manager's line of questioning and reasoning would mainly relate to lending propositions, put to him by people of integrity... mostly, anyhow. An inspector's mind would be attuned to the seamier side of human nature. And all inspectors would have seen too many examples of apparently-upright citizens falling dramatically from their pedestals. Of course, that had happened here in Barnmouth – last year with Miss Harding. It had certainly opened David's eyes and made him beware of treating things and people at face value. But he still hoped this would not extend into an in-built cynicism which must feature in many a bank inspector's make-up.

"You're absolutely right," he replied. "But I wouldn't want to take it too far. After the trouble we had last year, I can't believe some kind of conspiracy might now be going on in the branch."

Parker nodded – as if in agreement? "But I think I've made my point," he said, opening up his notebook to a fresh page. "We'd better see Mrs Bolton now."

When the supervisor was sitting in front of them, she did not seem to be in any better humour than she had, apparently, been when she met Trevor Smith on the pavement. But that was not really surprising. In the two and a half years David had been manager of the branch, she had never been less than ultra-efficient. Because of this, she tended not to suffer fools gladly and these last three hours must have played havoc with her patience.

As with the others before her, Parker studied her closely. David posed his first question and she immediately proved his assessment of her to the inspector. "I can't believe how stupid Bernard's been," she exclaimed, as though she could hold back her opinion no longer.

"You mean with the cash?" David asked. "Leaving it on the counter?"

"Of course."

"Didn't you see it there? Couldn't you have warned him?"

"Firstly, I didn't see it. I was dealing with the council man. I needed all my concentration taking in his credit. You know what a mess it's always in."

So, things had not improved since last Wednesday. At least, the man had come in earlier today.

"And secondly," Barbara continued, "have you ever tried to point out his deficiencies to Bernard?"

As a matter of fact, yes; last year, which resulted in his formal reprimand and, very nearly, his sacking. But David knew what she meant. It would take a brave member of staff, even one as senior as Barbara, to challenge Bernard about his work practices. It was something Norman Charlton should be on the lookout for, but even Norman would shirk such a duty for the benefit of an easy life. It was something over which David had taken Norman to task, but it was unlikely to bear fruit. That was why the man would never achieve promotion above his chief clerk's status.

"What about the man Bernard saw in the banking hall?" he asked. "Did you see him – or anyone else lurking around, for that matter?"

"Yes. I saw the man, but nobody else. He was short and stocky, with dark hair. I agree with Bernard about that. He was also wearing a jacket... not an overcoat. Bernard thought it was Harris Tweed and he might well be right. I'm not sure, but it was definitely a jacket."

"Colour?"

Barbara frowned in concentration. "It could have been greeny-brown."

"That sounds as though it could be Harris Tweed."

Barbara nodded. "I suppose so, but I'm not really sure. It's not the sort of thing my husband wears. I don't take much notice of what other men do."

That was not really surprising. Barbara could never be deemed to be fashion conscious. Frumpy, was more like it. So why should she notice what men wore? Not every wife was like his Sarah – constantly nit-picking his choice of clothes and accessories. But thank goodness she did, otherwise he might end up being turned out like Parker. And what was the inspector making of all this talk about men's appearance? He certainly looked as though he was taking it all in, but it was hardly likely to change his own style. Style?

That was not something he had to offer – sartorially, anyhow.

"Would you recognise him again?"

"Yes, I think so. No, I'm not so sure. But I'd do my best."

"You might have to," Parker suddenly interjected. "The police will be quizzing you, for sure."

Barbara looked alarmed. "The police?"

"Of course," David replied. "They'll be here shortly."

"I'm sorry," the supervisor said. "I didn't think. I've been so wrapped up with the inconvenience of it all."

Despite the bank having been robbed, it would seem Barbara was more concerned about the disruption caused to normal office routines. And, for once, her usual self-assurance seemed to have deserted her. "Don't worry about the day-to-day work," he tried to assure her. "The missing money's the most important thing at the moment. Is there anything else you can think of?"

Barbara Bolton shook her head. "No. It's just that I'm finding the whole thing so upsetting."

You can say that again. What with the previous warning of a raid, then an actual robbery, following on from the deaths of two elderly customers. But all this paled into insignificance when compared to the threat against his own family. In that respect, thank goodness it was the school holidays. At least, Sarah would have Mark strictly in tow. And with the four-day Easter break almost upon them, he would be able to take over from her. She certainly deserved that. Perhaps he could persuade her to go on a shopping spree, while he and Mark were at football on Saturday.

It was clear Barbara had nothing more to add, leaving Bernard Groves to come in and give his version of events. Not that anything new materialized from his confession, for that was what it amounted to. Everything seemed to point to the 'Harris Tweed Man'. Groves's description certainly seemed to tally with Barbara's – or was it the other way round? It would have been far better if they had not, apparently, colluded. The police would probably be disconcerted about this.

But, for this particular interview, Parker had, at last, come into his own.

David had not previously witnessed such an assassination job – without, of course, any blood and gore.

A demolition exercise might be more apt – the complete destruction of all that, apparently, made Groves tick. The man could not have known what was about to hit him. But he deserved everything that shot his way. At one point, he offered to resign, but Parker would not give him the luxury of taking such an easy way out. Everything Groves had done during that fateful lunch hour deserved the whole rule book being thrown at him. And Parker certainly did that. In the end, it seemed the missing £2,500 was almost incidental to all the offences the cashier had committed.

Bernard Groves eventually left the room like a broken man, the threat of the police interrogation now hanging over him. Parker may have kept in the background during all the previous interviews, but he had made up for it with the first cashier. And rightly so. David could not think of anything which could have been said in mitigation of the cashier's misdemeanours. The man had broken all the rules and must now suffer the consequences. It was difficult to see how he could possibly retain his employment with the bank. And it could well be worse – once the police got their teeth into him.

That just left Norman Charlton to see, but he was not able to be of any help. Although he had returned early from lunch, he had been closeted in the interview room with one of his many elderly ladies who sought him out for investment advice. A quite irrational thought flashed across David's mind. In other circumstances, the likes of Mrs Martingale and Mrs Whytechapel would be just the sought of account holders to relish dealing with his chief clerk. In fact, could the transfers from Mrs Martingale's account have, indeed, been related to some form of investment – as recommended by Norman? No, this was too fanciful. Until last week's visit, she had been 3,000 miles away in New York.

When DC Pound arrived, he proved to be almost kindly, not only to the other staff, but also to Groves. He believed the bank should deal with all the technical deficiencies of the cashier and he concentrated almost entirely on the likely thief. The police would now put all their efforts into trying to trace the person who Pound was happy to dub the 'Harris Tweed Man'.

From what they had to go on, David was sceptical of their likely success, but DC Pound was surprisingly confident. They had, apparently, ways and means. Perhaps the man's description already fitted someone they knew.

With such comforting assurances ringing in his ears, David eventually made his way home. It was now past seven o'clock, but he had telephoned Sarah early in the afternoon to warn her he would be this late.

Being dark and with no sign of the moon, he had to pedal carefully, the faint beam of the bicycle's front lamp failing to pick out even some of the larger potholes which had arisen over the winter months. At least it was quicker than walking and he was already relishing the prospect of a welcoming light ale to help relieve the stresses of the afternoon. It was unlikely anything was soothing Bernard Groves's brow. Certainly not Celia. She would be devastated that their social status was about to suffer total disintegration.

As he turned the corner into his road, he almost fell off his bike. Their house was in darkness. And where was the car? The Minx could not be in the garage; that was full of junk, following Sarah's latest spring-clean.

More to the point, with the house being clearly unoccupied, where on earth were Sarah, Mark and Dad?

# CHAPTER 24

David shivered involuntarily as he inserted his key into the lock of the front door. 'Keep a close eye on Mark if you don't want him to come to any harm'. That was what the note had said. The words were ingrained on his mind. And they had done just that. Mark had not been out of the company of himself or Sarah. And it would stay that way.

But had it?

As he closed the door behind him and switched on the hall light, he knew it would need more than electricity to shed some light on the whereabouts of his whole family, never mind just Mark, himself.

The sheer bareness of the house enveloped him as he opened the lounge door. He looked inside and then went into the kitchen. But he knew already; he faced a vain attempt to seek out the missing bodies. Yet, everything else was in place. It was as if the house had recently been spring-cleaned; not a cushion or household appliance was out of place. Apart from atypical tranquillity, normality abounded. It proved that Sarah – with or without the others – had not left in a hurry. And there was no evidence of a forcible entry or exit.

He left the kitchen and made for the stairs to check the three bedrooms and bathroom. After his initial panic at finding the house unoccupied, his heart was pounding less hard. Not that his concern had receded, but the lack of any disorder downstairs provided a morsel of comfort. Please not let this be misplaced.

Their own bedroom echoed the orderliness of the rooms below, but Mark's room was its usual jumble of football programmes, Dinky toys and Hornby 'Dublo' train accessories. David could not even avoid stepping on a Dinky Foden lorry and accompanying trailer as he tried to enter the room. Even in the tension of the moment, he could not help smiling; the boy drove his doting mother spare at the chaotic state of his bedroom. But his smile soon deserted him. How would they cope if some harm befell the lad?

In contrast, Dad's room was something of an orderly shambles. Since his head injury, any powers of organization and method had deserted him. It was just as well that he had little interest in material things – apart from his beloved wireless and the evening newspaper. Otherwise, his room would not now be devoid of clutter. Only odd items of clothing lay around, as was the case in the bathroom. There, a dripping hot water tap was the only sign of movement in the house. That must have been down to Dad; Sarah would never have been so careless. And it was almost unheard of for Mark to get near the tap – unless he was under strict supervision. Ever-alert to energy costs, David turned the tap tight and made his way downstairs, wondering what to do.

He had always been the most rational one of the family, but that was more to do with day-to-day events and procedures. What he now faced was something quite out of the ordinary – a crisis, fair and square.

He moved into the lounge and sank back into his favourite armchair where he always seemed to be able to think best. He had wrestled with many a work problem there and he needed such inspiration now.

What about the police?

He was tempted to telephone DC Pound there and then, but… There was no actual evidence to indicate Mark had been abducted. The detective would certainly need something to go on. He would not want to launch into what might turn out to be a wild goose chase. And there was simply no sign that anyone had been forcibly removed from the house.

The fact that the car had gone was another consideration. Surely, no abductor would use the victim's own car? And three victims? All in the same car? No, that would be physically impracticable. On the other hand, the car might have been stolen separately – as some form of subterfuge.

What if Mark had been separately kidnapped? Sarah might have given chase in the Minx, with Dad there for support. But that was far too fanciful. Sarah would be hopeless in a car chase. Mark had, perhaps, wandered off on his own and Sarah and Dad had gone off in the car to look for him. But she would never have let the boy out of her sight – not with that threat hanging over him. In any case, with these scenarios, she would have rung him at the office. She would never have gone off on such a search without speaking to him first.

David sank further back in his chair and let his eyes close in concentration. This was getting to be like experiencing that bad dream situation – the one which had crossed his mind before he saw Charlie Hicklemaker on Saturday. But now was clearly the time when he needed to think rationally.

What else could have occurred? They might have all gone out shopping. But at this time of night? And it was Wednesday – early closing day. Or they might have just gone out for a spin; the weather had been good enough for Sarah to have considered this. Yet, they would have been back by now.

Unless they had met with an accident...

David was glad he was sitting down. The prospect of a car crash did not bear thinking about. They well knew the consequences of a crash could be unremitting. It had been bad enough, seven years ago, when Mum had been killed outright, but Dad's brain damage was enduring. Yet, his disability had only been diagnosed last year. Until then, they had put his increasing irrational behaviour down to some form of senility. But an X-ray had then revealed permanent brain damage. Heaven forbid the same thing happening to Sarah and Mark, never mind what else might arise from a serious road accident.

This was certainly a valid reason for contacting the police – also Torbay Hospital – and he rose from his chair and went to the telephone in the hall.

But the response from both quarters was negative. No accident had occurred anywhere in the area today. Incredible. But was that good news or bad? It had to be good, but some form of accident would, at least, have established the whereabouts of his family.

He returned to his armchair, appreciating, more than ever, how much they all meant to him. Dad, even after his head injury, had been such a good father to him and he was really no trouble living with them in the same house. It had made a huge difference knowing what was wrong with him. They had become far more tolerant of his eccentricities. Before, their patience had often snapped. Sarah, in particular, now greatly regretted her past outbursts when Dad's unreasonable behaviour had driven her to distraction.

As for Sarah... Well, he had always believed a good test of their strong relationship was when they were apart. Though such times were rare. On the few occasions Sarah had an evening out with her girl friends, he could never settle. He would pace around the house, wondering what to do next, almost aching for her to return. In contrast, other couples seemed to lead practically separate lives, taking the view that their independence added strength to their marriage. They hated being under each other's feet. But to him, that was a tacit admission of a questionable union.

Thank goodness, that was not the case with Sarah and himself. They always enjoyed each other's company, in or out of the house. In a restaurant – or away on holiday – they could still talk to each other, conversation never waning. Other couples – like Bernard and Celia? – always seemed to seek out friends to join them for meals. They claimed it stimulated conversation and bonhomie. Each to his own, he supposed.

Now, being alone in the house was excruciating. Not knowing Sarah's whereabouts was agony. And what about Mark? And Dad?

What was he to do?

Walking the streets was an option, or, better still, getting on his bike. At least, it would feel as if he was doing something tangible, rather than just sitting around the house. But it would be so hit and miss. He would only come across them if the car had broken down…

Of course! Why had he not thought of it before? A breakdown. The AA. He had been a member for years and had never called them out. But Sarah might have had a problem.

He rushed to the hall, yanking the telephone directory from its stand. The Organization's documentation was stowed in the car's glove box, but the AA's regional office would know about any specific call-outs involving their motorcycle patrols.

He felt his heart pumping hard as he waited for his call to be answered.

# CHAPTER 25

David took a deep breath. Thursday morning and it was a relief to be back at work. The job of banking could now dominate his thoughts.

It had not been so last night and he would not want to go through that kind of trauma again.

And it could have been worse.

Having returned home just after seven o'clock, he only had to wait until eight for the AA to give him the good news. Fifteen minutes later, Sarah, Dad and Mark had turned up. Before his call to the AA, he had feared his agonizing would have extended well into the night – and how much longer after that?

"But what made you go out in the first place?" he had asked Sarah, once he had released her from his embrace.

"It was such a fine day," she replied, defensively. Perhaps his question had been laced with admonition, but it was not knowing. He had been at the end of his tether. "And we'd all been cooped up in the house. It seemed like a good idea. And we hadn't been to Dartmoor for months."

That was true enough. They ought to take more advantage of breathing in the moor's desolate beauty. It was like living by the sea; they never seemed to make the most of it.

"Anyway, we went through Newton Abbot and headed for Bovey Tracey. That was down to Mark. He wanted me to get my foot down on the Bovey Straight."

"And you did?" That would have been most unlike Sarah. When she drove with him, he had to encourage her to get out of third gear. As for the Bovey Straight... Mark must have been listening to him recently. He had recounted to Sarah the exploits of a cashier at Torquay branch. The man had inherited money from an aunt and invested it in a Jaguar XK120. He became the only Jaguar-owning bank clerk in the region – much to the disquiet of his ostentatious manager. Anyway, the best place in the area where he could put the car through its paces was a long, straight stretch of road between Newton Abbot and Bovey Tracey. It was known as the Bovey Straight and proved to be a magnet for the owners of MGs, Austin Healeys and Jaguars.

But Sarah? Competing with sports cars? In their Hillman Minx?

"Of course, I didn't," she replied. "Much to Mark's disgust."

But it would have been a relief to Dad. Since his motor accident, he had become understandably nervous about car travel. It had been a wonder he had agreed to go on this particular jaunt.

"Mark wants you to take him there next time," Sarah added.

"I don't think he'd be impressed with my efforts, either. Can you imagine the Minx competing with an XK120?"

Sarah moved to the sink to fill the kettle. A cup of tea would certainly go down well. But a stiff Scotch might be better. "Anyway," she said, after lighting the gas burner, "we left Bovey and made towards Haytor, then on to Widdecombe. I promised to take our men to Dartmeet and we'd then come back through Ashburton. A sort of round tour."

It was a route taken by many tourists in the summer months, managing to jam the narrow lanes with their cars and charabancs. The locals must yearn for the arrival of autumn.

"But we never got past Haytor Rock. We had a puncture."

Relief had previously swept over him when the AA had told him on the telephone about the puncture. After having vividly imagined all the horrendous things which might have happened, he had actually laughed out loud. But it had clearly been no laughing matter for Sarah.

"Quite frankly," she admitted, "I didn't know what to do. I certainly couldn't have changed the wheel. Your Dad had a go, but the wheel nuts were too tight for him."

"Thank goodness for the AA," David replied, thankful at having joined the Organization. He had been a member for several years and it was almost a relief to get something back from his annual subscription. Until now, his only return had been courteous salutes from passing motorcycle patrolmen. Having said that, it was certainly a pleasant response to his having the yellow AA badge attached to the bonnet's grill of the Minx.

"Yes, but that was the next problem," Sarah said. Having now made the tea, she poured out three cups and then filled a glass with lemonade for Mark. "We were nowhere near a telephone and there was virtually no passing traffic. One motorist did stop and said he'd get someone to ring the AA when he got to Widdecombe But how could we really rely on that?"

"So, how did you get in touch with them?"

"That was your Dad, bless him. He remembered we'd passed the Haytor Hotel. It was a mile or so back down the road and he said he'd go and ring from there. But after he'd set off, I realized I'd forgotten to give him the membership details. They were in the glove box. I was about to send Mark after him, but then I remembered the threat we'd had. How could I have forgotten that? It was becoming a nightmare."

"And? What did you do?"

"I could still see your Dad in the distance and I just blared the car's horn. He eventually heard it and turned to see me waving frantically. So, he came back. But this all took up more time. And I was worrying about it getting dark."

It was certainly not an easy situation for Sarah. David was even starting to feel guilty about thinking it had 'only been a puncture'. What would he have done – if he had not been able to change the wheel himself? Probably little different. It was not as if they were able to carry a telephone around with them. On occasions like this, people had to rely on Good Samaritans, but it would seem they were in short supply on Dartmoor.

Now, this Thursday morning, with yesterday's problems resolved and everybody safe and well, he had a problem of a different kind.

Dormant accounts.

"Are we any further forward?" he asked Jane, who was sitting on the other side of his desk. This time, she had a number of day sheets in front of her, but no actual ledgers. It was clear she had transcribed the information from the ledgers on to the sheets which appeared to be crammed with figures and information.

"Not really, sir," she replied, frowning.

"But what about all this lot?" he asked, pointing to the day sheets. "It looks as though you've been working on this exercise for weeks – not just a couple of days."

Jane's smile matched the warmth of the familiar blouse she was wearing – primrose, with blue edgings at the cuffs and collar – her Torquay United outfit. She would hardly like it being described as that, but it certainly reminded him of his team. It also made him relish the coming opportunity to let off steam at tomorrow's match and the one on Saturday. It was rare to have matches on consecutive days and both he and Mark were excited about that.

"I've certainly got a lot of evidence," Jane replied, getting her sheets into some kind of order. "As you can see, stacks of it. But as for answers…"

"Is this where I come in?"

"I'd like to think so. I certainly need some help."

"Let's start with Mrs Martingale, then. You said there'd been six withdrawals from her account. In the last six months, wasn't it?"

Jane nodded.

"Each for £1,000? And did you say they were simply marked TFR on the ledger sheets? Have you managed to find the actual vouchers?"

Jane now shook her head, making her newly acquired bobtail swing from side to side. "You're right about the amounts and the symbols, but as for the vouchers... they're all missing."

"All of them? They can't be."

"I've searched everywhere."

"Then you'll have to go back to the day's work – for all six of those withdrawals. You need to check the corresponding entries."

This was something he had learnt very early in his career. In the best accounting traditions, every debit must have a credit. So, there must be recipient beneficiaries for the six debits on Mrs Martingale's account.

"I've done that," Jane said, justifying the high regard he had been developing for the girl. "Each transfer has gone to an account at Newton Abbot branch."

"Whose account?" The transfers did not now seem to be linked to investments.

"I don't know, sir. The only information in our work is the branch's sorting code number."

"I wonder... do you think that's where her sister banks? I know she lives in Totnes, but she could well have her account at Newton Abbot. Have you been in contact with them?"

"No, not yet. I thought I ought to see you first."

Yes, her judgement was spot on. Delve around first, get the facts and then seek his advice. Far better to do that than to exercise what might turn out to be false initiative.

"Maybe," he pondered, "this might have something to do with Mrs Martingale's visit here last week."

"It's possible, sir. But Barbara said she only asked for an up-to-date statement."

"That's fair enough. If she's been transferring funds from her account... let's say to her sister... she probably wanted to know how her account stood before she returned to New York."

"I just hope it's that simple," Jane said. "Wait till you see what else I've unearthed."

"Unearthed?"

"Discovered, then... first of all with Mrs Whytechapel."

Jane turned to her next day sheet and ran her index finger down a column of figures.

"I've already told you about the withdrawals from her account," she continued. "They were much smaller sums than those for Mrs Martingale... £300 and £500. And they weren't transfers to other accounts. They were all cash withdrawals. I'm sorry, sir," she added, frowning, "but I seem to have left the cheques outside on my desk."

"But the withdrawals were made here? At our branch?"

Jane nodded. "Yes, each one of them. The cheques were made out properly by Mrs Whytechapel and cashed here."

"But she was in the nursing home – the Riverside. She wouldn't have been able to come in here to cash her cheques."

"Unless someone did it for her. She might have asked someone in the Riverside to do it."

"But why?"

"To pay her fees?"

That was certainly possible. But why would the Riverside want cash, rather than take a cheque? In any case, the branch would not have been able to cash a crossed cheque for anyone other than the customer – unless a specific arrangement had been made. But, maybe, Mrs Whytechapel had been using uncrossed cheques. These could certainly be cashed by someone else – unless the circumstances were suspicious.

"Did she have crossed cheques?" he asked. Surely, that must have been the case.

"Yes," Jane duly confirmed. "But the crossings had been opened."

David pursed his lips and considered her words. Opening

a crossing certainly enabled customers to cash crossed cheques. Inside the vertical parallel lines, they needed to write the words 'please pay cash', followed by their signature. This effectively overrode the crossing, the purpose of which forbade encashments. But, even when opened, crossed cheques could only be cashed for the actual customers or their known agents.

"Which cashier cashed these cheques?"

Jane looked at him pointedly. "Bernard cashed them all."

He might have known it. Nevertheless, in itself, it was not unusual for a customer to seek out a specific cashier. It was just that all accusatory fingers these days seemed to be pointing at Bernard.

"Have you spoken to him about it?"

Jane looked aghast. "No, sir. Of course, not. You wouldn't have wanted me to do that... not before I'd put you in the picture."

That was true. If there might be a need for delicate handling, it had to be down to him... especially when Bernard Groves was involved. But why would someone in the nursing home be cashing Mrs Whytechapel's cheques?

"And there's possibly more to it," Jane said, before he could put this point to her. "Do you know a Mrs Blackstone... and a Miss Bassenthwaite?"

David shook his head. What was all this about?

"They've both been customers since the twenties, but their accounts became dormant some years ago. Then, last year, they suddenly started to be used again."

"And they're elderly ladies, as well?"

"More than that. They're both residents at the Riverside."

"What?"

David's mind now instinctively flashed from these unknown ladies to the account of the Riverside Nursing Home itself – not to mention its owner, Michael Farthinshawe. Did all Jane's findings have anything to do with the change in the way the Riverside's account had been operating?

"When you say the accounts of these ladies have started to be used again," he said, at this stage, keeping his thoughts about the Riverside's account to himself, "are you talking about credits and withdrawals?"

"No, sir, just cash withdrawals," Jane replied, confirming his expectation of that particular answer.

"Just like Mrs Whytechapel?"

Jane simply nodded.

"And the same cashier?"

Jane nodded again.

"And there's more to come?" he asked, pointing to the day sheets to which Jane had not yet referred.

"Quite a bit," she replied, turning to those particular sheets. "Altogether, I've so far discovered twenty-five other re-activated dormant accounts. They've all started to operate again in the last six months."

Twenty-five? How many residents does the Riverside have? "You're not going to tell me they're all residents at the..."

"No, no," Jane butt in. "The others don't seem to have any connection with the nursing home."

"There's no link at all?"

"Not that I've established."

"But there could be... if you dig further?"

"It's possible, but I doubt it."

"But what about the actual operation of these accounts?"

"The pattern on all of them is different. They're really active accounts – debits and credits."

"As opposed to just cash withdrawals?"

Jane nodded. "But I haven't had time to get out the actual vouchers. The debits might well be cash withdrawals. I just don't know yet."

But why should so many dormant accounts suddenly start to be used again? One or two might arise naturally, but twenty-five? And these were occurring at the same time as the three old ladies at the Riverside were cashing their cheques.

"Have you looked into the account of the Riverside Nursing Home, itself?" he asked.

Jane looked puzzled. "The Riverside's own account? No. Why should I?"

"It just seems there's something fishy going on. In recent months, there's also been a complete change in the way the account's been operating."

"In what way, sir?"

"It always used to run perfectly – swinging in and out of credit. That's always a good sign of a thriving business. But in recent months, credit balances have disappeared; the borrowing is often hard up against the limit. Remember? I told you about this sort of thing last year."

Jane frowned.

"Overtrading."

"Oh, yes, but..."

It was not really surprising Jane was hesitating. Cases of overtrading would not cross her desk frequently.

"Trying to do too much on too little capital."

"Oh, yes," Jane said again, this time looking as if she meant it. "I remember thinking it could hardly be a bad thing for a company to overtrade. I thought the more business it did, the better it would be."

"And that can often be the case – provided cash resources are sufficient."

"Or overdraft facilities?"

"Yes. The two things go together. But some companies forget

this. They just strive for increased business – looking for greater profits. They forget profits don't necessarily equate with cash."

"I remember now; it can take time for profits to be turned into cash. Is that right?"

David smiled in appreciation of the girl's perception. "Exactly. Cash, not future profits, pays the weekly wages. That's why even profitable companies can go bust. They run out of actual cash."

"And you think this might be happening with the Riverside?"

"I don't know, but I doubt it. A nursing home should be the epitome of a successful business. Just think about it. It has regular income... always paid in advance... and consistent outgoings. If they've got their profit margins right..."

"Maybe the Riverside haven't," Jane interrupted. It was an example of her increasing self-confidence. In no way was her interjection disrespectful; it was more an example of her forward thinking.

"But why should things change now?" David asked. "As far as I'm aware, they've got full occupancy. And there's no reason why costs might have increased. There shouldn't be any change in their profit margins – or in the pattern of the bank account."

"So, you're thinking that the individual bank accounts of three residents might have a bearing on the business's account?"

That was the big question. On the face of it, there was no reason to think this at all. But if skulduggery was going on in one area...

"I don't know what to think," he said, "but something strange is going on. And it all appears to have started in the last six months. It seems to me there must be a connection. But there's one thing we haven't considered. Could Mrs Martingale have had any connection with the nursing home? And did she have any link with Mrs Whytechapel?"

"The fact that both ladies have been murdered makes you wonder, doesn't it, sir?"

Incredibly, throughout their discussion, David had overlooked the actual murders. Yet, why should these have happened at the same time as strange transactions were taking place on the bank accounts of the Riverside and some of its residents?

# CHAPTER 26

As he contemplated going home to lunch, David felt as if he were in the midst of a giant jigsaw – with the salient pieces missing. But was it likely so many disparate matters could be intrinsically linked? Hardly; it was simply not the stuff of the real world.

But the two murders were real enough, even though there was no evidence they were connected. Mrs Martingale had been pushed under a train and it sounded as if Mrs Whytechapel had been smothered in her bed. Although Jane was now delving around to see if a link between the two women could be established, this seemed highly unlikely.

He had also asked Jane to get Barbara Bolton involved in her investigations. Having been at the branch for thirty years, the supervisor had such an extensive knowledge of their customers. He now felt it had probably been a mistake to rely simply on Jane to do the digging around. He still considered his original motive had been well-founded: to keep any internal investigation in as few hands as possible. He could not really believe in-branch duplicity was likely, but Bernard Groves seemed to be doing his best to disprove this point.

What was the first cashier up to? Could he really have simply been careless to let £2,500 be taken from his till? It was not the act of someone, like Barbara, who had thirty years' experience behind him. Although last year he had lapsed in taking in credits correctly, he had always been a stickler in his control of actual cash. So, was there more to it than that? And his name had now come up again this morning. Was it only a coincidence that he had cashed all those cheques drawn by Mrs Whytechapel and the other two Riverside residents?

One thing for certain, another interview with Bernard was

called for. But this must await the outcome of Jane's latest task: to look more deeply into the twenty-five dormant accounts which had now been re-activated. The way things were looking, it would not be surprising to find Bernard drawn into that lot, as well.

David used his fingers to help recap what had happened in the last week: a threatened raid; two murders; a bank robbery; numerous unusual transactions on accounts; a well-established business account going awry; and, from a personal point of view, the most disturbing thing of all, the threat to his very own family.

As he rose from his chair to don his coat and cycle clips for the ride home, he was thankful the threat against Mark had arrived at the onset of the Easter holidays. It had enabled Sarah to maintain constant watch on the boy, but in a week's time, the school would have to be put in the picture. Next week, he would need to have a meeting with DC Pound in order to make the necessary arrangements. It might be sooner, if the detective got in touch beforehand with a progress report on their search for the 'Harris Tweed Man'.

But the ring of his telephone halted his progress to the door.

"I'm sorry, sir," Katie said, when he lifted the receiver, "but Mr Farthinshawe's outside. He wants to see you urgently."

"But I'm just off to lunch."

"I know, sir. I told him that. I'm not sure I should tell you what he said."

It would not be hard to guess. "All right, Katie, I'll be out in a moment. But would you mind ringing my wife? It looks like I'll have to skip lunch. I can't imagine this being a short interview."

He removed his cycle clips and hung his coat in the small wardrobe at the side of his desk. Farthinshawe's arrival was actually propitious; he was anxious to see the man, anyway. He needed to establish how the business was progressing and Farthinshawe might also give him some information about Mrs

Whytechapel and the other two residents. It would certainly be good to ascertain a satisfactory reason for the making of all those cash withdrawals. He only hoped the nursing home proprietor was in a better frame of mind than when they had last met.

Before an interview, he would normally get Jane to give him the up-to-date position of a customer's account. This would include providing him with the individual's Private Memorandum Card to remind him of the background of the account, but he had no need for this information with Farthinshawe. Even before the events of the last week, the account of The Riverside Nursing Home had loomed large in his mind for the reasons he had explained to Jane this morning. And these circumstances had only been compounded by the murder of Mrs Whytechapel and what had been happening on her account – never mind the sudden re-activation of the bank accounts of the other two residents.

No, he had no need for any background information this time and he already knew the current state of the Riverside's account. This morning, he noticed it was again bang up against its agreed overdraft limit. This was a further reason for wanting to see the man, but as he made his way to greet him in the banking hall, he pondered on why Farthinshawe wanted such an urgent interview.

They were soon sitting opposite each other in his room and he was shocked at the deterioration in the nursing home owner's appearance since the last time they had met. He had always considered Farthinshawe to be a bull of a man. Although not tall, he was thick-set and muscular. Craggy features included a skew-whiff nose which had probably been broken on more than one occasion. The man had always reminded him of an older version of Freddie Mills and he had not been surprised to learn from another customer that Farthinshawe had, in fact, been a more than capable amateur boxer. It seemed almost incongruous that a man like him should have ended up running a nursing home.

He hardly exuded tender loving care – something which all his residents would be seeking.

But this morning, any strength the man might have had, particularly of the inner variety, appeared to have drained from him. David knew immediately the hostile reception he had been given recently would not be repeated. Not unnaturally, Farthinshawe must be taking the murder of one of his residents particularly hard.

"I was so sorry to hear what's happened at the home," David said, once the initial greeting and opening small talk had taken place. "You must all be in a terrible frame of mind."

Farthinshawe pursed his lips and, at first, seemed unable to respond. "A terrible business," he eventually muttered. "A truly terrible business."

David felt at a loss as to how to continue the conversation. How do you try to console a man whose whole livelihood might now be at risk? The remaining residents were hardly likely to be sleeping easily in their beds, while the chances of attracting new residents in the immediate future were probably non-existent. Who would want to live in a nursing home tainted by murder? Even more to the point, who would want to take over a murdered woman's room?

"It's the not knowing that's the major problem," Farthinshawe continued. "Not knowing who could have possibly done it, never mind why. How could anyone kill such an old woman in her bed? Especially someone as sweet as Mrs Whytechapel."

And what about Mrs Martingale? How could anyone push that old lady under a train? The two murders must be connected. Surely? But why? And how?

"I think I'm going to have to close down," Farthinshawe added, now looking even more disconsolate. "A lifetime's business taken away. At a stroke. It's a disaster."

"How have the other residents taken it?"

"How do you think?" Farthinshawe snapped, some of his old fire returning. David could kick himself. The man's reaction was fully justified. It had been a stupid question and got its deserved response.

"I'm sorry," he said. "That was a crass thing to ask."

Farthinshawe nodded his acceptance of the apology. "The problem is," he said, "if they want to leave, there's nowhere else for them to go. At this stage, anyhow. As far as I know, all the other nursing homes are full up. So, for the time being, they're having to live with it. And for that reason, I can't close down yet. We've got to keep going, as best we can. I only hope the police will get their act together – and quickly."

"Do you know how they're getting on?"

"No, except that... Put it this way, we must all be under suspicion. They reckon it's got to be an inside job."

David shook his head. That must make things even worse. All looking over their shoulders, wondering who it is – and who might be next.

"Anyway," Farthinshawe continued, "as I said, we've got to carry on – for the time being, anyway. And that's why I've come to see you. I need more money. I want an increased limit."

What a time and in what terrible circumstances to be asked for increased facilities. Quite apart from the huge question mark which Farthinshawe had just admitted now hung over the business, the way the account had operated in recent months did not justify any further help – unless a totally convincing case could be put forward.

"You'd better have a good reason," he answered. "From what you've just said, it's hardly the most appropriate time for me to consider lending you more money."

Farthinshawe actually gulped before answering. "If you

don't, it won't be me who'll be kicking the old dears out on to the street."

Moral blackmail, eh? That was never a feasible case for requesting bank assistance, but it could still prove to be a banking dilemma. Should innocent people suffer from a commercial decision made by a bank? Except it was more personal than that. It would be the bank manager, on behalf of the bank, who made the necessary judgement – in this instance, David, himself. And some people considered a bank manager's job to be a sinecure?

"Look," Farthinshawe continued, when David made no comment, "the end of the month's coming up. That means the payment of salaries and monthly accounts. The residents' fees won't be in until the 1st May and I'm already up to my limit. That's it, in a nutshell."

But it did not make sense. With fees paid in advance, he should never be in this position.

"Your account never used to be under such pressure," David said, looking hard at the man. "Why is it now?"

Farthinshawe actually looked sheepish. Freddie Mills, this was not. "The fact is," he muttered, almost too indistinctly for David to hear, "I don't know."

"You don't know?" How could the man be asking for increased facilities when he did not know how he had got into such difficulties?

"No, I don't actually know," Farthinshawe simply repeated.

"But you must check your figures? Your income and expenditure? You must know why your overdraft's under so much pressure?"

Farthinshawe looked even more sheepish. "I've not been checking anything recently," he admitted.

What an admission. An apparently successful businessman not checking his figures? If this was the case, lending anything more would be out of the question. It would be utter madness – whatever the situation concerning the residents.

"Does that mean you don't even check your bank account?" he asked, not attempting to hide his incredulity.

Everyone should check bank statements. David even did it himself – and he was manager of the branch. Perhaps that was eminently apposite; he knew how easily mistakes could arise. But business customers, especially, should always carry out a reconciliation of their own internal books with the entries shown on bank statements. What if one of their credits might have been innocently credited to someone else?

Farthinshawe looked even more glum. "I used to – quite religiously. But for the last six months, I've left it to Mrs Flintshire."

"Mrs Flintshire?"

Farthinshawe nodded enthusiastically. "Yes, she been with me for years. Originally came as a domestic, but she was so good I made her one of my carers. It was amazing, really. She'd no nursing qualifications, but you'd never have known it. Best worker I ever had. Because of that, in no time at all, I promoted her to be my head carer."

"But a carer's not qualified to do your books."

"As I said, she was my best worker. She could turn her hand to anything. And, six months ago, I promoted her to manager. She deserved the promotion and I needed a break – from all the paper work. So, I left it all to her."

David could not stop his eyes closing in disbelief. This Mrs Flintshire – a carer, made into the manager? Just like that? What managerial experience did she have? What accounting experience? You don't just step into this sort of work. There must be more to it than that. But, apart from this extraordinary situation, ominous thoughts were now circulating around his mind.

"You're not going to tell me Mrs Flintshire's a signatory on the bank account?" he asked, certain of the answer he would get.

"No, not at all," Farthinshawe replied, thankfully proving him wrong. "I sign all the cheques. She makes them out, but I sign them."

"And you leave her to do the statement reconciliation?"

Farthinshawe had no need to answer, his actions speaking for him. He simply looked down into his lap behind the desk where, David imagined, his hands were probably wringing in despair.

"But she's not been doing it," David said, effectively answering his own question.

"She thought I was doing it," Farthinshawe admitted, looking up, but not being able to make eye contact.

"But you knew about the pressure on the overdraft. I spoke to you about it, only a little while ago. Remember? You even got hot under the collar when I dared to question if anything odd was going on."

"That couldn't have been the case... not then and not now. I trust Mrs Flintshire implicitly. In any case..."

Farthinshawe stopped abruptly. Not only did he look crestfallen, but he seemed positively embarrassed.

"Mr Farthinshawe, I don't think you should hold anything back. We might as well get everything out into the open."

"It's nothing to do with the bank account."

"What isn't?"

"It's a personal matter."

Did he have to drag it out of the man, piece by piece?

"What is?"

Farthinshawe concentrated again on his hands. "Mrs Flintshire and I... we're... we're planning to get married."

Of all the answers David might have expected, this possibility had never entered his mind. He knew Farthinshawe was not married, so extra-marital dalliance on his part was not a question.

And Mrs Flintshire might well be widowed or divorced. But, if a relationship had developed between them, it could well explain her elevation within the business. Infatuation, on the man's part? But no matter what the reason, it had led to Farthinshawe's laxity in checking on what Mrs Flintshire was actually doing.

"Far be it for me," David said, "to want to know about your personal situation... and I certainly don't want to pry into it... but is this the reason why things have been going awry with the business's finances?"

"No!"

Farthinshawe's answer was almost too emphatic – certainly ultra-defensive.

"In any case," the man immediately added, "you've been giving Mrs Flintshire all the guidance she needed."

"Me?" What was he talking about?

"Not you, personally. Your staff. Mrs Bolton, to be precise. She's known Cynthia... Mrs Flintshire... for years. You ought to be proud of the way she helps your customers."

"There's no doubting that, Mr Farthinshawe," David agreed. "I am. It's just that I didn't know she'd been helping out. But if she has, why have things been going so horribly wrong?"

With Barbara's assistance... whatever that might have been... Mrs Flintshire should have had no trouble in handling the book-keeping. So, what had the woman been up to? Was she really the paragon that Farthinshawe had so enthusiastically described?

"Anyway," David continued, Farthinshawe appearing reluctant to reply, "We'd better get back to your original request for more help. How much do you actually need?"

The question seemed to surprise Farthinshawe. Perhaps he had been so caught up in the activities of his lady friend that he had completely overlooked his reason for coming into the bank.

"£1,000," he eventually said. "Possibly two."

"It's one or the other, Mr Farthinshawe. It's not a case of plucking a figure out of the air."

He was getting rather tired of the man's apparent lackadaisical attitude towards the business's finances and his choice of words and tone of voice probably betrayed his feelings. Not that Farthinshawe appeared to notice anything untoward. No doubt, he would neither mind what was said, nor how, provided he obtained the help he seemed to think he needed.

"I've not worked it out exactly," he replied, unconvincingly.

"Well," David said, "it's only the 18th today, so you've got over a week before you need to make your end-of-month payments. What I want you to do is go away and prepare a proper cash flow forecast for the next couple of months. That means setting down... on paper... all your expected items of expenditure against your fee income which will come in at the beginning of May and June."

Farthinshawe nodded, enthusiastically. Did he think he was now halfway towards getting what he wanted?

"And in addition to that," David continued, "I want you to check all your bank statements for the last six months. If, for whatever reason, these haven't been reconciled with your own books, I want you to do this now. And I want you to do it, Mr Farthinshawe – not Mrs Flintshire."

He doubted if this would turn out to be the case, but he was experiencing nasty vibes about this Mrs Flintshire. All the problems on the nursing home's account seemed to have arisen since the woman's involvement as manager and would-be bookkeeper. It would appear that, despite any help that Barbara Bolton may have given her, Mrs Flintshire was either incompetent, or... Could it be worse than incompetence? His mind suddenly switched from the Riverside's account to those of Mrs Whytechapel and the other two residents, whose names had slipped his mind. The withdrawals from those accounts also started about six months ago. Was it possible these things were all linked in some way?

"Why not Mrs Flintshire?" Farthinshawe asked, interrupting his thought processes.

"Simply because it's your business. You need to take full responsibility. And let's face it, there weren't any problems when you were doing the books. I certainly don't want to cast aspersions on Mrs Flintshire," (Oh, no?) "but any investigation must be down to you. It's got to be you to sort out what's been going on. Don't you agree?"

He was relieved to see Farthinshawe nodding his head. Perhaps doubts were also crossing his own mind. He certainly seemed to have accepted it was down to him to take personal charge of the forthcoming investigation.

"One further point," David continued. "How do the residents normally pay their fees?"

"The residents?" Farthinshawe seemed to be confused at the change of subject.

"Yes, their monthly fees. Do you insist on standing orders, or cheques? And do any residents actually make their payments in cash"

"They nearly all pay by standing order. That way, I know the payments will be made regularly and on time. That's not always the case with cheques. And cheques can bounce."

"And cash?"

"No, never. We try to keep as little cash as possible on the premises. We don't want to encourage burglars. And we get a lot of visitors around the place… coming in to see the residents. We never know who they might be. So, it's better to be safe than sorry."

"And what about Mrs Whytechapel? How did she pay?"

"Poor Mrs Whytechapel was different from the others. When she came… it must have been five or six years ago… her late husband had set up a trust fund – specifically to pay her fees."

"And that came to you from the trust's bank account? By standing order?"

"Yes, but she'd been facing a problem. The funds were running out. She used to joke that her husband hadn't expected her to live so long. It seems like a bad joke now. Anyway, she told me she'd sent an instruction to your bank – to set up a replacement standing order from her own account."

David bit his bottom lip, recalling that Hopkins had said they had found a note in her diary that she had written to the bank. Yet, no-one in the branch had seen any such missive. Perhaps it had gone astray in the post.

"So, she never paid with cash?" he asked.

"Never. What makes you think she might have?"

"No reason, really," he answered. For confidential reasons, he could not divulge anything about Mrs Whytechapel's account. That also applied to the other two old ladies who, it would seem, did not pay in cash, either. "Anyway, you know what I need and let's meet up again next week. When you've got the information. I can consider what the bank might be able to do."

When Farthinshawe had gone, David sat back in his chair and wondered if there might still be time to pop home for some lunch. But it was now well past two and he had much to do. It was always hectic before the Easter break – four days for him this year, because Norman had volunteered to come in on Saturday morning. And apart from carrying out his actual banking work, he needed time to marshal his thoughts – now dominated by a certain Mrs Flintshire.

# CHAPTER 27

David was hardly in the mood for a few pints at Coombe Cellars, but, with it being Easter weekend, he and Greville had agreed last week to meet up for their weekly get-together this Thursday, rather than on Good Friday. On the other hand, it would do him good to relax for a couple of hours with his old friend and Sarah had certainly encouraged him to keep the meeting.

He had already unburdened himself on Sarah as to the day's events. From a banking point of view, he would now be interested in getting Greville's perspective on the dormant account situation and what might be going on with the nursing home's finances. Sarah had been more interested in the relationship between Farthinshawe and Mrs Flintshire than with the question marks over the nursing home, itself. She had rubbed her hands with glee at the intrigue. It had certainly been a relief to have experienced a bit of levity in the house and he had to admit he shared Sarah's curiosity about the apparent charms of Mrs Flintshire. It was almost worth stopping at the Riverside on the way to the pub. If he could check out this woman, it would certainly make Sarah envious.

But he kept his Hillman Minx pointing in the direction of Coombe Cellars, taking the narrow winding road on the other side of the river. Dusk had turned into night and, without any street lamps, he often needed his headlamps on full beam to pick out the road's twists and turns.

He neared his destination and turned off the road into the even narrower lane which ran down to the pub. He immediately saw a good number of vehicles in the car park. It must be on account of Easter. Trade was likely to be busier than usual and he hoped Greville and he would be able to find a quiet corner to themselves. Public houses might comprise bricks and mortar, but they effectively had ears. There was no doubting many customers became all agog at what might be under discussion at an adjoining table. And the noisier a pub became, the louder people had to talk to make themselves heard. No, Greville and he would have to use the utmost discretion to avoid any risk of unwittingly divulging confidential information to others.

As with last Friday, he was the first to arrive. After ordering a pint of Red Barrel, he found a table for two which overlooked the river. During the day, these window tables would be snapped up for the splendid views of the gulls, ducks and other wild life which inhabited the river. But when he occasionally brought Sarah and Mark, the boy was far more interested in the goings-on across the river – the steam trains plying between Newton Abbot and Barnmouth. But at night-time, there was nothing to see outside and most customers were more interested in being near the actual bar, or alongside the comforting log fire.

Greville arrived within five minutes and David rose to greet him and get him a drink. But he stopped in his tracks as GG approached. His best friend looked to be at death's door. At the best of times, he gave the impression of being weak and scrawny, but, tonight, he hardly seemed to have any flesh covering his bones. His cheeks appeared to be hollowed out of his skull and his sunken eyes had dark rings around them like a pair of Michelin tyres. When he struggled out of his overcoat, it was as though it had been several sizes too large for his body. The change in him from only last Friday was startling – and immensely disturbing.

"GG," David gasped, "What's happened to you?"

He was reluctant to suggest his friend looked in mortal peril; the last thing sick people needed was to be made more conscious of their condition. But this man was more than just unwell; he looked to be needing immediate hospitalization.

"I shouldn't have come," Greville just about managed to say, his words slurred, as though he had already been drinking. "And I certainly couldn't take a drink."

"What you definitely need is a seat," David answered, putting an arm around his friend and guiding him to a chair at their table. In doing this, he was shocked at how emaciated Greville had become in less than a week. It was as if he were starving to death.

"What on earth has happened to you?" David repeated, as he sat down next to his friend.

But Greville remained silent, slumped in his seat, at high risk of slipping off and sliding under the table. David put a hand on his shoulder – just in case – and repeated his question.

Greville stayed silent, staring blankly into space.

"Greville?"

Still no answer.

"Let me get you some food."

"No!" A response at last. "I can't eat. I've tried, but I can't keep anything down. I've not eaten all week."

No wonder he was staring death in the face. But why? What had happened?

"Have you been off work?"

Greville was back in a trance, staring at unseen images through the window.

David tried to rationalize about what might have happened, never mind what he was going to do. It must be something to do with work, if only because Greville had never enjoyed a social life of any note – apart from these weekly sessions at the pub. It was not as if there was a woman in his life – one who may have ditched him and sent him into a depressed state. As far as David was aware, GG had never had a girlfriend.

So, it must be to do with the bank. But Greville never had a problem at work. He was always on top of his job. He must be one of the best technicians in the bank, intimately knowing all the laws related to banking. His knowledge far outshone his own, but it did not necessarily equip him for management. It was the only thing that could occasionally sour their relationship. Greville could not seem to grasp why he had not also become a manager.

Work should not, then, be a problem, unless... The current inspection of his branch? Parker? Had something serious cropped up at Newton Abbot? The inspector had certainly not yet made another appearance at Barnmouth, nor had he been on the telephone. He must be pre-occupied elsewhere and that place was likely to be Newton Abbot.

But before David could raise this with Greville, his friend eased himself out of his chair and stood up precariously, leaning heavily on the table. David immediately got up to try and steady him, but Greville shunned his attempted help.

"No, David," he said. "Stay there. I've got to go."

"But, Greville..."

"No. I'm going – alone. I don't want you to come."

"But, Greville... you need some help. And how will you get home? You can't possibly drive."

"I'll manage. Now, promise me... just stay where you are."

This was crazy. What was GG thinking about? He would hardly make it to the door – never mind get himself home.

As Greville started to move towards the door, David made to accompany him. But Greville pushed him back, his weak arm making more of a gesture than a thrust.

"No, David," he said, his dull eyes imploring David to do as he asked. "Please, I beg you to do this for me. Please stay there. And David, one last thing: I'm sorry. I'm terribly, terribly sorry."

And with that, he hobbled as quickly as he could towards the pub's door, leaving David utterly bewildered by his parting words. But there was no way he could let GG go off on his own like that and, once he had left the pub, with the door closed behind him, David quickly followed and looked outside. He was just in time to see a woman helping Greville into the passenger seat of her car. They were too far away for him to recognise her, but as she moved around the back of the vehicle to reach the driver's door, he could see she was wearing a dark three-quarter length coat over a tartan skirt. But her head was covered by a scarf and he had no chance of seeing her face.

He stood there, not believing what he was seeing. Greville with a woman? And it could not be a casual relationship. She must have brought him to the pub in the first place and then waited in the car park for him to come out. No wonder he had not wanted to stay long. And no wonder he had insisted on leaving the pub on his own.

When the car had driven out of the car park, David felt totally alone with his thoughts. Although he never liked drinking by himself, he returned to their table and took a long swig from his pint of Red Barrel. He certainly needed that, but as he sat back in his chair, he knew that no amount of beer was going to help explain what he had just seen.

And there were simply too many other conundrums going on. Until tonight, he was coming to the conclusion they might all be intrinsically linked, but how could that also apply to Greville and this unidentified woman? Quite irrationally, he now wished he had indeed called into the Riverside Nursing Home. He simply could not get the image of Mrs Flintshire out of his mind.

And nor could he forget Greville confessing that he was "terribly, terribly sorry."

## CHAPTER 28

Ted Calland scored his second goal and Trevor thought he was in heaven. Calland was mobbed by his team-mates and the crowd of over 8000 went wild with excitement. A 2-0 win against Southampton yesterday and another win against Newport County today could send United to the top of the league. It would be a nail-biting end to the season. Promotion might well be settled by the result of the final game – away to Crystal Palace. It was a match not to be missed. But that could present a problem. The game would be played on the 1st May – a Wednesday. Would Mr Goodhart let him have time off?

And there was another problem: the manager was United's number one fan; he would want to go himself.

With others possibly on holiday, could the office be depleted by the two of them? Or would they have to spin a coin? More likely, the manager would pull rank. That might, actually, be better than having to accompany him. A manager and his second cashier on a 400-mile round trip together?

And who else might want to share in the jamboree? This rare opportunity to share in United's possible success was likely to bring into the open alleged supporters who would swear their undying allegiance to the team. Yet those same would-be fans would not have attended any previous match during the season. This could well apply to one or two people at the branch. Oh, well…

But, for now, Trevor was in heaven, though not from the celebrations going on around him and on the pitch; it was far more intimate than that.

Katie's reaction to the goal had been to jump into his arms, throw her own arms around him and kiss him squarely on the lips. Heaven.

Yet, he had approached the match with some foreboding. All right, Katie had agreed to come, but would she enjoy it? Did she know anything about football? It would be purgatory if she was bored stiff with it all, making her feelings patently clear – especially at a time when he was trying to put his heart and soul into supporting the team's efforts.

He had suffered from 'bored girlfriend syndrome' once before. Stan Kenton's band had come to Torquay, of all places, playing a single concert at the Town Hall. As an aspiring jazz saxophonist, in no circumstances could he miss what must be the jazz event of the decade, never mind year.

The only problem was Yvonne.

Egoistical, self-centred, wrapped-up-in-herself Yvonne.

She had set her stall out on their first date, dragging him along to see The Red Shoes, for God's sake. She had not even had the prior decency to ask him whether he would like to see the film. Looking back, he supposed the Stan Kenton follow-up date was a case of getting his own back. But it backfired. How could he revel in such magnificent stirring music, while Yvonne sat immobile at his side. It was as if her feet and toes were set in concrete.

They never did get around to a third date.

So, Katie was very much on trial. But he had no need to worry. It got off to a good start when she greeted him wearing a United scarf; she must have gone out to buy it specially, so as not to feel out of place. Very impressive.

As for her knowledge of football… 'Could do better' might feature, if he had to write an end-of-match report. But she did try! And, truly, he never expected her to understand the offside law. But it was her celebration of that goal that made the game for him. Heaven. And that was not all. When Sammy Collins slotted in a penalty, Katie's conversion into a United supporter was signed and sealed – with another kiss.

He was feeling quite light-headed as they left the ground – and not just from the 4-0 win. Katie skipped along beside him and then slipped her hand in his as they negotiated their way through a line of Devon General double-deckers. They were parked adjacent to the ground, ready to take supporters home. And her hand remained in his as they made their way towards the centre of town. Bliss.

They headed for the Strand which was some distance away, but neither of them suggested taking a bus. The weather was fine and Katie seemed to be enjoying the walk as much as he.

They soon came to Ellacombe and passed the primary school where he had taken his 11-plus. By some miracle, he had scraped through and then progressed to Torquay Grammar. He did not yet know where Katie had been educated, nor did he care. But he chose not to broach the subject, just in case she was in the anti-grammar-school brigade. On the other hand, if this were so, her opinion might now change by the way she was hanging on to his arm.

They soon reached Market Street and its indoor market. It was still open and he persuaded Katie to have a quick browse at one of the stalls which specialized in gramophone records. He did not expect her to share his taste in music – even though she had enjoyed his jazz at the Walnut Grove – and while he pored over records by the likes of Sonny Rollins and Count Basie, he noticed her eyes light up at seeing covers depicting Elvis Presley and Buddy Holly.

Resisting the urge to buy a record or two – they might only prove to be a hindrance on this date – he guided Katie into Union Street and then on to Fleet Street. The route took them into the Strand and one of his favourite parts of Torquay – the harbour area.

His love of it had started when, as a lad, he was taken to Pelosi's ice-cream parlour. Then, as he got older, he was indulged in Devonshire cream teas at the Tudor Rose café. More recently, he had enjoyed visits to the 400 Club, listening to bands led by Sid Phillips, Chris Barber and Acker Bilk. Not that he would inflict this on Katie tonight – she had already done him proud by going to football with him.

"Do you fancy a drink?" he asked, as they approached the Queen's Hotel at the end of the Strand.

Katie looked at him mischievously. "Are you trying to lead me astray?"

"I did that this afternoon – taking you to football."

Katie squeezed his hand. "And wasn't that exciting?"

"I'm just thankful you enjoyed it. I was really worried before the match."

"Well, I did. And I am a bit thirsty – after all that shouting."

"Let's go in here, then," he said, guiding her into the lounge bar of the Queen's. "What'll you have?"

"Just a lemonade. If I have anything alcoholic, I'll start talking too much."

They both laughed out loud at the irony of her words. This really was turning out to be a rather special day. To celebrate, he actually ordered himself a pint.

"I'm still worried about Mr Goodhart," Katie said, when they were settled with their drinks at a table near the bar. She looked uncommonly serious and was clearly harking back to her concerns last Saturday.

"Has something else happened?" Trevor asked.

"I'm not sure," she replied, sipping her lemonade. "There's been so much going on…"

"You can say that again," Trevor agreed, tasting his beer and then licking the foam off his lips. Although he never drank beer, always being undecided whether he actually liked the bitter taste, he was pleased he had ordered himself a pint. Like Katie, he was thirsty and having a lemonade might not have impressed her.

Goodness knows, the way she was being tactile with him, he most definitely wanted to impress her. And the alcohol might give him the confidence to match her own natural inhibition.

"But has something else happened since the robbery?" he added. Had he missed anything?

"I'm not sure," Katie repeated. "This lunchtime, Mr Goodhart had an awfully long interview with Mr Farthinshawe."

"I can't stand that man. He's as bad as Mr Hicklemaker."

"I know what you mean. I don't like him, either. But they're not as bad as Mr English."

"English? At the Esplanade?"

Katie nodded. "He's awful."

"I know there were all those problems with him last year, but I can't say I dislike him."

"That's because you're a man."

Trevor frowned.

"He likes the ladies," Katie explained, as though he were a dumb-bell. "He can hardly keep his hands off anything in a skirt."

"Including you?" Trevor asked, appalled at the thought. This might only be his second date with Katie, but he was already starting to feel possessive.

"No, thank goodness. I just glare at him. And he knows I'm now Mr Goodhart's secretary."

Trevor was not really sure why that might stop English trying his luck – if he had such inclinations. But he was now feeling relieved the man had not succeeded in pawing Katie's gorgeous body.

"I can't imagine Hicklemaker and Farthinshawe being ladies' men," he said.

Katie shuddered, albeit theatrically. It was clear how she viewed these two men. "I don't know about Hicklemaker, but Farthinshawe's got a bit of a reputation."

"He's not been ogling you, as well?"

"What do you think I am?" Katie shrilled, good naturedly, but making one or two people in the bar turn round.

"Shh..." The last thing he wanted was to become the centre of attention – of others, that is. Katie was another matter, altogether.

"But us girls," Katie continued, mischievously, " reckon he's got a thing going for Mrs Flintshire."

"His manager?" Trevor exclaimed, prompting Katie to mimic his 'sh'. But he could not keep his amazement out of his voice. Whenever Mrs Flintshire came to the counter, he was struck by her singular unattractiveness. How could anyone, never mind Mr Farthinshawe, be drawn to her... in that sort of way?

"And Barbara keeps going to the nursing home," Katie continued, almost rubbing her hands at the possible salaciousness of the supervisor's motives. "She says it's because she's friends with Mrs Flintshire, but..."

Katie deliberately failed to finish her sentence in the best nudge-nudge-wink-wink tradition.

"But she's happily married."

Katie grinned wickedly. "What about last Saturday? We saw her – with a man."

"But we agreed this could have been just a friend... or her brother."

"Oh, Trevor, you've no sense of fun. Let's have a game. Let's try and guess who it might have been. I'll go first. How about Mr Goodhart?"

What was going on? This was daft. While he was on a date with Katie, why would he want to talk about any hypothetical dating by Barbara?

"All right, then," Katie said, clearly gauging his reaction which he had no need to voice, "but I wouldn't put it past Mr Farthinshawe making a pass at Barbara."

Whether he liked it or not, Trevor could not stop himself

casting his mind back to Torquay railway station last Saturday night. The man with Barbara was certainly short, but was he as thick-set as Farthinshawe? He was wearing an overcoat, so it was difficult to tell. It was certainly intriguing. And despite his disparaging of Katie's little game, he now wished he had taken more notice. At the time, he had been more concerned about Katie and himself not being seen by Barbara.

"Do you think it could have been Farthinshawe last Saturday?" he could not help himself asking.

"You see?" Katie cooed, her eyes sparkling. "You're as bad as me."

She was probably right and had certainly got him thinking.

"But, getting back to Mrs Flintshire," Katie continued, almost disappointing him at the change of subject, "when Mr Goodhart dictated his PM note after his interview with Mr Farthinshawe, he said he thought there was something wrong with the nursing home's accounts. He didn't spell it out exactly, but I got the distinct impression he was worried about Mrs Flintshire."

"I can't say that upsets me too much. I don't like the woman."

"You don't seem to like anyone," Katie said, attempting to feign apparent sadness.

"Are you fishing, or what?"

"Don't be daft. I know you like me. Else you wouldn't have invited me to football."

"You're teasing me, now."

It was so unfair. Why could he not be as uninhibited as her? Was it down to the stars? His mother was an expert on astrology and, although he was naturally sceptical, he had a sneaking belief there might be more to it than he would care to admit.

"But what about Barbara and Mrs Flintshire?" Katie asked, becoming serious again. "We know they're friends and Mr Goodhart says Barbara's been giving Mrs F advice on the nursing home's book-keeping. On that basis, he says there shouldn't be any problems with the accounts."

"I'd go along with that. But what if that's all a front for her visits? Perhaps she's going to the home because of Mr Farthinshawe and not Mrs Flintshire."

Katie frowned. The look did not suit her. He only wanted her to smile. No, she was not a smiler; she was a grinner. She was far too outgoing just to smile. "I'm sure that never entered Mr Goodhart's mind," she said, then feigning outrage. " But you see? You're now playing the game I suggested."

*Touché*. But it was intriguing – even if it did sound far-fetched.

"But, going back to when we sat down," he replied, "you said you were still worried about Mr Goodhart. This business at the nursing home... with Mr Farthinshawe and Mrs Flintshire... it can't be anything to do with that, can it?"

"No," Katie answered. "I thought it was something more personal than that."

"He's not said anything?"

"No. He never really talks about his personal life."

"Perhaps it's just the accumulation of everything else. God knows, there's been enough happening at the branch – never mind those dreadful murders. And Mrs Whytechapel was killed at the nursing home. You don't think..."

Katie now looked genuinely alarmed. "It can't be all tied up, can it?"

Trevor could only shrug his shoulders.

"But there is something else going on," Katie continued. "Jane's doing some kind of investigation. And she's keeping it to herself – her and Mr Goodhart."

"Have you asked her about it?"

"Course I have. You know me – old nosey-parker."

"And she's said nothing?"

Katie shook her head, as though it had been a personal failure on her part.

"But on those other matters," Trevor said, deciding to take Katie into his confidence, especially as there were now a couple of things concerning him, "there's something else that's bothering me."

Katie's eyes shone – no doubt at the thought of another intrigue developing.

"I really can't believe," he continued, "someone actually stole that £2,500 from Bernard's till."

"But it's gone. Someone must have taken it."

"I know, but…"

Ever since getting back that day from lunch with Katie, something had been troubling him. Something had been niggling at the back of his mind and steadfastly refusing to come to the front. He had gone over everything, time after time, but… but nothing. Perhaps he was just letting his imagination get the better of him. But, this discussion they had been having… it was almost as if something was staring him in the face. Yet, he still felt blind to it.

"Tell me what you're thinking," Katie urged.

"No, it's nothing." At this stage, he could only keep such fanciful thoughts to himself.

"In that case," Katie said, moving closer to him and taking hold of his hand, "why are we talking about work? It's Saturday – our day of rest."

"That's supposed to be Sunday."

"Saturday and Sunday. And why aren't you playing tonight? I just loved your saxophone."

So, she does like jazz – as well as Buddy Holly. "I don't play there every Saturday."

"Well, let's go there, anyway."

This was getting to be more than he deserved. A girlfriend who went to football with him and, now… at her suggestion, not his… wanting to go to a jazz club?

"You're on," he said. "But let's have something to eat first. There's a new Italian place just round the corner. Fancy spaghetti?"

"Spaghetti? We have that at home… on toast."

"That's Heinz, silly. I'm talking about spaghetti bolognaise."

"Bolog-what?"

And as he took her hand in his – Katie's self-confidence was, indeed, catching – he was still grinning at her sense of fun as he led her out of the bar's door. He would not spoil the rest of the evening by dwelling on the matters at work which were niggling him more and more. But he had decided to share his concerns with Mr Goodhart when they returned to work on Tuesday.

# CHAPTER 29

Football-wise, it had been an Easter weekend to remember. On Good Friday, David and Mark had seen United destroy Southampton, 2-0. The team had then thrashed Newport County, 4-0, on Saturday. The only downside was today, Easter Monday. Southampton, in the return match from Friday, achieved their revenge with an unconvincing 1-0 victory. All right, he had not been there, but for Southampton to win, it just had to be unconvincing. Anyway, all was not lost. Victories in the remaining two matches, at home to Queens Park Rangers and away to Crystal Palace, should secure promotion to the second division – for the first time ever.

Last night, the prospect of this should have enabled him to sleep peacefully, but those problems at work had re-surfaced. They had limited his sleep to far less than the eight hours he reckoned he normally needed.

Sunday's afternoon trip in the car had not helped. Buoyed on by winning the morning's monthly medal at the golf club, he had taken the family on what had proved to be a puncture-less trip to Dartmoor. He chose a similar route to the one Sarah had previously planned, but he also took in the area around Princetown.

A swirling, dank mist cloaked the region and made the forbidding prison even more cheerless than usual.

Perhaps, this trip had not been a good move.

It unnerved him to be in close proximity of this grim place. Convicted murderers were ensconced behind its iron-barred windows, but outside, at large, one other murderer, at least, deserved to join those inmates. And what about the perpetrators of the threats? Whether or not they ended up here, please God, let them be caught soon.

In bed, it had not been so bad while he lay awake – apart from Sarah disproving her contention that she never snored. But when he eventually succumbed to sleep, his dreaming was chaotic. It was as if he were in the middle of a play. Names and faces flashed before him: Bernard, Trevor, Jane, Barbara and Greville represented the bank; Farthinshawe, Flintshire, Hicklemaker, English, Martingale and Whytechapel took the part of the customers. But there was no logic to his dreaming; everything was mixed up. Some who were alive became dead, whereas the murdered ladies loomed larger than life. And then Hopkins, Pound and Parker entered the stage, stirring the whole pot into an incongruous mish-mash.

In the morning, he awoke, dripping with perspiration. It took several minutes to rid himself of these unwanted images. When this was done, he was able to lie quietly and it all started to feel rather odd. It was as if he really believed he was nearing the solving of the mystery. Had his dream helped in some way? And he was now convinced it was probably just one mystery; somehow, all the disparate parts – like those of a jigsaw – would come together into one solution.

But how? And when?

# CHAPTER 30

Despite his continuing worries, David had profited from his four-day Easter break. Somehow, he and Sarah had put to one side their concerns about the threat to Mark. It was not that their anxiety had diminished... nothing would do that... but they had succeeded in making their holiday weekend as normal as possible.

It was now nearly two weeks since Sarah had received the threatening note. Could the police have been right all along? That it was a one-off incident? That it did not justify exhaustive investigation? No, David could not agree with such thinking, but it was an enormous relief that a second missive had not yet been penned. The longer that continued, the better.

It had also been good to spend more time with Mark – and not just by going with him to football. Several times, they had been together on their hands and knees, creating main line operations and marshalling yards which would have done the GWR proud. And then, before bedtime, the Monopoly board had surfaced. Mark's eventual acquisition of hotels on Mayfair and Park Lane had sent him to bed happy and driven his parents into bankruptcy.

Yes, such relaxation had done him the world of good and he arrived at the office on Tuesday morning feeling able to face the rigours of the week. It was not something he had anticipated at the beginning of the holiday weekend.

The Tuesday after Easter was always busy at the bank, but David deliberately put to one side anything that was not urgent. Straightaway, he needed to learn about Jane's latest developments into her investigation into the dormant accounts.

"Did you have a good weekend?" he asked, when she had settled herself at his desk, having placed four separate piles of vouchers in front of her.

She nodded enthusiastically. "John's started to teach me to play golf."

"Really?" Now, that was certainly an advantage of having a golf professional as a boyfriend.

"You sound surprised, sir," Jane replied, then trying to feign mock disgust. "Don't you think women can play golf?"

"On the contrary," David said, attempting to forget the lady members at Barnmouth who consistently bobbled the ball fifty yards down the fairway to a chorus of "good shot" from their playing partners. "There are some very good lady golfers. So long as John doesn't start teaching you to pay football or rugger. I'm old-fashioned enough to believe some sports should definitely be left to men."

"There's no chance of that, sir. But I'm really enjoying my golf. John's even shown me how to draw and fade the ball."

This was now getting ominous. Draw and fade? He, himself, had been playing the game for over twenty years and he could still not do this to order. Hook and slice when it was not wanted, maybe. But to draw and fade, to order? He had better make sure Jane never challenged him to a game.

"But what about the dormant accounts?" he asked, getting down to business. "Any chance of those problems fading?"

"Not a chance, sir. It's getting worse."

It had only been Thursday morning when Jane had scurried away to do some more digging around. What else had she discovered?

"What have you found now?" he asked, fearing the worst.

"First of all," Jane replied, glancing down at the piles of vouchers, "what I haven't found out is any connection between Mrs Martingale and Mrs Whytechapel. I've looked at their PM cards and through their files. Although they've both banked here for so long, there's nothing at all to connect them."

"Apart from their accounts being dormant and then starting up again in the last six months."

"That's true. But there's no apparent reason why their murders might be linked."

David frowned. "Do you think the police might have got it wrong? That the ladies weren't murdered at all? Could their deaths have been accidents?"

Jane shrugged. "But that's their problem, isn't it? Not ours. Aren't we only concerned with their bank accounts?"

She was probably right there. Any detective work on their part must be down to banking activities; the police were the only ones qualified to deal with murder enquiries. Yet, the murdered ladies were customers of the bank and their accounts were included in the ones they were investigating.

"In that case," he answered, "let's again start with Mrs Martingale. Have you been in touch with Newton Abbot branch? That's where the transfers went, wasn't it?"

"That's right, sir, but no, I really haven't had time yet. In any case, as Mr Parker's doing an inspection there, I wondered if it might be better coming from you."

She had a point there. It would give him a good excuse to contact Parker again. What was the man doing? No sight or sound since Wednesday. Was Parker so unconcerned about what had been happening here? More concerned about completing his inspection at Newton Abbot on schedule? In many ways, it was flattering to be left alone... to carry out the investigations in his own manner, without outside interference. On the other hand, it would be nice to know that Parker cared about what was happening here.

"All right," he replied. "I'll contact him later. What about Mrs Whytechapel? Her cash withdrawals were all here, weren't they?

All cashed by Bernard? And you've got the cheques there?"

"Yes, sir," Jane replied, picking up one of the piles of vouchers in front of her and then passing half-a-dozen cheques across the desk.

David took them from her and looked carefully at each cheque. The amounts were either £300 or £500, a single cheque having been cashed each month since last October. They appeared to be correctly signed, with the crossings opened properly. And each cheque bore the rubber till stamp of the number one cashier, Bernard's initial being scrawled across each stamp. Before doing this, he would have had to have been satisfied as to Mrs Whytechapel's identity and, having cashed six of her cheques, she must have been well known to him. Yet, she was an elderly resident in a nursing home. That rather implied she might be confined to the home. And Farthinshawe had specifically said she had written to the branch to set up a standing order. Rather than come in? Even though she regularly cashed cheques here? It was all very odd and he would have to see Bernard about it.

"Everything looks all right with the cheques," he said, for the moment putting to one side the customer's ability to get into the branch. "Have you checked the signatures?"

Jane nodded. "The only problem is our original signature card's so old. But the signatures on the cheques still look all right to me. The writing's a bit shaky, but you'd expect that with such an elderly person."

That was fair enough and it was always surprising that signatures did not change much, even over many years. It was just as well. Customers' signatures to banks were like fingerprints to the police. They were a prime source of identification.

"You've not spoken to Bernard?"

"No, sir. We agreed I shouldn't."

"I'll see him later, then." Now he had the actual cheques, he was properly equipped to see Bernard and get the facts behind the encashments. But there was another curiosity. Even if Mrs Whytechapel had been able to come into the branch, why should a resident of a nursing home need to make such regular cash withdrawals? Especially when Farthinshawe had said he never took cash as payment for fees.

"What about these other items?" he asked, pointing to the three remaining piles of vouchers in front of Jane.

"These are the cash withdrawals made by Mrs Blackstone," Jane said, picking up the first pile.

David took them from her – about ten, in all. They were for varying amounts, mainly £50 and £100. Once again, they appeared to have been made out correctly and each one had again been cashed by Bernard.

"And this pile," Jane said, when he had finished scrutinizing them, "are cheques cashed by Miss Bassenthwaite."

This was getting to be like playing a gramophone record over and over again. Apart from the actual signatures and amounts, it was the same old tune. And to compound matters, both these ladies, and not forgetting Mrs Whytechapel, were residents of the Riverside Nursing Home.

It just did not add up. And those thoughts of his in bed... the answers which would not come into the open... were still gnawing away in his mind.

"And the rest?" he asked, motioning to the remaining pile of vouchers.

"These relate to the twenty-five or so other accounts which used to be dormant," Jane replied, picking up the vouchers which must number well over a hundred.

David shook his head. Jane had certainly done well to retrieve so many vouchers covering so many accounts. "And until a few months ago, these accounts were all inactive?"

Jane nodded. "And I haven't yet managed to find all the

vouchers. But there're enough here to go on."

"You can say that again. And did you get Barbara involved… to help out?" It did not seem possible for Jane to have done this on her own.

"I tried," she replied, now looking a little annoyed, "but when I told her what it was all about, she didn't want to know. She said she had too much work on her own plate."

"I suppose that was fair enough," David said, "with Easter coming up."

Jane seemed unconvinced. "Perhaps. But when I got out all the vouchers, I was pleased to be doing it on my own."

David looked at her directly, the fingers and thumb of his left hand stroking his chin. As he studied her face, curious at her choice of words, he was conscious of not having shaved closely enough that morning.

"You saw how those other cheques were all cashed by Bernard," Jane continued. "Well, all the credits in this lot went through Barbara's till."

That was odd. "What about the cheques? Were they cashed by Barbara?"

"No. Not by Barbara – or by anyone. Yet, they look as though they should have been."

What was she talking about? "Let me have a look," he said, stretching his hand across the desk.

He quickly saw that none of the cheques had actually been made payable to a specific person. Each payee had been annotated as 'cash' or 'self' – as if the customer was, in fact, intending to cash each cheque. But none of the cheques bore a cashier's till stamp to confirm that it had, indeed, been cashed.

David looked up at Jane. "No till stamp on any of them."

"No, sir. And no crossing stamp, either."

David looked back at the cheques, quickly flicking through

them. If a cheque had been paid into an account at another bank, that bank would have impressed its identification stamp on its front. That was important if the cheque could not be paid, for technical reasons or for lack of funds.

"So," he said, "all these cheques must have been paid into accounts here. But they're all payable to 'cash' or 'self'.

"Yes, sir. But now look at the backs of the cheques."

David turned the cheques over and immediately saw that each one had been signed on the back by the customer. "They've all been endorsed," he said, as much to himself, as to Jane.

"But why, sir?" Jane asked.

It was a pertinent question. Cheques which had been endorsed on the back by the payee could be paid into another person's account, title effectively being transferred to that person. But why should all these customers have done this on so many occasions? Why not make out the cheques in favour of specific payees. That would be far simpler, rather than this 'cash' and 'self' business and subsequent endorsements. It did not make sense.

"I've no idea why," he replied. "But what it also means is that we don't know which accounts have been credited with these cheques. If we knew that, we might have some idea of what's been going on."

Jane nodded her head, but seemed reluctant to venture an opinion on how that could be achieved.

"You're sure these people aren't residents at the Riverside?" David then asked, though knowing this was not possible. The nursing home was simply not big enough to accommodate so many people. But there might still be a connection. Everything else seemed to be leading to the Riverside.

"No, they're not," Jane replied. "As far as I could find out, there's no link at all."

"And going back to the credits," David mused, "they all went through Barbara's till." He could see the supervisor's till stamp clearly embossed on each credit slip and he then looked back at the cheques. "And the cheques have all been cancelled by Barbara."

Any cheque drawn on his own branch had to be examined to ensure it was technically in order. Once confirmed, the scrutineer authorised its payment by cancelling the cheque with a red-ink initial through the signature. All the cheques in front of him bore Barbara's unmistakeable initial. That, in itself, might well be feasible, if she had taken each credit into her own till. But for some twenty-five different customers? Especially as she was only a relief cashier.

"We now need to find out about the cheques," he said. "Who's actually been credited with them. Any chance you could do that this morning?"

"Sir!" Jane exclaimed, spreading her arms across all the vouchers which now covered most of the desk. "This morning?"

"I'm sorry," David hastily replied, smiling apologetically. He was thinking of her as superwoman again. Goodness knows how long it would take her to do what he wanted. "I'm getting ahead of myself."

Jane looked relieved. "There must be over a hundred cheques here – drawn over a six-month period. That means digging out the work for every day an entry went through. That would take hours."

David raised his hands in mock surrender. But this job needed to be done as soon as possible. And he now realized there was only one way to achieve it.

But it was time for Jane to get on with her normal work and, after he had sent her on her way, he sat back in his chair and contemplated all she had discovered. Things were hotting up; there was no question about that. Something rotten was going on and he was getting more concerned by the minute.

And there was another thing.

Something was now bothering him about the original threat that the branch would be raided. But what? The note's phraseology? The perpetrator's choice of words? Or was it just another instance of something gnawing away at him, but obdurately refusing to surface?

As he was mulling this over and castigating his mind's stubbornness for not revealing the answers, a knock on his door heralded the arrival of Trevor Smith.

"I'm sorry, sir," the cashier said, "but could I have a quick word with you?"

## CHAPTER 31

Trevor had been aching to return to work on Tuesday.

It was not really physical, but his heart was pumping with a yearning like never before. He had not seen Katie for two days. It felt like a lifetime.

Yet, had he been so afflicted with previous girlfriends? No, never. And most certainly not with Yvonne. Others had just been companions: friends with whom to share the escapism of the cinema; to have a knock-up on the tennis court; or to stroll with along Torquay's promenade at sunset. He would never have considered taking any of them to football or to the Walnut Grove; these were his male preserves. Yet he had not hesitated to share such masculine fields with Katie. It had led to consequential emotions he could never have previously imagined.

Now, at work, Katie was certainly there, but only at arm's length. He would also have to maintain only surreptitious eye and vocal contact. They had agreed to that on Saturday. Otherwise, the teasing would be excruciating.

If… what a big little word that was…if their relationship was to develop, he would not put it past the bank to transfer one of them to another branch. And he was certain he would be the one to go. After all, Katie had only just been promoted here. No, far better to keep everything under wraps – even if they needed to act as strangers between the hours of nine and five. His only doubt was whether Katie would be able to maintain such secrecy.

But, this morning, he had more on his mind than Katie and he was not relishing the prospect.

On Saturday night, he had made up his mind to see Mr Goodhart. He could not get the Riverside Nursing Home out of his mind. What might be going on between Mr Farthinshawe and

Mrs Flintshire? When he thought of his own new-found feelings towards Katie, he could not imagine such ardour being matched between the nursing home's owner and his manager. What could the man possibly see in Mrs Flintshire?

Ugh!

But why was Barbara so friendly with the woman? And why had she been helping with the business's book-keeping? Perhaps the two of them were old school friends; they were certainly of a comparable age. And was Barbara's friendship limited to Mrs Flintshire? Or did it also extend to Mr Farthinshawe? And romantically?

But it was not just the possible shenanigans at the nursing home that were troubling him. What was it about the theft from Bernard's till? Something about it continued to niggle him. But what?

Yet, when could he see Mr Goodhart? First thing had been impossible; he had to deal with the night safe wallets. And there had been so many, all crammed to capacity. At weekends, traders found the outside wall's night safe particularly helpful. But it had kept him busy until nearly opening time at ten o'clock.

He did not want to wait until after closing time before seeing the manager; he needed to share his concerns well before then. The first hour after opening had then proved to be hectic on the counter, but there was a lull at about eleven. The trouble was that he had seen Jane go into Mr Goodhart's room earlier and Katie now appeared to be desperate to get to him for her dictation. Dare he try to nip in before her? She would not be best pleased at that, though he could make it up to her later. Or was that wishful thinking?

Jane suddenly emerged from the room and it was his opportunity. Bernard had already agreed he could take a break from the counter – without being told the reason why – and as soon as he had locked his till, he made for the manager's room. He reached the door just before a determined-looking Katie. Was she being deliberately provocative by clasping her shorthand notebook and pencil to her Lloyds Bank- green figure-hugging jumper?

"Just give me a couple of minutes," he pleaded, not really knowing where to look.

He would not have got away with it if it had been Miss Harding. But, there again, he would never have given Miss Harding his undivided attention on Saturday. That gallantry on his part clearly clinched it for Katie. She grinned saucily.

"That might be all you'll get from me, next time we go out," she whispered in his ear.

As he knocked on Mr Goodhart's door, he was much-relieved that Katie was, indeed, expecting them to have another date.

# CHAPTER 32

"Of course," David said. "Come in and sit down."

He did his best to sound welcoming, but he could well do without being a shoulder to lean on this morning. That must be what this was about; Trevor would hardly want to see his manager about anything else. Mid-morning – on a busy day after Easter? On the other hand, it might simply be a query on an account; a black-list customer wanting to cash a cheque? No, he would have seen Norman about that. It must be a personal matter. To do with the threat of the raid? That must, surely, still be preying on Trevor's mind.

"How was your Easter?" he simply asked, once Trevor was sitting down opposite him.

"Losing to Southampton yesterday, didn't help, sir."

David pursed his lips and shook his head. "That was so frustrating. Promotion probably won't now be decided until the last day of the season."

And, if so, that game at Crystal Palace was one not to be missed. For a while, he had been wondering how to broach this 400-mile-round-trip with Sarah. He was sure she would not object to his going, but to take Mark with him? Being an evening match, they would probably not get home before three in the morning. During term time? No, there was no chance of that being allowed. But how would Mark react if he went on his own? The only answer would be for United to have secured promotion before that last game.

"But I know you're busy, sir," Trevor quickly said, "and I don't want to take up much of your time."

What a tactful way to shut his manager up from talking about football! But it was typical of the boy to gauge the appropriate moment for idle chit-chat. He was turning into an impressive young man and if he got moving with his Institute of Bankers diploma, he should have a successful career ahead of him. Whether Parker would agree with that was another matter.

"Shoot away, then," David said, now knowing this was not to do with a query on the counter.

"It was over the weekend when I decided…" Trevor said, then pausing, his eyes betraying a concern over something important.

"Go on," David coaxed. He was eager to help if he could, but this now had the makings of being anything but a quick word.

"I'm sorry, sir," Trevor said, acknowledging the prompting. "It's just that I'm not sure how to put it. Part of it's rather delicate, if you know what I mean."

It would be easier to know what he meant, once the lad had said something concrete.

"Why not start at the beginning?"

"Well," Trevor said, taking a deep breath, "this business with the nursing home… we reckon something funny's going on there."

"We?" If any word could eclipse all others in a sentence dealing with funny goings-on at the Riverside, it was this particular two-letter word.

And Trevor's response was to blush to the roots.

"We?" David repeated, when no immediate reply was forthcoming.

"She's going to kill me for that," Trevor eventually confessed.

"She?" Would his responses always be one-worded?

"I'm sorry, sir, but please… will you keep this bit to yourself?"

David nodded, although he was not thrilled at the prospect of becoming a confidant over something of which, at present, he knew nothing.

"It's Katie and me."

"Katie?" That staccato response again.

"You won't let her know I told you, sir. We promised to keep it to ourselves."

David could not now stop himself grinning. Trevor and Katie dating? That really was very good news. But if there had been a secrecy pact between them, only one of them was in danger of breaking it; and that would not have been Trevor. No wonder he was so embarrassed at having spilled the beans.

"I still don't know what you're talking about," David said. Why not string the boy along for a while?

"You've not heard anything, then?"

David shook his head.

"Katie's said nothing?"

Another simple shake of his head.

"She really is going to kill me." But, this time, Trevor said it with a smile. And was that a look of pride in his eyes? One thinking that Katie, the most outward-going, uninhibited chatterbox in the office had kept a secret which he, the reserved one, had blurted out?

"No, Katie's said nothing," David said, becoming serious again, " but, as you said, you didn't want to take up much of my time."

"Of course, sir. Sorry. Anyway, on Saturday, I took Katie to football, then we had a drink and a meal down by the harbour. That's when we got talking about some of the things that've been going on here…"

"Quietly, I hope," David interrupted. GG and he knew the dangers of pub talk, but did that apply to Trevor and, in particular, Katie?

"Most definitely, sir," Trevor answered, genuinely indignant. "We made sure no-one could overhear."

"Go on, then. What did you mean by funny goings-on at the Riverside?"

"It all seems a bit odd," Trevor continued, frowning, "and it's not just that I don't care for either Mr Farthinshawe or Mrs Flintshire, but are they up to something?"

"I don't know. What do you think?"

"Katie says you're concerned about how the account has been operating recently."

"Go on."

"Yet, Barbara's been helping Mrs Flintshire sort out the books."

David simply raised his eyebrows.

"In which case," Trevor continued, " the books should be in apple-pie order."

It was all very well for Trevor to come in and simply tell him things he was perfectly aware of…

"And," Trevor continued, "Katie says the girls know Barbara spends quite a bit of her spare time at the nursing home."

Now, this was something new.

"No doubt, helping with the books?" he suggested. But was there more to it than that?

"This is where the delicate bit comes in," Trevor said, looking concerned and, again, embarrassed. "I hope you don't think I'm telling tales… but it might be important."

"You just tell me what you think you should," David answered. "Then let me be the judge and jury."

"I also took Katie out last Saturday," Trevor said, as if it were an enforced admission, the lump in his throat bobbing up and down. "I was playing at the Walnut Grove and I invited her to come."

So, this dating had probably started then… and continued on Easter Saturday. It could be getting serious… especially if Katie was prepared to go to football and to a jazz club. But this was not the time to quiz him on this.

"Anyway," Trevor continued, "we were waiting on Torquay station for a train to take us home and we saw Barbara – with a man. The first thing Katie thought was why? But I said that just because her husband was in Spain didn't mean she couldn't go out. And then we thought it might have been her brother."

"You didn't recognize the man?"

"No, sir," Trevor replied, now looking a little sheepish. "We were so concerned about not being seen, ourselves... so we moved out of the way. In any case, at the time, we didn't think that much of it."

"And now?"

"We got talking about it again this Saturday. It was this business of Barbara often going to the nursing home. You see, the only thing I'm sure about that man on the station was that he was short." Trevor paused, as if for dramatic effect, before adding, "And Mr Farthinshawe's short."

Now, this could put a different slant on things. But was it feasible for Barbara to be having a liaison with Farthinshawe – especially as the man had said he was planning to marry Mrs Flintshire. Or was there something more complicated about his love life?

"Is that it?" he asked, seeing Trevor sit back in his chair, as if relieved to have got the story off his chest.

Trevor nodded. "I hope I've done the right thing, sir."

"You certainly have," David said, smiling, to help put the boy at his ease. "And I'm saying that as judge and jury."

But, as Trevor's account had evolved, he could not get Jane's on-going investigation out of his head. She had done sterling work in giving him the information to contact Parker about the transfers from Mrs Martingale's account. Now, after what Trevor had just told him, it seemed even more important to see Bernard Groves about the cash withdrawals by the residents of the Riverside. But it was going to take Jane some time to trace all the entries on the other twenty-five dormant accounts and he was now certain how this could be achieved more quickly.

"Who are the main key holders this week?" he asked.

Trevor looked almost startled at the change of subject.

"Bernard and I have the keys to the inner cash grill."

"And the outer strong room door?" This was the answer he was seeking.

"That's me and Jane. It would normally have been me and Bernard, but Jane said she expected to work late this week. She needs to get to the ledgers and voucher boxes in the main strong room. It didn't seem fair to ask Bernard to stay late, just because he was one of the key holders. So, he swapped with Jane. He'll do her stint next week."

Good. That could not be better. "So, you'll be staying late with Jane?"

"Yes, sir. I agreed to give her a hand, if she wanted it."

"That's why I wanted to know who the key holders were. Jane definitely needs some help; she's doing a big investigation for me… into dormant accounts. And I now need to know the results as soon as possible. Do you think Katie might be prepared to stay and help, as well?"

"I'm sure she would," Trevor replied, a couple of pink spots surfacing on his cheeks.

"And, if I stay, too, that'll make four of us and we can work in a couple of teams. I reckon we'd then get the work done in no time."

"What sort of work is it?"

"We need to trace the destination of over a hundred cheques drawn on about twenty-five previously dormant accounts. It seems that these cheques were paid into other accounts here. What we'll have to do is get out the day's work for each of these entries. And credits have also gone on to these accounts; we need to find out what cheques were included in those."

"How many days' work are we talking about?"

"It goes back for six months and if all those cheques and credits were processed on different days, we'll have to get out the work for well over a hundred days."

"Phew." Trevor could not hide his assessment of the enormity of the task. "That'll take ages."

"But much quicker than if Jane was doing it on her own. I reckon, if we get a good system going…"

"In pairs, you said?"

"Yes," David replied grinning. Was this a leading question? "And I'd better be with Katie."

"And you promise not to tell her…"

"Yes, yes, yes. What we'll be doing is not linked to anything you just told me. So there's no need for her to know that I know. I'll leave that to you. But I want tonight's investigation to be kept between the four of us. I don't want Norman, Bernard or Barbara to know… at this stage, anyway. That's why I was keen to know who the main key holders were. The others can go off home as normal, not knowing we're staying on to do the checking up."

"It's all rather intriguing, sir."

"And it also sounds melodramatic. But I have a feeling it'll prove worthwhile. So, off you go…"

"Just before I go," Trevor interrupted, leaning forward earnestly, "there is one other thing."

So, there was more to come; to do with what they had been discussing, or was it another aspect to his new-found romance? It was, surely, too soon for them to become engaged?

"Something's been niggling at the back of my mind," Trevor continued, "about that money stolen from Bernard's till. But I can't put my finger on it."

So, it was still about the problems at the branch. And Trevor was having premonitions, as well as himself. Why would both of them have such feelings beavering away at the back of their brains, yet doggedly refusing to surface? In his own case, it was a general foreboding, but with Trevor? Was it just specifically linked to the robbery?

"In what way?" he asked, making a mental note to ring DC Pound to see how they were progressing in their search for the 'Harris Tweed Man'.

"It's that man in the banking hall," Trevor answered. "The one who stole the money just before I got back from lunch. Incidentally, sir, I couldn't tell you before, but I can now… I'd been having lunch with Katie. That's why I was back late; we lost track of time."

That clears up that one, then. But it was understandable why he could not have come clean about it at the time. Perhaps, that would ease Parker's concerns about the boy.

"Anyway," Trevor continued, "if he had just stolen the money, wouldn't I have seen him coming out of the branch, or running up the High Street? I doubt if he'd just calmly walk away, as though nothing had happened."

That was logical enough, although it was difficult to contemplate getting into the mind of such a thief.

"Yet, that was what must have happened," Trevor added, "but something is really bothering me about it. It's as if I just need something to trigger my mind…"

His words tailed off, as he shook his head in apparent bemusement.

"Well, keep thinking," David said. "If you come up with anything, come and see me straight away. In the meantime, I'm going to ring the police… to see if they've made any progress. Now, off you go. I'll then speak to Jane about tonight. And I'll make sure it's all right with Katie. No doubt, she's outside now – chomping at the bit for her dictation."

Trevor grinned, almost as if he knew this was, indeed, the case.

## CHAPTER 33

With the prospect of late-working that evening, David did not want to miss out on lunch again. At one o'clock, having pre-warned Sarah on the telephone, he donned his overcoat, scarf and trilby. He left his cycle attire in the cupboard; Jane had returned from her own lunch hour and said a cold easterly had blown up. In any case, with so many thoughts scurrying round in his brain, a brazing sea-air walk might do him good.

Jane's prognosis had been spot-on. As soon as he stepped into the street, he had to grab his hat to prevent it joining the squawking gulls which were circling overhead. The chill wind soon made his eyes water and he was glad he was on foot, rather than being buffeted about on his bicycle.

Still clutching his trilby, he passed through the short tunnel under the railway line to reach the promenade. He then stopped to lean on the iron railing which separated the walkway from the beach.

The sea was awesome.

Fortunately, the tide was out. Fearful waves would, otherwise, be breaking over where he was actually standing. They could, even, cascade over the railway line behind him. It was at times like this that he admired the fishermen from nearby Brixham. They would always brave the elements to provide holidaymakers and residents with pieces of cod to accompany their soggy chips. A seafaring life was definitely not for him; he had even been seasick on the Isle of Wight ferry.

But here, on dry land, the exhilaration of the moment was sweeping through him and he moved off, invigorated by the salty air having cleansed his sinuses.

Not that such a brine-laden atmosphere aided the hotels and

other buildings which overlooked this part of the sea front. The salt would already be etching into the new paint work which adorned several of the properties. Their owners had taken advantage of a mild, dry spring to carry out their annual re-decoration earlier than usual.

One such hotel proprietor was John English. The Esplanade's gleaming woodwork was a credit to the quality of Dulux. It had not been so last November. Then, when English had requested a loan to expand the hotel, the building had a tired and hungry look. That in itself had not put David off, but he certainly expected re-decoration to have been completed before the summer's avalanche of visitors.

David looked closely at the hotel as he passed by. He did not want to have anything to do with English, but the hotel itself was an impressive three-storey building in a prime location. Although he did not trust the owner, he was convinced he had nothing to do with the written threats. Because of the past, he would simply not want to draw attention to himself in this way.

As he left the hotel behind him, making his way to the cherry-blossomed road which eventually led to his house, he decided he could also dismiss Charlie Hicklemaker as a possible perpetrator. Almost everything seemed to revolve in some way around the Riverside Nursing Home, yet Hicklemaker's only tenuous link to that business, appeared to be the nearby plot of land he wanted to develop. For all David knew, the man might not even have met Farthinshawe, never mind the questionable Mrs Flintshire.

The bracing air may have cleared his mind on these particular points but, although it was a start, it had not yet provided him with the overall clarity of thought he was still seeking.

Maybe, a piping hot bowl of vegetable soup would help. He reached their house and unlatched the front door, the wind almost taking it off its hinges. The aroma of Sarah's home-made broth then immediately caressed his unclogged nostrils. Exquisite!

"Careful!" Sarah shouted from the kitchen, clearly not impressed with his undignified entrance. Yet he could now see from the hall that she had opened a kitchen window, effectively creating a wind tunnel from the front to the back of the house.

He hung his overcoat on the oak stand by the front door and removed his trilby which, miraculously, had not been lifted from his head during the walk home. That done, he entered the kitchen and was pleased to see Sarah's admonishment had been in good humour. She seemed genuinely pleased that he had been able to make it home for lunch and a warm embrace accompanied her welcoming kiss.

"How's your morning been?" she asked, already starting to ladle their lunch into two large rustic pottery soup bowls.

"Only two bowls?" he asked, frowning. Where were Dad and Mark?

"Don't panic," Sarah said. "They've gone train spotting at Newton Abbot."

"Dad has?" He never did that.

"It was me… I suggested it… that he should do a grandpa thing."

"Was that wise?" Notwithstanding Sarah not wanting to allow Mark out of her sight, Dad's head injury did not make him the ideal chaperon.

Sarah shrugged and let out an untypical world-weary sigh. "I just feel I've had it up to here," she said, raising a hand to her eyebrows. "School holidays seem to be getting longer and… this time… having to keep a constant eye on Mark… Quite frankly, it's starting to get me down. In any case, nothing's happened since that first note. I now reckon it really was a hoax."

"If you're right," David replied, "it was a pretty poor one, at that." But he was not convinced that Sarah was convinced. More likely, it was wishful thinking on her part. The danger of that could lead to complacency. "But what about the travelling?" he asked. If Dad was in charge, they could end up anywhere.

Sarah smiled at that. "Don't worry. You didn't have the car, so I took them. I said I'd pick them up at three. Mark said the Cornish Express would have gone through by then. I was just thankful not to have to stop. Anyway, they appreciated the door-to-door service. Seriously, that arctic wind had got up and I didn't fancy them walking to the station… to pick up the train. I'm surprised you made it home, without catching your death."

"It was a bit rough," David admitted, shivering involuntarily. "But what are they going to do for lunch?"

"I did them a picnic: sandwiches; boiled eggs; crisps; and a Mars bar each. Your Dad took a flask of tea and Mark's got dandelion and burdock."

David pulled a face. That was his least favourite fizzy drink. "And you're sure they'll be all right?" He was not convinced that he was convinced.

"You know Mark," Sarah said, drawing him to the table where the soup's aroma now vied with that of the crusty loaf which lay already cut into chunks on the bread board. "He won't leave his spot on the embankment. And he'll enthuse your Dad with the excitement of it all. By the way, what is the *City of Truro*?"

David grinned and explained about the Bulldog-class locomotive which, along with the King-class *George V*, was the most famous engine in the GWR.

"Anyway," Sarah said, as they sat down at the table, "I just asked you how your morning's been."

"You might say, interesting," he answered, smacking his lips in appreciation of the soup. He then told Sarah about his meeting with Trevor and that four of them would be working late tonight.

"He's a canny boy, isn't he?" she said, when he had finished.

"You mean, managing to date Katie?" he asked, grinning.

"That, as well... although I'm not sure how he'll be able to handle her."

"That depends on how you interpret your choice of words."

"David! Be serious. No, Trevor's got a lot about him. In many ways, he reminds me of a younger you."

"He certainly has the same interests... and I'm not talking about Katie. And it's funny, he also seems to have a similar instinctive hunch about what might be going on at work."

"And do you think you'll discover anything tonight?"

"We'll definitely find out where the money's gone from all those dormant accounts. Whether that tells us anything significant is another matter. I just hope it doesn't take too long."

"If necessary, I'll keep your meal warm in the oven."

"Thanks. Is it hot-pot?"

"Of course."

What else? He could live on his favourite dish for a month.

"One other thing happened this morning," he said, dragging his spoon round the bowl for the last drop of soup, then wiping the sides of the dish with a wedge of bread, "I spoke to Parker... after I'd seen Trevor."

"Parker? I'd forgotten all about him."

"I'm not surprised. I had, except that I kept remembering I hadn't seen him. He said he'd been pressing on with his inspection at Newton Abbot. He probably wants to get it finished before you go back."

Sarah could not hide her indignity.

"Anyway," David added, quickly, "I gave him all the details of the transfers from Mrs Martingale's account. With luck, he'll have the answers to these tomorrow. He certainly said he'd ring me then."

"Do you think it's all starting to come together?"

"I really don't know. But one other thing I've got to do is see Bernard Groves this afternoon. I can't understand how those nursing home residents could have been coming into the bank to cash their cheques."

"And you said… before… that Bernard had cashed them all?"

David nodded and wiped his mouth with his serviette. "Yes, it's odd, isn't it?"

And he was still thinking this as he left the house, thankful the wind seemed to have calmed down. He would not be able to see Bernard until the bank had closed and after the first cashier had balanced his till. He would also quiz him again about the stolen money. Before then, he would try and speak to DC Pound. Had he made any progress with the 'Harris Tweed Man'?

But the answer to that turned out to be 'no'. Nor were the police any further forward in solving the murders of the two ladies. What were they doing? Not a lot, by the sound of it.

And the detective did not seem to be concerned any more about the two original threats that had started everything off. It was as if the police had now taken the view that no news was good news and there was little likelihood of the threats turning into reality. It was a point of view with which he was now inclined to agree.

He had to wait until half past four for Bernard Groves to balance his till – an errant one pound note being found in, of all places, a bag of copper. It was amazing how some differences arose, but at least this one had turned up. Bernard could normally be relied upon for unfailing accuracy with his cash. For that reason, the loss of £2,500 must have hit him hard. It certainly showed in his face and general demeanour when he sat across the desk from David.

Gone was his former arrogance. To give him his due, this had diminished after his dressing down last year. Yet, in recent weeks, David had felt it was still lurking beneath the surface, as if time would be the factor when it would be given its head again. But the robbery had cast such concerns aside and Bernard sat slumped in his chair. He stared down into his lap, where his hands were clasped, steeple-like, as if he were in silent prayer.

"I suppose you're going to interrogate me again about the robbery," he mumbled, before David had posed his first question. It made him feel more like a policeman or a bank inspector, rather than Bernard's branch manager.

"As a matter of interest," David replied, "no, I'm not. But, as you've raised the subject, have you had any further thoughts?"

At this understated reply, Bernard looked up acutely and his eyes actually exhibited some form of life. "The more I think about it," he said, his voice almost pleading for his manager's support, "I feel certain the man in the banking hall was casing us."

If it had not been for the fact that they had previously received warning of a raid, David would have thought that it was now Bernard who had been seeing too many gangster films or had been reading graphic crime novels. He could imagine Bogart talking about casing a joint, but Bernard?

"Don't you think," he replied, "the man would have been more of opportunist thief?"

"Is that what the police think?"

"I don't know what the police think."

"But have they found the man yet?"

"Not to my knowledge."

"Why ever not? For God's sake, what are they doing?"

Bernard's passive air had been short-lived. Anger now burned in his eyes and his inflamed cheeks matched the tone of his outburst. It was as if he were trying to shift the blame for the episode on to the shoulders of the police. He had, perhaps, forgotten it was he who had carelessly left the money on his till for the man in the banking hall simply to help himself.

"I'm sure they're doing all they can," David replied, his measured tone not really reflecting the fact that he had no evidence to justify his statement. "Anyway," he continued, "that's not what I mainly wanted to see you about. I'd like to know what you can tell me about Mrs Whytechapel, Mrs Blackstone and Miss Bassenthwaite."

Bernard's look betrayed his astonishment at the raising of these names.

"Mrs Whytechapel? The woman who was murdered?"

David nodded.

"You think I had something to do with that?"

David had to take a mental step backwards. Such a thought had never crossed his mind. But why not? Bernard had suddenly been cashing all of Mrs Whytechapel's cheques. Was that because there was some connection between them? If so, had there then been a dramatic falling out? No, this was absurd. How could he contemplate anyone in National Counties, never mind Bernard, being caught up in such a lurid affair?

"Of course, I don't," he replied. " But you clearly knew her – and you must also know Mrs Blackstone and Miss Bassenthwaite."

"I've never met any of them."

Oh, dear. What was the man trying to hide? Maybe, he was involved , after all. But how? Thank goodness Jane had rooted out all the cheques – categorical evidence that Bernard had cashed them all for the three ladies. For the moment, they could remain in the top drawer of his desk. If necessary, he could spirit them out of it in due course – like a rabbit out of a conjuror's hat?

"But… for the last six months," David said, conscious that he was enunciating his words precisely, rather like Joyce Grenfell in her best schoolmistress mode, "you've been cashing cheques for all three of these customers."

"I know I have."

So, how can he say he's never met the women?

David had no need to pose the question; it must have been apparent from the incredulous look in his eyes.

"I cashed them for Barbara."

"For Barbara?" What was this all about?

"Yes, There was nothing wrong with that. The ladies always opened the crossings. And Barbara was their known agent."

David leant forward in his chair, elbows splayed on the desk, his own hands now steepled, with each forefinger brushing his upper lip. Was he missing something here? Was Bernard's glib explanation deliberately trying to make him look stupid?

"I'm sorry, Bernard," he eventually said, "I don't get it."

The cashier actually sighed, damn him. "You know Barbara's involved with the Riverside…"

"I'm sorry?"

"Barbara's been helping Mrs Flintshire… helping with the accounts… for some time now."

At least, he already knew this – originally thanks to Farthinshawe and then to Trevor, via Katie, this morning. But what had that to do with Barbara cashing cheques for the residents?

"Anyway," Bernard continued, as though it was now his turn to impersonate Joyce Grenfell, "about six months ago, Barbara became a friend."

"A friend?"

"Yes, one of Mr Farthinshawe's volunteers. He's always encouraged people in the town to become friends; he calls them 'Friends of the Riverside'. It's to provide the residents with a bit of outside companionship… especially residents who don't have any visiting relations."

"And Barbara's one of these friends?"

Bernard nodded. "Mrs Flintshire persuaded her. They've

been friends... personal friends... for years. And with Barbara's husband away, she had time on her hands to help out."

"In what way?"

"The friends... there must be a dozen or so... Celia does it occasionally... they do shopping for the residents; take them out if they want it; or just go and visit and talk to them. As I said, it's all about companionship."

It was starting to make a bit of sense now. And good for Farthinshawe for trying to bring some quality of life to the residents. They might, otherwise, just stay in their rooms, or sit silently in chairs around the walls of the communal sitting room. And, it would seem, from what Bernard had previously said, that Barbara also provided another particular service.

"And when the residents wanted some cash," he said, "Barbara brought in their cheques for you to cash?"

"Yes. She couldn't cash them herself, of course. That wouldn't have been right... so I cashed them all. She then took the money back to the Riverside on her next visit. It was all above board. She told me she had the full approval of Mr Farthinshawe."

That was something, anyway. But why had he not been told about the arrangement? It was a matter he should have known about, if only for everyone's protection – not least that of Barbara. Suppose something had gone wrong? If there had been a dispute of some sort?

"And did this arrangement apply to others?" he asked. "Or just the three women we're talking about?"

Bernard first shook his head and then nodded. It was the sort of double-headed question Sarah often put to himself – one requiring a yes and a no answer. Now, he was doing it. "Just the three," Bernard said. "Probably because the other residents banked elsewhere."

"But why didn't anyone tell me about it?"

"I can't speak for anyone else," Bernard replied, "but I assumed you knew. It had become such a regular occurrence, I thought everyone knew."

Everyone, it would seem, apart from the manager. But what he did know was that he was getting increasingly concerned. More than ever, he had a gut feeling that this evening's late working would not be a waste of time.

But before that, he really must see Barbara.

## CHAPTER 34

" I think she's gone home," Katie said.

David had asked her to see if Barbara was free to come and see him and he now looked at his watch. Five-to-five. "That's early for her."

"Everything's balanced," Katie replied, "and I heard her say to Norman... on her way out... she said she might as well go. She wasn't holding any keys, so she could have an early night – for a change."

He could see Barbara's point. She was often last to leave, even when she did not hold the strong room keys. But he really needed to see her about those withdrawals – never mind find out her story about what was actually going on at the Riverside. Now, it seemed, this would have to wait until the morning.

"What about the others?" he asked. If everything was balanced, there was no need for anyone else to stay. His dormant account team could then make an earlier start than he had expected.

"You're thinking about our cosy foursome," Katie trilled, smiling in a wicked, though quite inoffensive, way.

Cheeky girl. He only hoped she would be in the right frame of mind to take part in this investigation. Her natural ebullience could easily get the better of her.

"I'll ignore that one," he said, grinning. "Anyway, let me know when everyone else has left. We can then make an early start."

Katie skipped out of the room. Was it Trevor's influence? She seemed even more exuberant than usual. Sarah was probably right; the lad might well find her something of a handful. On the other hand, Katie must have a lot about her to share in his pastimes, so early in their courtship – if that was the right word for what was going on. It was a special sort of girl who would go to football matches and jazz clubs when neither activity was likely to have attracted her before.

Casting such thoughts from his mind, he pondered on what the evening's investigations might hold and what might be revealed. It was certainly an unusual arrangement for him to join three of his more junior staff in an exercise of this sort. But he could not think of a better team, especially as Trevor and Katie were taking more than a passing interest in what might be happening. In particular he hoped something might trigger Trevor's mind over what was clearly niggling him. It was strange, and rather comforting, to know they were sharing similar feelings.

By five-fifteen Katie returned to say everyone else had left. The only person to show any interest in what might be happening was apparently Norman. Without painting the broader picture, David had already warned him he would be working late and the only concern Norman expressed to Katie was whether he might be able to be of any help.

Jane had already done a sterling job, having established that they might well have to examine each day's work for the last six months. Documentation such as day sheets, machine listings and batch summaries were stored in long cardboard boxes which were kept in the strong room. The actual cheques and credits were filed in drawers under each customer's name. Jane had taken the appropriate boxes from the metal shelves which lined the walls of the strong room and she now asked Trevor to help bring them out into the general office on a trolley.

The back-office desks were clear of the normal daily clutter of vouchers, day sheets and ledgers, leaving them plenty of room to spread out. But with so many old vouchers and forms to examine, it was important to have in place an effective, workmanlike system.

David had deliberately left the organization of the exercise to Jane, making it clear to the others that she, and not he, was team leader. She had done all the preliminary work and knew exactly what they should be looking for. It would be a good test of how well she could handle such an operation.

The only thing he stipulated was that the teams of two should comprise Trevor with himself and Jane with Katie. It was not just a case of splitting up Trevor and Katie, but if he and Trevor were together, it was possible their minds might feed off each other – to reveal answers to their respective conundrums.

Jane already seemed to be revelling in the lead he had given her. It was not something, only a few months ago, he could have imagined her relishing. The change in her had been immense.

What an advert she was for imaginative staff training.

He had always believed such training was not simply a question of acquiring technical knowledge – knowing banking rules and regulations. He had learnt that from his time as a clerk – when some of his managers seemed to have tunnel vision over technical accuracy outweighing all else. He had vowed that, if he ever became a manager, he would not fall into that trap. He would give his staff their heads; let them learn from their own mistakes. He had always tried to instil confidence in them – not always successfully, he had to admit – and making Jane tonight's team leader was a case in point. If she veered from the required path, he could always guide her; and if she knew he had confidence in her, she should learn to have confidence in herself.

"We've an awful lot to do tonight," Jane said, when they were all sitting around her. "Until now, I've been on my own... I think you know that... so I'd better set out what this is all about."

David noticed Katie give Trevor an excited glance, as if they were about to be let into a big secret.

"Each year," Jane continued, "we always do a check on dormant accounts and this time... probably for the first time ever... the number's actually reduced. This isn't a case of accounts having been closed; instead, over twenty-five accounts have suddenly become active again. We hope to find out why tonight – especially as these accounts include those of Mrs Martingale and Mrs Whytechapel."

Mention of the two murdered women had the desired effect. Jane had their undivided attention.

"Over the last six months," she explained, "a number of cheques were drawn on all these accounts. We've already looked into the withdrawals on the murdered women's accounts and, tonight, we're going to deal with the rest."

She paused and drew two piles of cheques towards her.

"These are the cheques concerned and we need to know which accounts they were credited to. The cheques don't have other banks' crossing stamps on them, so they must have been credited to accounts here. Our job now is to find out which accounts."

Trevor tentatively raised a finger. "Excuse me," he said, Jane then giving him a nod to carry on. "Can't we simply tell which accounts were credited from the payees' names on the cheques?"

"You'd think that, yes," Jane agreed, "but no payees are actually named. That's one of the strange things about it. All the payees are just recorded as 'cash' or 'self'."

"But the cheques weren't actually cashed?" Trevor asked.

Jane shook her head. "No, none of them. Not one has a till stamp on it."

"In which case," Trevor persisted, "the cheques should have been endorsed on the back… endorsed over to the customers who were being credited. At the very least, the cashier should have written the names of such customers on the backs of the cheques."

"That's why we have a problem, Trevor. The only endorsement on the back of each cheque is by the drawer. It's an open endorsement – not made out to a specific person. And when it was paid into an account, no mention has been made of the account holder's name."

David listened to the exchange with interest... and with some disquiet. Jane's opening explanations had grabbed, and retained, the full attention of the others. She had also made it abundantly clear that something unnatural had been happening... that normal banking procedures had not been adopted. Was Trevor now thinking along the lines of himself? Had that elusive trigger been sprung?

"So," Jane continued, "what we have to do is take each cheque in turn and, for each date, dig out the day's work from these boxes. We'll then be able to establish how the entries were actually processed. Once we find out which accounts have been credited, we can dig out the individual credit slips from the voucher drawers."

She paused, as if to let the scale of what they had to do sink in.

"This is going to be quite a task," she said, glancing at David, possibly seeking his support, though this went without saying. "We'll work in pairs – Mr Goodhart and Trevor taking this bundle of cheques and Katie and I'll deal with the others. I've already jotted down the names of the drawers of the cheques on the day sheets in front of you. Against each name I've written the dates and amounts of the cheques. What you need to do is to write down... alongside each item... the accounts into which these cheques were paid."

"Do you think a pattern will emerge?" Trevor asked.

"I don't know, but if this looks likely... early on... for goodness sake, shout. The thing is, dormant accounts normally remain dormant. That's why this situation's so extraordinary. And because of that, we might discover something even more extraordinary tonight. So, let's get on with it now."

Jane had made it clear what was required of them and David and Trevor moved to a clear desk, with their bundle of cheques. Jane and Katie took up a desk behind them and David was impressed with the way Jane started to explain to Katie – someone who did not normally get involved with clerical tasks – exactly what they had to do.

The pile of cheques he and Trevor had in front of them related to about a dozen different accounts. He flicked through the cheques and immediately saw that each one was payable to either 'cash' or 'self'. Normally, customers would only do this if they were to cash the cheques themselves. Yet, in no case, had this actually happened. Instead, these different and diverse customers had all endorsed their cheques over to unnamed individuals. The whole business was now looking decidedly ominous. Had a deliberate plot been hatched to conceal the identities of the beneficiaries of all these cheques?

He gave the date of the first cheque to Trevor, who delved into the box containing the work for that day – the 2nd November, last year. They soon established from the appropriate batch of work that the cheque had been paid into the account of a Mrs Bishop.

And the second cheque, drawn a couple of weeks later by a completely different customer, was also credited to the account of the same Mrs Bishop.

How odd.

The next half a dozen cheques had been debited to their respective accounts between last December and January. They had been mostly paid into different accounts, but Mrs Bishop's account also came up again.

"We better check the PM card for this Mrs Bishop," David said to Trevor. "And can you check out the cards for these other accounts?"

But when they checked the box of Private Memorandum cards, none was there for Mrs Bishop, nor for any of the other accounts. Yet, this should not be possible. Whenever an account was opened, a PM card was always raised, recording all the available details of the customer concerned.

"Jane," he called across to his assistant, "we have a problem here."

The girl did not seem surprised. "Have you come across a Mrs Bishop, sir?"

"Yes, and the absence of her PM card – and those for other customers."

"Katie and I are hitting the same problem," Jane replied, coming over to him. "What's going on, sir?"

"I don't know," he said, "but let's get out Mrs Bishop's ledger sheet."

"Right, sir" Jane said, making for the strong room, where the ledger cans were kept overnight on a metal trolley. She soon emerged with the A-D can and thumbed through the sheets until she came to Mrs Bishop's account.

"Look at this, sir," she immediately said, beckoning him to her side. "It's a really active account… but look… almost every time a cheque has been paid in, another one has been drawn out for the same amount. You can see there's never much of an actual balance on the account."

"We need to get out all of Mrs Bishop's cheques," he said, a foreboding now hanging over him. Was Trevor feeling the same way? And Jane, for that matter? "And get out the ledger sheets for the other accounts. Let's see what's been happening on those."

Jane went to get the other ledger cans and was eventually able to give him the answer he was expecting. "It's the same pattern on all these accounts."

"Now, let's get out the actual cheques," he said. "We need to see who they were payable to. We'll start with Mrs Bishop."

But, even before seeing these cheques, he knew in his heart what had been happening. And it appalled him. And the perpetrator? He felt sure he also knew the answer to that one.

"The cheques have all been cashed," Jane eventually told him, having retrieved them from the voucher drawers.

"Let me see." David said, taking the cheques from her. Leafing through them, he immediately noticed two things, but, for the moment, he would keep one of these to himself. First, though, there was something else he needed. "Those cash withdrawals for Mrs Blackstone and Miss Bassenthwaite," he said, looking at Jane, "have you still got them out?"

"Yes, sir," she replied, moving to an adjacent desk and retrieving two piles of vouchers. "They're here. Do you want to see them all?"

"Please," he replied. Taking them from her, he scrutinized them carefully.

There were half-a-dozen for each account and he immediately jotted down the numbers of each cheque, then doing the same for the questionable Mrs Bishop.

"Have a look at this," he then said to the others who were now grouped around him.

There was no response.

"Look," he repeated. "Look at the cheque numbers."

Jane was the first to react. "They're very similar. Are they from consecutive cheque books?"

"If they are, why shouldn't they be?" Trevor asked. "Their names all start with the letter B."

"But that's too much of a coincidence," Jane said. "That would mean all these women would have asked for a new cheque book at about the same time."

David listened keenly to the exchange and he agreed with Jane. As cheques were not personalized with printed names, replacement books were kept in numerical order, any customer requiring a new one being allocated the next available. It was hardly likely these three customers would have needed new books at exactly the same time. In any case, Trevor and Jane had not spotted the answer he was seeking.

"They're not consecutive books," Katie suddenly blurted out, her eyes sparkling. "Look at the numbers. I reckon they're all from the same cheque book."

That's more like it. David felt like clapping her on the back. "Exactly! But how can that be possible?"

No-one answered. He did not have a definitive answer either – only grave suspicions.

"Could it be," Trevor volunteered, tentatively, "that this particular cheque book was issued to someone who then forged the customers' signatures – to draw out the cash?"

They all pored over the cheques and Trevor was again first to speak. "These cheques drawn by Miss Bassenthwaite don't seem right. The signatures are all slightly different and… look… look at this one… the 'h' is missing from the signature."

"That one must be a forgery, then," Katie exclaimed. "Customers would never sign their own cheques wrongly."

David was content to stay quiet and listen to their theories develop.

"It must be all tied up with the nursing home," Trevor said, then looking anxiously at David. "You don't think it's down to Mrs Flintshire? She's not got hold of a cheque book and been forging the signatures of the residents?"

"Is that Mrs Bishop a resident?" David ventured, looking round at the others who seemed agog at Trevor's suggestion. The lad's idea was certainly feasible, but it was not what he thought, himself.

"We don't know anything about Mrs Bishop," Jane answered.

"And I don't think we're going to," David replied. All they knew about her were the entries on her account. When he had originally looked through her cheques – and those that had been drawn on the other previously-dormant accounts – he had noticed two things. One was the numbers of the cheques – the sequential numbering which now included the cheques drawn on the accounts of Mrs Blackstone and Miss Bassenthwaite. The other team members had not yet picked up the second thing he had noticed. For now he would still keep this to himself; the fear that was spreading through him was too hot to share at the moment. One thing for sure, they need not explore these dormant accounts any further; they already had all the evidence he needed to take the next step forward.

It was now approaching seven o'clock and time to call it a day. He asked the others to pack things away and Jane and Trevor were soon able to lock up the strong room. As they put on their outdoor clothes, he made it clear that they must keep to themselves everything they had discovered that evening and they then all left the building by the front door.

After thanking them for all their help, David bade them goodnight on the pavement. But as they made off in their different directions, Trevor backtracked towards him, leaving Katie standing on her own, some twenty yards away.

"Look, sir," Trevor whispered in his ear, "across the road."

David peered through the gloom of the dusk and saw a shadowy figure scuttling away.

"That woman, sir," Trevor added, his voice actually cracking. "I'm sure she was watching the building – as we came out. And, sir, it's just dawned on me what's been bothering me so much."

David looked at him sharply. Whatever Trevor's revelation turned out to be, he was already pondering his next move. He had not recognised the person across the road, her head being covered by a thick woollen scarf. But he certainly noticed the woman's other attire. He had seen it before at Coombe Cellars – a tartan skirt under a dark three-quarter length coat.

# CHAPTER 35

On arriving home, it was a question of which telephone call David should make first. In the end, he plumped for Michael Farthinshawe; he might then have further information for his second call. He only hoped that the man would be receptive to a call at this time of the evening.

It was now eight o'clock and, in the half-hour he had been home, he had recounted to Sarah all that had happened that evening. She had listened intently and it had been good to get his theories off his chest. They sounded even more fanciful in the snug confines of their house and he was relieved that Sarah agreed with his conclusions.

She had always been a good sounding board and, with her banking experience, she was often able to give him a second opinion on technical matters – particularly those related to back-office operations and routines. In this respect, he was particularly pleased to have her practical knowledge on the issue of new cheque books – something that came within her own job function at Newton Abbot. Some branches – especially large ones – might have different systems in operation, even though general principles remained the same, and Sarah was able to confirm his view that if a person was determined enough to violate the cheque book system, there was not much, as a manager, he could have done about it.

When he rang the nursing home, Farthinshawe actually answered the telephone himself and said he was still working in his office – on the task of reconciling the nursing home's accounts.

"I'm sorry to trouble you like this in the evening," David said, pleased the man was doing as he had asked.

"I'm glad you have," Farthinshawe answered. It was not

the answer he could have expected. "It'll save me ringing you in the morning."

"Oh?"

"I'm not liking what I'm seeing," Farthinshawe said. "No wonder you were mad at me for not reconciling our bank statements. But it was a genuine error. I really thought Mrs Flintshire was doing it. And ... as I told you... she thought I was doing it."

It might have been a genuine misunderstanding, but such incompetence was totally unacceptable in an on-going business like the Riverside.

"What's the problem?" David asked, expecting the worst. There had been so many missing pieces in this jigsaw and another one now looked like turning up.

"There's been no problem with our normal income and expenditure. Mrs Flintshire's clearly done a good job. I've reconciled all the credits and cheques in our books with the entries on your bank statements."

"So, what's the problem?"

"The trouble is we don't get our paid cheques back with our statements. There's never been a need for this until our year end – when the accountant wants them."

"But if everything's reconciled, why do you need them now?"

"Not everything is reconciled."

"I thought you just said..."

"I said that all the entries in our books had been reconciled."

Farthinshawe was getting as pedantic as Bernard Groves at his best. *Come on, man, what are you trying to tell me?*

"So?"

"So," Farthinshawe replied, himself now seeming to be exasperated, "there are a lot of cheques on our statements which we don't recognise. They're not out of our cheque book."

"We?" David asked, fearing the worst, after having implored Farthinshawe to do this reconciliation on his own. "Did you say 'we'?"

"Yes, I did," Farthinshawe replied. "And I know what you said, but... but, you must see, I had to ask Mrs Flintshire about this."

That was probably fair enough, but without the cheques to hand, Farthinshawe might not have got any satisfactory answers from her... especially if she was involved in some way. After this evening's findings, he now doubted this. On the other hand...

"And what did she say?" he asked. He was now feeling thankful he had made this telephone call, but as to the way it was progressing... It would have been better sitting face-to-face with Farthinshawe and being able to have a look at the nursing home's books and bank statements.

"She had no idea what they were," Farthinshawe said. "And that's why I wanted to speak to you tomorrow... to arrange to come in and have a look at those cheques."

"So, they hadn't been made out and signed by Mrs Flintshire?"

"No. Although she makes out the cheques, I told you before... she never signs them. I sign them all. And she knows nothing about this lot. As I just said, they certainly didn't come out of our own cheque book."

"How many of these cheques were there? And how much were they for?"

"It's been going on for about six months now and there've been dozens... all between £300 and £500."

That certainly had a familiar ring to it. And for it to have been happening to this extent, no wonder there had been pressure on the bank account. As it was, Farthinshawe may be wanting to see these cheques, but it was also going to be high on his own agenda when he got into the office tomorrow.

"I'll look them out in the morning," he said, " as soon as I get in. I'll then give you a ring and we can take it from there."

"Good," Farthinshawe said, sounding relieved. "But this isn't why you rang. You clearly wanted to speak to me about something – presumably nothing to do with this."

"Yes, I did," David replied. "I wanted to ask about the Friends of the Riverside."

"What about them?"

"Am I right in thinking they're volunteer visitors?"

"Yes, not that we have many these days."

"Is Barbara Bolton one?"

"Yes, she comes occasionally."

"Only occasionally?"

"She comes to the home quite a bit, but that's mainly to help with the accounts. I told you before… she's been a great help to Mrs Flintshire."

"But she does visit the residents, as well?"

"I'm not really sure. I'd have to ask Mrs Flintshire about that."

No… not yet, anyway. In any case, a different message was coming across from the one Bernard Groves had given him.

"Would part of her visiting," David asked, instead, "include a cheque-cashing service for the residents? To save them having to visit the bank themselves."

"Why would the residents want to have cheques cashed for them? They hardly spend any money here."

"I'm thinking specifically of Mrs Blackstone," David persisted, "and Miss Bassenthwaite."

"Those two never have a need for cash. It's as much as they can do to get out of their chairs."

"And Mrs Whytechapel? When she was alive?"

"Poor Mrs Whytechapel," Farthinshawe replied, with feeling. "Of all the residents, she was the most lucid. But she didn't have a need for cash. I told you before, she recently wrote to the bank to set up a standing order for her fees. So, cash was certainly not needed for those. But, why do you ask?"

"Oh, something's cropped up. But you've given me the answer I wanted. I better let you get on. But I promise to ring in the morning… about those cheques."

With some relief, David finished the call; he did not want to answer any further questions about the cashed cheques. His next telephone call was now most urgent – to Chief Inspector Hopkins. Especially as he now knew what had been bothering him about the threat on the blotting paper.

# CHAPTER 36

The next morning, David sat in his office, door firmly closed. He needed solitude as he contemplated last night's extraordinary happenings. He had already made it clear to Katie and Jane that he must not be disturbed. Having been sworn to secrecy by Chief Inspector Hopkins, it was far better, at this stage, to try and avoid any further face-to-face contact with his staff. Earlier in the morning, he might easily have given the game away, unintentionally, before being given the all-clear from the police.

When he had rang Hopkins last night, the Chief Inspector was not at his desk. As soon as DC Pound got the gist of David's theorizing, he demanded David's presence at the police station. Hopkins would need to see him personally about such a critical development.

But in no time at all after his arrival at Torquay police station, David was ensconced in the back of a black Wolseley squad car as it careered along the coast road to Barnmouth. David felt the adrenalin pounding through him as the car took hairpin bends at speeds which he felt sure would see the vehicle crashing through the barriers – how flimsy they now seemed – which separated the road from the precipitous cliffs that cascaded down to the sea, far below.

With tyres squealing and the car's strident bell demanding others to create a clear path, it was, for David, the ultimate in white-knuckle rides. Only when they neared their destination did the car slow down and the bell got switched off to avoid any forewarning of their imminent arrival.

"Where now?" Hopkins asked, turning round in his front seat to look at David.

This was why David was in the car. Parts of old Barnmouth

comprised a maze of narrow streets, many bearing a numbering system which might baffle even the most perceptive postman. Hopkins had not been at all confident in finding the right house, especially as he was convinced that time was now critical.

"Turn left at the end of this road," David replied, his eyes then straining through the windscreen which was now smeared from a light drizzle. "Now take the next right and then right again."

The car slowed to almost walking pace as it entered a road which was barely wide enough for cars to pass each other. Terraced houses on either side were only distinguishable by their differently-coloured front doors and, without adequate street lighting, it was impossible to make out the numbers.

"I knew we'd need you with us," Hopkins said. "We'd never have found the house in time."

If he had not felt such foreboding about the outcome of this exercise, David would have wallowed in the sheer excitement of such a chase. As it was, he could only steel himself for the leading role he was about to play.

"That's the house," he said to Hopkins, pointing his finger at a red-painted front door which actually stood ajar on the opposite side of the road.

Hopkins told the driver to pull into a space on the nearside and then leaned back to face David.

"Right," he said. "Off you go. It looks as if we've just made it in time."

Hopkins had decided that David – a friendly face, just in case – should be the first to approach the house and David eased himself out of the car and made towards the front door. But why was it open? At this time of night? Perhaps Hopkins was right. They were just in time.

As his hand reached for the knocker, the door swung fully open and Barbara actually dropped the heavy suitcase she was carrying. She was all dressed up in outer clothes for a journey and David immediately recognized her three-quarter length coat. He would also never forget her look of astonishment at seeing her manager standing on her doorstep.

"What are you doing here?" she managed to gasp, then turning white when she saw Hopkins and his burly, uniformed driver approaching behind David.

Then she collapsed on the floor, sobbing uncontrollably, and leaving David at a loss as to what to do.

But there was no need to do anything. Hopkins was now firmly in charge and, with the help of his driver, he lifted Barbara gently up from the floor and moved her into the front room. He settled her on to the sofa – her sobbing now resonating round the small room – and then turned back to David.

"I think that's enough proof," he said, "don't you?"

Now, the next morning, David awaited the arrival of DC Pound who was coming round to put him fully in the picture. Last night, in her small house, which they now knew she had already sold, Barbara had been in no fit state to answer any questions and she had been taken to Torquay police station where she had been questioned well into the night.

Earlier that evening, David's account of events had certainly been enough to convince Hopkins that the murky goings-on with customers' accounts had been down to Barbara. Added to that, were the revelations of Trevor's long-awaited intuitive suspicions about the 'raid' and Farthinshawe's discovery of bogus cheques being debited to the account of the Riverside Nursing Home.

While he waited for DC Pound, David also wanted to hear from Parker about the transfer of funds to Newton Abbot. Were his investigations proving to be more difficult than expected? Or had he discovered something else? Something which might have a bearing on what had been happening at Barnmouth?

The links between the two branches were certainly strange. Even the threatening note against Mark had arisen at Newton Abbot. If something else was happening there, it was just as well the Easter school holidays had not yet ended. At least, that was delaying Sarah's return to the branch.

In the meantime, an unquantifiable buzz had been circulating around his own branch.

"Barbara's not yet turned up," Jane had told him about half an hour ago. She had then deliberately paused, as if reluctant to speculate on the reason for the supervisor's absence. It was certainly not something David wanted to discuss and he simply asked her to provide cover. Her own work could be dealt with later.

When Katie had completed taking down his dictation, she had also been reticent in expressing a view. Was a conspiracy of silence going on out there? Last night, all of them must have formed a verdict on what they had discovered. Yet, he could imagine their reluctance to share their thoughts with their manager. Apart from Trevor, that is; he had done just that on the pavement last night.

As he pondered on this, his telephone rang and Katie said DC Pound was in the banking hall and wanted to see him urgently. Good. At last.

"Needless to say," the detective said, as soon as he was seated, "we couldn't be more grateful to you. We had been hitting one dead end after another... until your call last night. Now it looks as if the case is solved."

Solved? The case? Did he mean the murders? He would hardly use that phraseology in respect of the dormant account exercise or Bernard's alleged raid.

"Having been literally caught on her own doorstep," DC Pound continued, clearly noting David's raised eyebrows, "Mrs Bolton has confessed to nearly everything. You arrived at the house only just in time. A few minutes later she would have been on her way to London Airport. She hoped to get on the Malaga flight in the morning."

"But if she'd planned this, did she know things were building up against her?"

Pound nodded. "That's what she said. She's clearly a very intelligent woman. That's why she nearly got away with it. She reckoned if she got to Spain, that would be it. She'd be safe. And I think she's right. I don't think there's any extradition agreement with Spain."

"But how did she know we were on to her?"

"Even though you hadn't said anything, she sensed that was the case – even before last night. That's why she was outside the bank. She was wondering what was going on. When you came out, she saw your Trevor Smith whisper in your ear. She was then certain. She'd already got her bag packed – in case she needed a speedy getaway. If we'd been any later, she'd have gone and we wouldn't have known where."

So, how long had Barbara known he had his suspicions? It must have been all down to the dormant account exercise. Although he had restricted the investigation to himself and Jane, it was only a small office and Barbara had been a core constituent for so many years. She had probably made it her business to know what was going on – at all times. And when Jane had asked her to help out, she must have known her skulduggery was at serious risk of being exposed. No wonder she had made an excuse not to help.

"So, she's admitted everything?" David asked. That would certainly make things simpler – rather than having to prove everything, chapter and verse.

"Almost everything," Pound replied. "First of all, you were right about her opening all those fictitious accounts."

Last night, he had come to the indubitable conclusion that

the accounts of Mrs Bishop and so many others were a figment of Barbara's fertile imagination. Once he had established she had been purloining cheque books from the branch's central stock, it was the only possible answer. Forging customers' signatures on cheques and then paying these cheques into accounts she had opened fictitiously was a risky exercise, but she had almost pulled it off. It had been clever, but not clever enough; otherwise she would have taken more care over the cheque books she used – being more selective with the numbers. The other incriminating factor – which he, alone, had noticed last night – was that all the cheques drawn on the fictitious accounts had been cashed by Barbara herself. Likewise, the credits paid into those accounts had been processed through her own till. That way, no-one else would be involved – to raise any suspicion. She had certainly used Bernard to cash other cheques, ostensibly on behalf of Mrs Blackstone and Miss Bassenthwaite. But being a Friend of the Riverside, she had a logical reason for that. This would not have been the case with the fictitious accounts.

"But what did she do with all the cash?" David asked. "The cash she drew from the fictitious accounts?"

"We don't know about it all," Pound replied, "but there were wads of it in her suitcase."

"To be smuggled into Spain?"

"It seems like it."

"And did it include the money she took out of Mrs Blackstone's account... and Miss Bassenthwaite's?"

"We don't know yet. She hasn't said. But she certainly duped your first cashier."

A Friend of the Riverside, indeed. Some friend. But it was a lesson for them all to learn – not just Bernard. Anything out of the ordinary – even carried out by the most trusted employee – needed to be questioned. It was only fair to everyone concerned.

"And," Pound continued, "she also duped everyone with the theft of £2,500."

This really had been Trevor's masterly breakthrough. For so long, something had apparently been troubling him – until it clicked last night. When he saw the woman outside the bank, it had reminded him of his encounter with Barbara on the day of the robbery. He had returned late from lunch and had been berated by her on that same pavement – because he had made her late for her shopping. But even if he had been on time, she would not have started her lunch hour until just after one. To do her shopping? On early closing day? When all the shops would, by then, have been closed? And Trevor had recalled that she had been clutching her shopping bag to her. She would not have done that if it had been empty. No doubt, it had been stuffed with £1 notes, all 2,500 of them. So much for the alleged 'Harris Tweed Man'.

"Has she admitted the theft?" he asked.

"Oh, yes," Pound replied.

"But why did she do it? She couldn't have planned the robbery."

"No. It was on impulse. The opportunity was suddenly there. She saw the money lying on the counter. And when your first cashier went to the back of the office… No wonder she then wanted to get off to lunch quickly. I hope it's a salutary lesson for Mr Groves."

"And for everyone else," David agreed. "But why did Barbara decide to take the money?"

"She said it got her to her target."

"Her target?"

"Yes, £30,000. I'll come back to that later. But another big chunk of the money came from the Riverside's account. That was a good deduction on your part. You don't fancy being a policeman, do you?"

David smiled at that one, but this really was no laughing matter. The Broadman affair last year had involved his secretary's criminality and it was hard to believe another senior member of his staff had now travelled down the same unscrupulous route. But, last night, it had become clear to him that this was, indeed, the case.

Barbara had clearly been milking the Riverside's account, forging cheques which she either cashed herself, or whisked into various of her fictitious accounts. She had assured her old friend, Mrs Flintshire, that, each month, as part of her help with the accounting, she would carry out the company's statement reconciliation, so neither Farthinshawe nor his manager knew what was happening on the bank account.

Then, it had finally clicked as to what had been troubling David with the wording on the piece of blotting paper. Almost certainly, a member of staff had written the note. Anyone else – any outsider – would, surely, have used the word 'bank', not 'branch'. Such a person would have written 'this bank will be raided at 2.30'. Staff working in a particular banking branch would consider it to be their branch; customers would tend to refer to their bank.

But when Pound had arrived, he had said the case had been solved. Until now, he and the detective had been talking about fictitious accounts, forgeries and theft. But what about the murders?

"When you came in just now," David said, hardly able to get his words out, "you said it now looked as if the case was solved." He took a deep breath before adding, "You mean the murders?"

DC Pound nodded and his eyes actually shone, as if from the exhilaration arising from the eventual catch. "She's admitted everything. Well, almost everything."

"Barbara has?"

It was the answer he feared, but could not actually believe. Manipulation of bank accounts and theft was one thing, but murder? A double murder, at that. What could have possibly motivated an upstanding member of his staff – until six months ago, that is – to do such a thing? Now, her previous thirty years of outstanding service counted for nothing. How could she have been capable of carrying out the ultimate crime?

"Mrs Bolton had a plan," Pound replied. "She had given herself six months to raise £30,000 – taking it in dribs and drabs, to avoid suspicion. She decided the best way was to target dormant accounts. She selected elderly people, preferably in their eighties and nineties. If they hadn't made use of their accounts for some years, they were unlikely to do so during this six-month period. Mrs Martingale was a case in point. She had lived in the States since the war, during which time she had not used her account at all. The chances of it being re-activated during the six months were probably non-existent."

"And then she suddenly turned up," David interjected.

"Yes. It was an enormous shock to Mrs Bolton, made worse by Mrs Martingale asking for an up-to-date statement of her account. For the last six months, your trusted supervisor had been making fraudulent withdrawals and then suppressing the issue and despatch of Mrs Martingale's statements. Now, her whole operation was about to be blown sky-high."

"And because of that, she killed her?" It simply did not sound feasible.

"Something like this can unbalance a person's mind. That's what happens with most murders. They're seldom pre-meditated. Mrs Bolton panicked – she knew the old lady was going to the railway to catch her train home and she nipped out of the branch and followed her. The general melee on the platform gave her the perfect opportunity and she was back in the branch within fifteen minutes. Apparently, nobody missed her."

"And she told you all this?"

"Once we got her back to the station, it all came flooding out. It was as though she'd been burst like a balloon – everything spilling from her."

"And you believe her?"

"Of course. It makes sense… especially when you take Mrs Whytechapel into account."

In the horror of learning about Mrs Martingale's murder, David had momentarily forgotten about Mrs Whytechapel.

"This elderly lady," Pound continued, "was marooned in her nursing home. She was a perfect target for having her account milked. With no activity on it for many years, Mrs Bolton assumed it would continue that way. Then the lady wrote to you to set up a standing order to pay her nursing home fees."

David shook his head. "Mr Farthinshawe told me about that. Before then, you'd said it had been in her diary – that she'd been in touch with us. But no-one here received the letter."

"Mrs Bolton did – and suppressed it."

"And then decided to murder her?"

DC Pound now appeared to be enjoying himself, as if he, personally, had solved the crimes. "She told us she was a regular visitor to the home," he said, "and she knew the layout and routines. In her state of mind, it was simple for her to go to Mrs Whytechapel's room and smother her. It would have looked as if she'd died in her sleep."

This was almost too much to take in. What was everyone else in the office going to think… when they heard? Some of them might, even, need medical help to get over the shock. Some could be traumatized, having worked with Barbara – and been friends with her – for so long.

And something else was bothering him…

"Why did she start all this dirty work in the first place?" he asked. "Why did she need £30,000?"

"You're not going to like this," Pound said. "but in her view, it was because of you."

"Me?" What was going on?

"Do you remember turning her husband down for a loan – for £30,000? I gather he wanted to build holiday homes in Marbella."

"I certainly did. It was an untenable banking proposition."

"Maybe. But both he and, especially, his wife were outraged. Having worked for the bank for thirty years, Mrs Bolton couldn't believe you turned them down flat. From then on, all they could think of was revenge and retribution."

Could his logical banking decision really have led to so much criminal activity? For the rest of his life, was he going to have to live with the deaths of two innocent old ladies?

"On no account, need you berate yourself," Pound said, as if reading his mind. "You simply can't legislate for how people might react to what they think is a personal slight."

It was all very well saying that, but this really was going to be difficult to get over. Yet, he could not dwell on it now. What about the threat to Mark? Surely, Barbara could not have been responsible for that?

"And the threat to my son?"

"We haven't cracked that one yet," DC Pound answered, shaking his head. "Mrs Bolton's keeping mum about that – for the moment, anyway. But we believe she had an accomplice… someone else who had a grudge against you."

When the threats first raised their ugly heads, the police had been keen to know if a customer might have borne him a grudge. With the help of Sarah, he had racked his brains on this, but none of his possibilities had proved to be feasible – especially as his recent concerns over Mrs Flintshire would now seem to have been misdirected. On the other hand, he had not even considered Geoff Bolton. So, was there someone else lurking in the background?

But before he could explore this further, the telephone rang. He picked up the receiver and told Katie he could not really be disturbed.

"But it's Mr Parker on the phone," she insisted. "I told him DC Pound was with you. He then said it was even more important to speak to you."

"You'd better put him through, then." At least, this would give him the opportunity of telling Parker the outcome of all the problems at this end. Because of what had happened, he also felt sure that Barbara must, somehow, have set up fictitious accounts at Newton Abbot to receive the transfers from Mrs Martingale's account.

"I'm going to have to come over and see you," Parker immediately said, when he was put through. "These accounts – the ones you asked me to look into – they're all fictitious."

"That certainly doesn't surprise me," David answered, unable to suppress a weariness in his reply. "And I also need you to come over here and…"

"But there's more," Parker interrupted, "I think you know the head of securities here, Greville Gladstone."

Ah, GG. After all David had been told this morning, it was good to hear a friendly name. What a lot he would have to tell him at their next meeting at Coombe Cellars. "Of course," he said. "How is he?"

"Not good, at all," Parker replied. "He's just committed suicide. He's hanged himself from a beam in the staff rest room."

# *EPILOGUE*

Two months on and David had still not got over GG's death – compounded by the apparent reason for his suicide. According to Barbara... and there was no cause to doubt her... Greville had been consumed by jealousy. It did not simply rest with David's promotion within the bank; he was also green with envy at the Goodharts' settled family life and a son to be proud of. What was more, he had always been infatuated with Sarah. In which case, how could he have possibly wanted to hurt her, as well? They would never know the answer to that one.

All this had spilled out of Barbara when she learnt of his death. They had been partners in crime, both harbouring all-consuming grudges against David.

It was little comfort to hear Barbara say that Greville had meant his revenge to be harmless. How could he have possibly thought that? It was he who had penned the threat against Mark. What could be more harmful than that? He had left the note on Sarah's vacant desk to await her return. Despite the conclusion of the handwriting experts, he had also written the threat on the blotting paper, leaving Barbara to place it in the banking hall. There had never been any intention of a raid – nor of an actual kidnap. They just wanted to inflict David with one headache after another.

At that stage, Greville had not known about Barbara's fraudulent activities, but once she had drawn him in, he had no way out. She had even persuaded him to fly with her to Spain. He would provide financial and legal expertise in the holiday homes business.

But, it would seem, even GG had a conscience. When he learnt of Barbara's murders, he went to pieces, culminating in his strange apology in the pub. He could not reconcile himself to be a party to what had become fatal retribution.

Barbara was due for trial in July. There could be only one outcome. But David would not be in Barnmouth when it happened. As a prime witness at the trial, he would be in much closer proximity to the Old Bailey.

His changed circumstances had arisen on the day United played their last match at Crystal Palace. He had not been able to attend. Trevor and Katie, their romance blossoming, went instead. They had witnessed a 1-1 draw, meaning that United missed out on promotion to Ipswich Town, on goal difference.

On that day, David had been in Head Office, earning a different kind of promotion – quite the reverse of Bernard Groves who had been given a final disciplinary warning. David's investigatory prowess had been recognized by the Chief Inspector, though this had almost been thwarted by the Regional Manager. Spattan had, apparently, been singularly unimpressed that his least favourite manager should receive further plaudits from the Chief Inspector. Since then, David had established that these two men had always been bitter rivals. Could it be that Spattan was another man consumed with jealousy?

But the Chief Inspector had won the day and had appointed David as one of his inspectors, based in Tunbridge Wells. Now, he and Mark would have to start supporting another football team.